PRAISE FOR SERVES YOU RIGHT

Must Read!

A gripping mystery thriller with a compelling lead - smart and flawed. Embedded with emotional punch to keep readers hooked.

— BOOK NERDECTION - 5/5 STARS

A well-written thriller filled with enough twists and turns to keep any avid mystery/crime reader engaged. The author's ability to keep me second-guessing was amazing.

I highly recommend to anyone who loves a good mystery they can't put down. There isn't anything I disliked about this thought-provoking, fun read.

— ONLINE BOOK CLUB
(ONLINEBOOKCLUB.ORG) - 5/5 STARS!

The edge-of-the-seat suspense, spell-binding cliffhangers, and jaw-dropping plot twists hooked me, leaving me turning through page after page. Once this whodunnit pulls you in, it never loosens its grip, relentless until the final word.

— READERS' FAVORITE - 5/5 STARS

Loved it. Pacing is well-done with no chapters feeling like they're lagging. Gregory does a beautiful job of drip-feeding us the details. The final reveal felt satisfying, while leaving the reader with lasting questions to think about.

— BADLY ANNOTATED READERS
SOCIETY - 4/5 STARS

A gripping story that kept me thoroughly engaged...I found it difficult to stop reading...fast paced and filled with so much action that it never let up. The writing style was captivating and the characters genuine and relatable...exceptionally well-written…the ending was an absolute surprise

— READERS' FAVORITE RATING: 5/5
STARS!

The pacing is relentless. Twists drop like thunderclaps and just when you think you've figured things out, boom, Orion Gregory throws another curveball.

— ADRIFTINAFICTIONALWORLD
REVIEWS

Gregory has created a phenomenal kick-@$$ main character. You'll be on the edge-of-your-seat with this one.

— BOOKGIRLBROWN REVIEWS

ORION GREGORY

SERVES YOU RIGHT

BECAUSE WAITING FOR KARMA TAKES FOREVER

A SYDNEY LIVINGSTONE DETECTIVE NOVEL

Publish Authority

Editor: Teresa Evans
Cover design lead: Raeghan Rebstock

ISBN 978-1-954000-97-1 (Paperback)
ISBN 978-1-954000-98-8 (eBook)

Published 2025 by Publish Authority,
300 Colonial Center Parkway, Suite 100
Roswell, GA, USA
PublishAuthority.com

Printed in the United States of America

I dedicate this novel to the following individuals:

My wonderful wife and two daughters, who refused to give up on a struggling writer who sometimes was better at procrastinating and making excuses than producing actual material.

Uncle Ron, a beloved member of our family who may not have shared our blood but was still just as much a part of us. You were a wonderful role model to our daughters, and I will never, ever forget you.

Tom Mitsoff, a fellow novelist whose friendship I will cherish for a lifetime. He's not nearly as bad as his namesake in this novel. In fact, he's significantly better. His latest novel, "Artificial Awakening," will make a lasting impression on you.

Also, Jerry Boyd, Steve Milano, Jr., Coach Brad Hagan, and my wonderful canine friends Ariel, Neptune, and Daley. You were all here at the start of this project, but your heavenly journey began before it ended. I love and miss each of you.

CHAPTER 1

He didn't even bother burying his wife's body.

Part of it was due to being in a hurry. He had a time window of three hours. But there was another reason, too. She had disrespected him.

First, there was the audacity of asking for a divorce just before he was scheduled to take his girlfriend on vacation. But that wasn't the worst thing, although Frank McBride wasn't thrilled about the idea. The ultimate act of disrespect? She wanted half of everything, including the thousands Frank had recently inherited from the death of his mother. Dividing the house would be painful, but Frank could accept that. But he couldn't fathom her stealing his inheritance.

Mom would turn over in her grave if Sheila walked away with half of that money. She designated that money for me. And for me only.

Frank had been blindsided by Sheila's announcement that she was leaving. He believed they were both content in their suburban lifestyle – the modest home in Green Haven, Ohio; the way he handled his stepdaughter Carmen and their own daughter Ashton; and their open marriage. Yeah, she had been reluctant at first, but eventually, she had warmed to it. They had agreed to keep each other appraised of other partners, to keep communication open and, more importantly, not to let any relationship escalate to the point that it became a threat to the marriage.

But then Andrea came along, and Frank broke his side of the agreement. Frank hadn't planned on falling in love, but she'd slowly won him over. She was as pretty as Sheila had been before the weight gain and short haircut. And while his wife was boring and practical, Andrea was spontaneous, willing to drop even important things to seek out a good time. They made love in parks, cars, and even behind a stack of boxes in his warehouse at work. She was quick-witted and made him laugh.

He began to spend less time with Sheila and their kids and more with Andrea and her son. He and Sheila stopped talking about other things, like finances and household decisions. He guessed the final straw had been when he canceled the annual family vacation so he could take his girlfriend and her kid to Six Flags over Georgia.

On a cool, clear Thursday morning in late September, Frank strangled Sheila to death.

He'd asked Sheila nicely to rescind the request; the money had been slowly growing in value, safe in Frank's separate bank account. Sheila didn't just say no. She laughed at him. She mocked him with an imitation of his own deep voice: "My mom wanted me to have that cash! I need that money to take my slutty girlfriend and her autistic son on vacation." At that moment, she signed her own death warrant, as far as he was concerned.

Frank didn't initially respond to Sheila's rant. He waited

fifteen minutes, smiling silently while ignoring his pulsating temples. He wondered if his lack of response surprised her; it certainly wasn't the norm. She knew what her mocking did to him.

She sat with her back to Frank, working on an email. Pounding the keyboard harder than usual. She was a few minutes from leaving for work. Was she trying to elicit a response from him? He did nothing yet.

But Sheila had to know this would end badly for her. Didn't she? She was not only disrespecting him. She was disrespecting the final wishes of his late mother, the only woman Frank had truly admired in his life. Yet, Sheila plodded away at the keyboard, her back turned to him. Did she think he'd never have the guts to take her out?

I'll show this bitch.

Sheila's typing was interrupted by Frank's right forearm enveloping her neck. Frank had refined his behind-the-back chokehold during hand-to-hand combat sessions during his two-year stint in the Marines. Then, he'd been dishonorably discharged for assaulting a fellow soldier. He'd been baited. Railroaded. Thrown out of a military career for an act beyond his control. And now he was being railroaded again…by someone who had promised to honor, love, and cherish him until death.

As he tightened his grip, Frank's thoughts turned to Andrea. She had predicted that Sheila would one day make this very demand for half of what he owned. She even jested about killing Sheila. Frank had gone along with Andrea's gag. Where would he place her body? Where would they ditch her car? How could they make it appear the killer originated from one of her trysts from their open marriage? But it would never happen. Harmless banter, really. Well, at least as far as Andrea was concerned.

Still, Frank felt he had more than gotten the message across. And he knew once the news of Sheila's disappearance hit the streets, Andrea would be smart enough to figure it out. And she would be 100 percent behind him.

As Frank's grip twisted to the right and tightened around Sheila's neck, her reaction surprised him. There was no screaming, gasping, flailing, or even pleading. Instead, she went into battle mode. She grabbed his arms with both hands and attempted to dig her nails in.

He released his grip on her throat before her nails could penetrate and grabbed her below the armpits. Frank shoved her against the living room wall. Her head hit with a thud, shaking every vertical structure. Two family pictures crashed down, glass cracking in the frames but not shattering. Dazed, she jumped to her feet and attempted to lift her right knee into Frank's groin. His left thigh absorbed most of the shock, although he felt some residual pain in the targeted area.

In full military training mode, Frank shoved her back into the wall with his left hand and struck her squarely in the throat with his cupped right hand. The fleshy area between his thumb and forefinger thrusted into her larynx. She looked into Frank's eyes, gasped, and crumbled to the floor.

Frank straddled his unconscious wife, placing both hands around her neck. He strangled her for a full two minutes. After detecting what might have been an exhalation, he continued the assault for another minute.

Until she was 100 percent, unequivocally dead.

On the side of his right arm, near his triceps, Frank felt a burning sensation and noticed a dime-sized portion of skin missing, possibly a rug burn from the struggle.

Not a good injury, but one that could be easily explained. He worked most of his time in the warehouse of the superstore. So many things can happen in that setting.

He inspected his forearm for scratch marks. The area was a little red, but none of his skin was broken. Thank goodness he had released that first chokehold.

He glanced at Sheila again, blue-faced, dress torn, lying on the floor with her hands outstretched. She'd never spend one dime of his mother's inheritance.

Thankfully, no blood was spilled. Not a drop. Cleanup would be a lot easier now. He was aware of what police investigators could do with Luminol, a substance that lights up blood spills like the Vegas strip.

He'd simply need to remove Sheila's body and ditch the picture frames. Like he'd described to Andrea, Sheila's car would "arrive" in a tattoo shop parking lot to make it appear that one of her trysts had turned deadly.

Frank left Sheila on the living room floor as he backed his car into the garage. He placed the body - wrapped in an old gray sheet he found in the attic - in the back seat.

He planned to drive to a remote area near the city of Youngstown. Frank nearly forgot to leave his cell phone at home for the journey. *I'm a dolt. I should roll up my sleeve for the injection now.*

When Frank reached his destination, he felt like someone was following him. Logically, this didn't make sense, but he couldn't shake the feeling. He pulled onto a semi-hidden dirt road that led to a decrepit white farmhouse.

Perhaps Old McDonald died, and the place wasn't up for sale yet.

Once Frank was certain no one was around, he lifted Sheila's body out of the car and walked several hundred feet to a densely wooded area. He wasn't sure if he was still on Old McDonald's property.

The entire experience was becoming too surreal in his mind. He carried the body of a woman he'd been married to for 14 years through a now misting rain toward an embankment. Frank's heart raced, and he found it difficult to breathe. He needed to focus his mind on something that would keep him sane. He had to block everything out of his mind except one thought.

Andrea.

If he got away with this, he and Andrea would keep everything – the house, all the money in the bank account, Frank's inheritance, and 100 percent of his retirement. Even Sheila's car would be returned to him, and he was pretty sure there was a life insurance policy of at least $50,000. He looked to the future because thinking about the present was unfathomable.

He heard his feet angle down the embankment. Was he far enough in the woods where no one would notice him? Yes, he was sure of that. He made one final check by swiveling his head in all directions. Once satisfied that he was in the clear, Frank rolled Sheila's body toward the bottom of the hill.

Midway, her body became stuck. Perhaps there was a rock underneath her. He couldn't be sure.

He picked his way down the slope and - using the strength of his sizable arms and chest - sent her rolling. During her bumpy descent, the sheet came away from her face. Frank could see Sheila's formerly closed eyes had opened.

Was his mind playing tricks, or was she smirking, albeit subtly? Was she mocking him from the bottom of the hill?

He needed Andrea here with him. Right now. She would tell him everything would be okay. She'd remind him about their future life together. And she would tell him - in no uncertain terms - that Sheila's eyes staring at him from the bottom of the ravine was simply a coincidence. Pure happenstance.

God, he needed Andrea so much.

Frank wished he had time to at least cover Sheila's smug face to let her know that *he* finally had the last word. Eventually, the ravages of time would take care of Sheila. No one would discover her out here for a long time - if ever. The maggots and other creatures of decay would wipe the grin off her face soon enough.

Frank climbed back up the hill and made the five-minute walk back to his car, relieved that nobody had pulled into the driveway behind him. As far as he could tell, no one in the world knew he was there. Everything had gone according to plan.

CHAPTER 2

Not guilty.

The verdict from the Frank McBride trial reverberated through the Walsh County police station where detective Sydney Livingstone had just begun her new career as a police detective.

At 8 am Monday morning, on a cloudy day in mid-May, acting Police Commissioner Ed Lasek addressed his officers. Sydney knew it was Lasek's first meeting as the department head. With graying hair and thick-rimmed glasses, she thought he bore a slight resemblance to Dustin Hoffman in his later acting years. His gray-and-white pinstriped suit seemed somewhat outdated.

"If I could have your attention," said Lasek, scanning the room. The rumbling quickly died down.

"As I'm sure you've already heard, McBride was acquitted last week in Green Haven. I felt the evidence was substantial, but the defense attorney successfully planted a seed of doubt in the jury's mind."

Several officers shook their heads in dismay.

"Juries have minds?" interrupted Detective Tom Mitsoff. "I might beg to differ." He looked around, grinning. Sydney watched Captain Wilma Griffith roll her eyes while she maintained a neutral expression. "You can make fun of juries all day long," said Lasek. "But keep in mind that the investigation was botched from the get-go by the Green Haven Police Department. And while this wasn't our investigation, I feel that we all can learn a lesson from their shoddy investigative work.

"The prosecutors were dealt a crappy hand from the very beginning of the case. Their hands were tied because the investigators on the scene did not do their jobs correctly. Over the next few months, we are going to review Green Haven's actions in this case, from start to finish. Be prepared to put in some late hours in the next few months."

A low groan reverberated.

"We must make sure that we process evidence correctly, interview the right witnesses, and use the resources that we have. This guy, McBride, is now free to walk among us, although we all know he probably killed his wife and dumped her body like a stinking bag of trash. I can assure you, Walsh County will not make the same mistakes as Green Haven."

Lasek shot Mitsoff a look, then stacked his papers against the podium. He walked back to his office without another word.

The rest of the meeting was neutral. Police Chief Delvin Pratt took over for Lasek, going over the assignments of everyone in the division. Reports of a peeping Tom in the south side of town were increasing, despite a neighborhood watch. A reserve generator was stolen from the back side of Lipscomb Corporation on Blair Street. And someone was entering garages in the east end, stealing beer from residents' refrigerators, and leaving the empty cans behind.

"Hey, Livingstone, how's that beer case going?" Once again, Mitsoff.

"Maybe if you can crack that case, we can assign you to something a little less important. I think someone's been removing tags from mattresses in department stores."

Syd felt her heart quicken as several officers chuckled. She was surprised to see Sergeant Stu Montenegro among them. She had thought they were becoming friends, at least as far as a friendship can develop during one week of working together.

"That's enough," said Pratt, shaking his head. "But since you're so chattery today, Mitsoff, I have a question for you. Are you still seeing that little red-haired girl or have you decided to…"

Pratt cupped his ear and waited for the congregation to finish his sentence. They all replied in unison. "Keep your mitts off."

The room exploded in laughter. Syd smiled, feeling somewhat vindicated, although Montenegro's initial reaction still stung. She still wasn't sure if the ribbing she received was a sign of acceptance or something else.

Getting through the police training academy proved difficult for Syd, despite her former career as a professional tennis player. As a well-conditioned athlete, Syd had expected to breeze through the academy. But the 800 hours of training in six months made her appreciate the dedication it takes to become a police officer. Besides the physical requirements of weight training, running, and martial arts, Syd had to become proficient with firearms, de-escalation techniques, and non-lethal apparatuses such as tasers and pepper spray. She even had to endure a taser shot from another recruit, an event she hoped to never experience again.

The most difficult part of the academy was the extreme lifestyle change. Pro tennis had been physically and mentally challenging. But she enjoyed the flexibility. You could adjust your sleeping habits to your lifestyle - practice early, in the middle, or late in the day. You could decide which tournaments you wanted to enter and which ones you wanted to forgo. If you weren't getting along with your coach, you could terminate them and find another.

The academy turned Syd's once-flexible world upside down. She went to bed and woke up at designated times. She ran, lifted weights, and fought hand-to-hand at a time and place chosen by someone else. She even ate and used the bathroom at a time of someone else's choosing. For six months, she'd given up control of her life. And it wasn't easy.

As the others filed out of the meeting, Syd flipped over the yellow page on her writing pad to reveal a fresh one. She penned a note to herself.

Research the Frank McBride case.

Syd had lived in the area long enough to understand that this was a town with few secrets. Something told her the Frank McBride story was far from over.

CHAPTER 3

T he feeling of being followed.

Frank McBride knew that feeling well after serving overseas in Afghanistan for two years. If serving in hostile enemy territory did anything to you, it made you constantly look over your shoulder.

Despite what he had said in media interviews after his trial, Frank was surprised by the verdict. He had admitted to police that he was home at the time police estimated that Sheila disappeared. Police took photos of the rug burn on his right triceps early on in their investigation.

"I'm always working in the warehouse," he told the police, "Carrying boxes, loading trucks, and loading pallets. This injury is mild compared to what I'm used to."

The jury didn't seem impressed either way by Frank's injury. Sure, it was odd that it appeared so close to Sheila's disappearance. But it certainly wasn't damning.

Frank's lawyer did a commendable job of creating reasonable doubt based on Sheila's affairs. Several witnesses had testified that she had returned home with men on several occasions.

The shoddy work of the Green Haven Police Department also played a major role in Frank's acquittal. They hadn't searched the house for several weeks after Sheila had been reported missing. By the time Sheila's body was discovered by a hunter fifteen months after her murder, it had been so well consumed by animals and the elements, there was no identifiable cause of death. The coroner could only list the cause of death as "Suspected Homicide."

The 'not guilty' verdict meant everything to both Frank and Andrea. They could now move forward with their lives. No more late-night trips to the police stations to answer questions that had already been asked hundreds of times. No more meetings with lawyers. And certainly, no press vans stationed outside his home. He was finally free.

Or so he thought.

The trip to Cypress Theme Park would hopefully be the beginning of a long and prosperous life for Frank and Andrea. They'd spend the day there before heading to their rented log cabin at Kellys Island State Park, where several bottles of champagne were being delivered. They would enjoy an evening of total freedom from everything that had burdened them for the past two years. While imbibing, they'd enjoy the whirlpool on the deck, which faced the scenic woods. They'd look up at the stars and discuss dreams of the future. And the next day would be open for parasailing, and maybe exploring local sites.

But Frank still couldn't shake the feeling of being watched. Hundreds of people scurried around him. He sensed a presence, though he saw nothing when he looked behind him. Perhaps it was the press trying to milk one final story about the troubled man who was fortunate enough to get away with murdering his wife.

Frank didn't mention the feeling to Andrea. If he had been 100 percent sure that someone was tailing him, he would have said, and they would have left. But Frank had been diagnosed with PTSD several years after returning from Afghanistan, so it was within the realm of possibility that he was imagining things. He needed a drink. That would calm him down and ease his paranoia.

Frank turned to Andrea and said, "Why don't we head out to Kellys Island now so we can begin celebrating? The longer we're here, the more I realize this place is for kids."

Andrea moved her short black hair away from her face and wiped a bead of sweat from her forehead. "But we were going to ride the big coaster. And you promised to win one of those big stuffed animals for me."

Frank looked around again but saw nothing. "I know I promised, but I'm looking forward to our time alone. Maybe we can come back tomorrow. We've got a week off, and we can do anything we please."

Andrea looked up at the gigantic roller coaster. "All right," she said with a smile. "But promise we'll come back tomorrow?"

"Promise," said Frank, wrapping his arms around her shoulders and kissing her on the mouth. "One quick bite at the food court, and then we're out of here. The champagne and hot tub are calling."

Surrounded by food vendors' stalls, Frank could no longer distinguish the aroma of greasy hamburgers from the coiled fried messes, stale coffee, light beer, and cotton candy. Instead, they melded into a smell of their own - the sweet, coppery scent of death.

In his mind, Frank had compartmentalized the murder of Sheila. She'd pushed him too far and had practically asked for it. Almost immediately after she had died, there was a sickening odor - subtle at first but growing the longer she remained with him. First, on the floor of his house, while wrapping her body in a sheet, then during the 30-plus minute drive in her car.

He hadn't thought about that smell in years, but now it surrounded him again. Maybe there was something to this afterlife thing. Was Sheila reminding him that she would never go away, at least not until justice had been served?

He looked over at Andrea, who was happily finishing a chili dog next to a side of circular, mangled fries. She was saying something about changing the drapes in the front window of her house, but Frank wasn't listening.

His hamburger looked nauseating. Even the idea of taking a sip of beer made him want to vomit. The smell was now all-encompassing.

A pair of young boys chased each other, darting between tables. One bumped their table, causing some of Frank's beer to spill.

"Undisciplined brats," he muttered. "Can you imagine what kind of adults they're going to be?"

Murderers? Spouse killers?

There goes Sheila again, funneling bullshit into my mind.

"We were all there once," said Andrea. "Just ignore them."

Frank smiled, wondering how Andrea wasn't overcome by the disgusting smell. "You know what, I'm not really hungry," he said. "I'm going to throw this stuff out."

Distracted by the unpleasant odor, Frank forgot about the possibility he was being followed. He fell into line behind two teenagers who were attempting to shove their trash inside an overflowing receptacle. The park seemed to be growing more crowded by the minute.

The park noises consumed Frank's thoughts. Ice cream machines revved crazily in a high pitch, barbeque grills hissed louder than usual, and soda machines buzzed. Kids squealed at their parents while nearby game operators hollered at customers to step forward and win prizes.

He glanced upward, noticing hot-air balloons in the distance, moving toward the theme park. They were decorated with bold, contrasting colors. The late afternoon sun cast its light onto them, creating a living rainbow of color in the open air.

Frank's eyes honed on one particular balloon, a white teardrop with silver accents and a printed logo. Four passengers waved cheerfully at everyone below. He struggled to read all the letters, but his mind was quick to fill in the gaps.

Murderer.

Frank was now trapped by the growing crowd. They jostled him, making it impossible to breathe properly. If he had the military sword that he found in Afghanistan, he could clear a five-foot radius around himself with a 360-degree swing. And what was that stinging sensation near his spine? Had a bee or wasp stung him? Or did someone accidentally jab him with a plastic fork?

But the stinging sensation was less noticeable than the

certainty that he was being taunted from the heavens by some bastard who had rented a hot-air balloon. How was that possible? Who would've even known he would be at this theme park at this exact time?

Frank saw Andrea walking toward him, carrying a hot-fudge sundae.

"Surprise!" she said. "I bought you a little treat. I figured maybe some ice cream would stimulate your appetite."

Andrea, he thought? *Of course. She was the only person who knew they were coming here today. But she would never betray him, would she? Andrea had stood steadfast by his side for two years. Had someone gotten to her? Was she gaslighting him so she could end up with everything? No, that couldn't be right.*

Andrea handed the ice cream to Frank. "Have some," she said. "It might make you feel better."

Why wasn't she looking skyward? Playing coy? Perhaps. But then again, maybe someone else was behind all of this.

Frank let the sundae fall out of his hands. It struck the ground, cracking its plastic container and oozing white and brown onto the concrete.

"Shit, Frank. I just paid seven bucks for that. What the hell are you doing?"

"Look up," said Frank. "That white-and-silver balloon to the west. Tell me what you see."

"Yeah, I guess it's nice," she shrugged. "They all are. Why are you acting so strange?"

"Read the message on the balloon," said Frank. "Tell me what it says."

Andrea squinted, looking upward.

"I don't understand why it matters, but I'll give it a go. Um - it appears to be a moving and storage company, I think.

Yes, 'Furderer Moving and Storage.' Now, why was that important enough to drop your ice cream?"

Furderer. Not Murderer?

Shit. In all the hullabaloo of the last several years, Frank had neglected to update his contact lens prescription.

"Andrea, I am so sorry," he said. "For some reason, I'm not feeling well."

Perhaps it was the combined smells of the food court, or maybe it was something else. The stinging sensation on his back was now more painful.

"I think I need to find a place to sit."

Andrea placed her hand on his shoulder and attempted to help him navigate through the tight crowd. In the distance, Frank could see a few vacant seats located around a water fountain. It looked inviting - water spraying upward in a fanning arc, sparkling in the sun's reflection.

He'd cool off near the fountain. Once he gathered his thoughts, they could leave and resume their romantic getaway. He grabbed Andrea by her outstretched arm and pulled her toward the fountain. When he was only steps away, Frank collided with a distracted man - holding four large translucent cups of beer - coming from the opposite direction. The impact caused the man to lose his balance, sending the cups tumbling out of his hand and onto the ground.

The man turned to Frank, his face red with anger. "Watch where you're going, asshole!" he shouted. "That's $36 of beer you spilled. You're either gonna pay me back or I'm going to kick your ass and take the money out of your wallet myself."

The stinging sensation seemed to be increasing by the second. He tried to focus on the man, but his vision blurred.

The man leaned in, transferring saliva into Frank's face as he continued his verbal barrage.

Frank understood the most logical solution would be to remain calm and pay the man for the spilled beer, especially after the last two tumultuous years. But between the insult and challenge to his manhood, Frank certainly wasn't going to back down now.

Frank's tormentor was about 6' 2" and would be fortunate to reach 160 pounds. He looked like someone who had experienced a few too many go-rounds with methamphetamines. With Frank's superior size and strength to go along with his hand-to-hand combat techniques, he knew he'd have this guy on the ground in a matter of seconds, begging for his life.

The man grinned, displaying two missing front teeth. His crooked nose had obviously been broken before. He sported a stained blue ball cap, a heavy-metal T-shirt, and his blue jeans displayed holes in the knees.

Andrea tugged at Frank's shirt sleeve. "Let's just go."

Frank moved closer. "I give you one free shot," he growled. "From that point on, I'm only defending myself."

Frank held his hands low. Even a direct shot didn't really concern him. He'd taken huge punches from some of the top instructors in the area during his martial arts classes. Surely, this guy wouldn't even come close to matching them.

Frank suddenly was seeing two images of the man in front of him. And then three. The world was rotating around him like a turbo-charged merry-go-round. He no longer was thinking about moving his head at the sight of an incoming fist. He couldn't focus his vision on any one thing. He could hear Andrea begging him to stop among the chats of a bunch of high school kids who were encouraging the other man to throw a punch. And the stinging pain in his back had become even more intense. He lost all feeling in his legs.

At the same time, the man barreled his head into Frank's face. He heard laughing from above him. Everything was a blur. And still, there was that stinging sensation in his lower back. He heard Andrea scream. And then, Frank lost consciousness.

CHAPTER 4

"Karma, Karma, Karma, Karma, Karma Chameleon!" Sergeant Stu Montenegro chortled as he slid into the Fourth Precinct, swaying hips from side to side and flexing both arms to display sizable biceps. He entered an open area - called the "bullpen" - where several officers were already seated at their respective desks. His booming voice, housed in a compact five-foot-eight frame, resonated from all four walls of the bullpen. Especially this morning, Montenegro appeared ruggedly handsome to Syd. An eight-year veteran of the department and just shy of 40, his wavy black hair showed no signs of graying or receding. A day's worth of beard growth made it appear that he wasn't concerned about how he was perceived.

The news had broken a few hours earlier about the assault on Frank McBride. McBride's heart wasn't beating when paramedics arrived at Cypress Theme Park, but resuscitation efforts yielded a faint heartbeat in the ambulance. At the hospital, he was placed on life support, with doctors offering little hope for any type of normal recovery.

Montenegro spotted Syd – who was trying not to react to his clamorous entrance - sitting in the second-to-last row. He took a seat to her left, saying, "Sleazebags like McBride may fool some of the public, and even jury members and judges. But eventually, they get what's coming. Karma, karma, karma."

A smattering of applause filled the room. Several officers commented on Montenegro's tirade.

"You're damn right."

"Douchebag got what he deserved."

"Justifiably FUBARed."

In her brief time as a Walsh County police officer, Syd had noticed there seemed to be something about the manner Montenegro talked about the McBride case that united everyone. There was something contagious about Montenegro's energy and enthusiasm.

Captain Wilma Griffith spoke from the front of the room. "Thank you for your input, Sergeant Montenegro, but technically, you are incorrect. The court doesn't deem anyone as innocent. But they may consider someone 'not guilty' if their culpability cannot be proven beyond a reasonable doubt."

Montenegro cleared his throat. "Captain, we all saw the evidence. It was overwhelming. If he didn't murder his wife, then I'm a red-headed Swahili boy. But as the old saying goes, 'Karma never loses an address.'"

Griffith raised both hands. "I'm going to clarify what's going on in case any of you haven't heard," she said. "It appears that Mr. McBride confronted the wrong person at a theme park," she said. "He is in McClinton Hospital now, battling for his life. The prognosis for recovery is grave."

One person clapped. And then another. Soon, the sound of applause dominated the room.

Syd scanned the room to see if anyone refrained from clapping. As far as she could tell, no one did.

After waiting for the room to quiet down, Griffith continued.

"While some in this room are probably pleased, we must conduct ourselves professionally. And as far as the law states, McBride is an innocent man who was now the victim of an attack."

Sighs and groans.

"He killed his wife and got away with it!" yelled Mitsoff from the second row. "Are we supposed to walk around sulking?"

Griffith shook her head. "We've all seen the evidence against McBride. But he was acquitted. He cannot be tried again. As law enforcement officers, we must abide by the law.

"The suspect in the assault of Mr. McBride is Rex Cutter, a local with a few items on his rap sheet, including a pair of DUIs, disorderly conduct, and a breaking-and-entering charge that was reduced to criminal trespassing. He's being held right now."

Griffith paused.

"I am assigning Montenegro - along with Detective Livingstone - to the McBride case. I have scheduled an interview with the suspect at 10 am tomorrow."

The room grew silent.

Syd tried to hide her surprise by feverishly scribbling notes on her pad. What role in the interrogation would she play? An active participant or a tag-along?

Despite her stellar performance at the police academy and her recommendation from then-Police Commissioner Bastille, interrogating a murder suspect was a far cry from pursuing beer-stealing juveniles. Still, she felt encouraged that upper management was placing their faith in her. Or were they?

Montenegro brushed Syd's shoulder and gave her a wink no one else could see. Syd's eyes scanned the room and met Mitsoff's. He shifted in his seat, shook his head, and began scribbling in his notebook. She could tell something wasn't sitting right.

CHAPTER 5

Gabriel Babson and his wife Bridget were on the brink of divorce. She had openly demanded change for nearly two years, but he could admit to himself he made no effort. Bridget had suggested marriage counseling, but Gabriel knew that nothing discussed in a counselor's office could solve any of the problems he'd created.

Gabriel had been a prick. He'd disrespected his mother-in-law, punched holes in the wall, and once destroyed their 100-gallon fish tank with a bar stool. And he drank too much every night - shots of whiskey paired with beer. But as far as Gabriel knew, Bridget had never guessed the truth about his behavior. His gambling addiction was controlling him. He had borrowed money from questionable individuals to finance outlandish bets. He lost most of the time, and the sharks were demanding payment. To make matters worse, he had forged Bridget's signature on financial documents, giving him access to her 401(k). Much of her money had vanished, and once the divorce process began, it would all come to light. Gabriel couldn't have that.

Someone was going to break his balls - either the loan sharks or his wife's attorney.

At this point, he could see only one option. Bridget would have an unfortunate accident. If everything went according to plan, the 401(k) would never even come up. He would be the beneficiary of his wife's insurance policy - nearly three-quarters of a million dollars. And all his current problems - both marital and financial - would be solved.

Gabriel begged Bridget to go on a rafting trip to the New River Gorge in West Virginia. "It's everything we need to rekindle the fire in our marriage. We'll rediscover why we fell in love in the first place." He was surprised when she agreed.

With its slow-moving rapids and long pools, the New River's 13-mile course was ideal for beginners. As it was late September, the water level was even lower than usual, and Gabriel bet it wouldn't attract many thrill-seekers. He was right. They had the course practically to themselves.

With only a couple miles left, he suggested a stop at an open area along the riverbank. He pulled a couple of wine spritzers from his backpack and winked at her. "We haven't seen anyone for hours. Let's take a romantic swim."

They ended up partially undressing in the waist-high water. Soon enough, they were entwined together in a powerful eruption of desire and longing. For a moment, Gabriel thought about abandoning his plan. If they could make love so passionately, why couldn't they work out their differences?

But as the lovemaking ended and his hormones returned to normal, Gabriel remembered the reasons for his plan. He'd dug too deep a hole, both with his wife and undesirable people. He had to move forward.

Bridget broke free from his grasp and began wading toward shore. Gabriel came up behind her, placing his arms around her waist. He pressed close and began to caress her.

She giggled, "Let's get back to the boat. Maybe we can be together again when we get home." She tried to wriggle free, but he tightened his grip.

She tried to turn to face him, protesting, "You're hurting me. I want to go to shore."

"No."

"What do you mean, no?"

"I mean, I'm not letting you go."

Now, Bridget really started to struggle. "Gabriel, please let go. What's wrong with you?" He held her tight. She kicked and thrashed. "WHY ARE YOU DOING THIS?!?" she screamed.

Gabriel was done talking. He wrapped his right forearm around her neck. She gasped as he pulled her head below the surface of the water. With the other hand, he reached and found what he was looking for: a large stone. He let go of her momentarily to get a firmer grip on the stone. As Bridget's head broke the surface, Gabriel brought the rock up and smashed it onto her head. A stream of blood flowed down her scalp. She tried to speak but could only gurgle.

Gabriel considered hitting her multiple times so that her pain wouldn't last. He wasn't enjoying watching her suffer. But he also knew that too many blows to the head would make it obvious to a medical examiner that a rafting accident hadn't been the cause of her death. He had to make his final blow count. He raised the stone high. Bridget's head cracked like someone took a hatchet to a frozen pond. Her body jerked, then went limp.

Gabriel towed Bridget's body further down the river into more turbulent waters and then let it go. Her lifeless form was carried downstream until it cascaded over a waterfall, tumbling against jagged rocks along the way.

Eighteen months later, Gabriel's lawyer - the confident and formidable Rebecca Woods - persuaded a worn-out jury of his innocence after three days of deliberation. In truth, she saved his life. Exoneration paved the way for a life insurance payout that helped him return to normal. He'd paid off some unsavory individuals, along with $15,000 in credit card debt. He'd sold their modest home and upgraded to a larger one in a better area of the city. He purchased a newer car and installed a modest, in-ground pool. And after an eight-month absence from work - due to incarceration - he was reinstated at his factory job.

THIRTY DAYS AFTER THE ATTACK ON FRANK MCBRIDE

Gabriel was certain he was going to make love tonight. After the last two years, he was ready.

Daphne Graham was new in town, a divorced mother of two. During the three hours they'd spent drinking together, Daphne told stories about two miscarriages and a heartbreaking divorce. Gabriel shared about losing Bridget, conveniently leaving out the details.

But Daphne wanted him. He would bet his life on it. He hadn't had sex with anyone but himself since that day on the New River, but tonight would be different.

Daphne mentioned that the kids were spending the night with friends and suggested he follow her home. She had given him the all-clear.

He watched her exit her car and stumble to the front door. When he reached her, she leaned in to kiss him, her body pressed tightly against his.

Whether their night together would become more than just a one-time deal, Gabriel couldn't care less. He was living in the moment. After making love, things would play out as they should.

As they kissed, Daphne turned her keys in the lock with her free hand, then pushed the door open with a shoulder. Gabriel stepped forward to follow her inside but met a firm right hand on his chest. "That's enough for tonight; thanks for a great evening."

As he heard the deadbolt click, Gabriel stood alone on the porch, feeling frustrated, betrayed, and extremely hard.

He fumbled with his car door, hoping that no one had seen him through their windows. Her perfume and the taste of her lipstick still clung to him. He had spent hours listening to her stories and life ambitions with no payoff at the end. He clutched the steering wheel in a death grip with his left hand while slamming his right fist against the dashboard, causing it to crack. From inside the glove compartment, he retrieved three antidepressants and swallowed them without water.

If he hadn't been so consumed with rage, he might have noticed a black sedan pulling behind him as he drove away from Daphne's home.

Once back at home, Gabriel popped a lorazepam and let his saliva dissolve it into nothingness. If he could wait only five or ten minutes, he'd begin to feel the effects. But the angry energy was still there. He spotted an old computer tower that he'd stuffed into a corner after it stopped working. He raised it over his head and sent it crashing onto the white and gray linoleum tile. Pieces exploded across the floor.

No harm, no foul. He didn't need defective equipment anyway.

Little prick-tease.

Gabriel reminded himself to breathe. The lorazepam was beginning to work, but not fast enough. He stared at the bottles of bourbon sitting on his kitchen counter, then found his favorite - a half-empty handle of Bulleit 10 - and poured himself a double shot. Usually, he threw in a couple of ice cubes, but not today.

Bulleit 10 didn't burn the back of his throat like cheaper brands. He filled the shot glass again and tossed back another.

He stared at the empty glass in his hand and tossed it into his kitchen sink, shattering it.

"Who needs a glass when you've got a bottle?" he muttered, grabbing the container by the neck and flopping on his living room recliner.

Within a few minutes, the bottle now held a few ounces of backwash, and he struggled to watch a televised hockey game between the Avalanche and Penguins.

Several scoring opportunities were squandered, and a nasty fight broke out on the ice. Slowly, the room started to spin, causing Gabriel to keep one foot on the floor.

Maybe he was going to be sick. Maybe not.

"Damn, Penguins. Put the puck in the bitch-ass net!" he mumbled.

With the Avalanche increasing their lead to 4-1 midway through the third period, Gabriel clicked off the television and headed toward his bedroom. After vomiting in the bathroom, he decided to soak in a hot bath.

As the tub neared capacity and he bent to turn off the water, Gabe felt a shadow in the doorway behind him. He thought he heard muffled footsteps.

Had he locked the door behind him? He couldn't remember. Could it be Daphne? Had she changed her mind and followed him home? Would she surprise him by coming around the corner?

Hell no. It's the bourbon and the drugs. Playing tricks on me.

Gabriel took another minute to listen intently. There was nothing except perhaps his crazy Imagination.

He scrubbed himself all over with soap, first his upper body and then the lower, imagining what would have happened if Daphne had let him in the door. He thought of her sweet smile and curvaceous body. Yes, Daphne would've been just fine.

As Gabriel leaned his head back, something in the mirror above the sink caught his attention. It appeared to be a raised arm, covered in a black sleeve. An echo stirred in his memory of his own hand raising, gripping a river stone.

A stone? No. The bathroom light was reflecting off it.

Damn! It's something metal.

The object was on its way downward, in the direction of his head.

It all had to be a hallucination. The alternative was too frightening to fathom.

CHAPTER 6

S yd hoped to interview Cutter after Montenegro, who had interrogated nearly a hundred suspects during his time with the department.

Montenegro placed his gun on a table outside the interview room and prepared to go inside.

"I'll rock this sonofabitch's world," he said. "By the time I'm done, he'll welcome you with open arms. If he tells us everything, there'll be no need for you to interview him. But I don't expect that."

She watched Cutter through the one-way glass, sitting alone at a table large enough for four. He fidgeted while chewing on dirty nails. He squinted at the glass as if to penetrate the barrier.

"What are you trying to get him to say?" asked Syd. "The report said there were plenty of witnesses."

Montenegro moved toward the door of the interview room. "I need to find out if this was really a random confrontation. Maybe he was targeting McBride all along."

Montenegro examined himself for a moment in the reflective glass.

"But something else is bugging me. How did a twerp like Cutter beat up a strong guy like McBride?"

"Maybe he's trained in MMA or something," said Syd.

"Just the opposite," said Montenegro, peering at Cutter. "McBride learned hand-to-hand combat in the service. He trains at a martial arts academy in Canton. All that came out during his trial. Definitely not someone to mess with."

Syd glanced back at Cutter. He did not appear strong or physically intimidating. "If you can't get anything out of him, I'm not sure what I can accomplish."

"Let's see how it goes," said Montenegro as he cracked the door open. "We'll try the good cop, bad cop routine. You know which one I'll be."

Montenegro's initial politeness during the interview turned to anger and finally to borderline physical intimidation. But Cutter offered only vague responses.

"Don't know."

"Never met him before."

"Barely touched him."

"Not my fault."

The door to the room swung open and Montenegro exited, shaking his head.

"Ten minutes I'll never get back. The asshole is acting like he's got no skin in the game."

Syd placed a folder inside her tan leather briefcase and picked it up by the handle.

"Let me see what I can do," she said, rising from her seat.

Montenegro, still standing in front of the door, shook his head. "No. Don't go in there. I don't like his vibe."

Lasek, who had also been watching the interrogation,

spoke. "Sergeant Montenegro, I think you should let Detective Livingstone interview the suspect."

Syd and Montenegro briefly looked at each other.

"We haven't gotten any real information, so how could it hurt? I'd be interested in seeing how she does."

Montenegro pulled up a seat next to Lasek. "It's your call, Chief but I don't think he's going to give us anything. And there's something about him…"

"I'll be okay," said Syd. "I'll befriend him. Maybe he'll open up."

Montenegro shrugged as Lasek gave her a nod to proceed. Syd opened the door and entered the room. Cutter was oblivious, still staring at the floor.

Syd took a seat across from Cutter and placed her briefcase on the table. She pulled out a pen and a notepad and began writing. Cutter didn't look up.

"Hi, Rex. My name is Syd Livingstone. I'm a detective here."

Cutter grunted.

"You've been through a lot," said Syd. "I can only imagine how hard this must be."

Cutter shrugged.

"But I'm here to help you, Rex. I want to get to the bottom of all this."

Cutter finally looked up. He peered at Syd. Nearly a minute passed.

"I didn't mean to hurt him," he said. "It was all a mistake.

Syd noticed three cameras located throughout the room. She knew all activities - every move, every word - were a part of the permanent record, subject to scrutiny from supervisors like Lasek and Pratt. And, in time, Cutter's defense team would have access to the tape. One day, it might be presented to a jury.

He was beginning to trust her, it seemed. She didn't want to make a mistake now. She felt a heaviness in her chest. The smell of perspiration, probably Cutter's, permeated the room. The odor nauseated her, making it even more difficult to breathe. She was sure she would vomit, with the act permanently on record. She could imagine Mitsoff's reaction.

Great job, Hurl Girl.

Well done, Detective Blow Chow.

A single drop of sweat - originating from the bottom of her hairline - trickled down the length of her spine. She shivered, hoping Cutter hadn't noticed. She felt a heartbeat in her temples. She didn't need a migraine now as she was beginning to break through.

Syd had played the mental game before. You can't compete in tennis without being mentally strong. But this was a different game. A blatant mistake now might allow Cutter to beat the charge on a technicality.

"I believe you didn't injure him on purpose. You seem kinda rough, but I sense a good heart."

Cutter looked up from the table slowly.

"It was an accident," he said, adjusting his shackled feet. "I didn't even hit the guy with a good shot."

Cutter leaned toward Syd.

"It was a little fight. Tempers flared and it was over quickly. I didn't mean to hurt him."

He closed his eyes tightly and sobbed. "I've heard that he might die. Is that true?"

When Syd hesitated, Cutter cradled his head and placed it on the table. He reminded her of a little boy attempting to appease his mother.

"Do you know if the guy's okay? I need to know."

Syd glanced back at the glass behind her but could only see reflection. "Rex, listen. I'm not sure about Frank McBride's condition - at least as of now."

Cutter raised his head from the table. "You said 'Frank McBride'? Wait. *the* Frank McBride?"

Syd paused and then glanced at the reflective glass. "Yes, that's right. You didn't realize?"

"The guy who waxed his wife and then got off. I never put it together. Is that why they were asking if I knew him?"

Syd shook her head. "Did someone hire you to assault him?"

"Hell no! I ain't no hit man. I work on cars, period."

"Are you friends with any family members of Sheila McBride?"

"Hell no. Never met any of them before. But I see what you're doing. You want to charge me with murder - the premeditated kind. Am I right?"

Syd remained silent.

"I asked you a question."

The intensity of Cutter's face and his raised voice made her even more nervous.

"As far as I know, no one has died," she said, omitting the fact that McBride's prognosis wasn't promising. "I just want the truth."

Cutter slammed both fists on the table and propelled himself upward.

"He's dead, isn't he? And you're not telling me."

Syd pulled back. "Rex, I never said McBride died."

Her stomach churned. She wanted to rewind and start the interview over.

"I know what's going on here. I get into a shoving match,

and some local dude dies. And now you want to charge me with premeditated murder. Well, bullshit. I don't kill for money. It just happened."

On the other side of the glass, Montenegro moved toward the door.

"I can't let her continue. He's erratic as hell."

Lasek grabbed Montenegro by the arm. "Give her another minute."

"I'm only trying to get answers," said Syd. "And McBride's still alive."

Cutter was now pounding on the table with both fists. He wasn't listening. "You guys have the resources to send me down the river, while I can't even pay my rent. But I ain't going down."

Syd stood up across the table from Cutter and placed her hands on his shoulders.

"I'm not accusing you of murder," she said. "I'm only trying to find the truth."

"Yeah, I get it," said Cutter. "And those answers will put me in the electric chair."

This is spiraling out of control. Where's Montenegro?

"No, no, no," said Syd, her arms still on Cutter's shoulders. "I am only exploring the possibility-."

Cutter placed both hands over his temples, like his head was about to explode. Then, his right hand darted toward the holster on her right hip.

Oh shit! Why did I bring my gun in here?

She attempted to push Cutter away, but she could feel the firearm slipping out of its holster. A moment later, it was in Cutter's hand, pointing at her head. His eyes were wide, his right hand shaking.

"I'm not going down alone," he said. "You're going with me!"

Lasek stood up quickly from his chair outside the interrogation room, unaware that his upward momentum had caused it to crash down behind him.

"She brought her fucking gun in there with her? What the hell. Montenegro?"

"I don't understand," said Montenegro, rising from his chair. "She watched me peel off my gun before I went in.

She's wearing a blazer. I didn't see it. I assumed-" Then his voice trailed.

Lasek stared at the glass. "This is now a life-and-death situation. Someone let Pratt know what's going on. And let's notify the emergency response team. This is spiraling out of control."

CHAPTER 7

It was four hours into the standoff, but time seemed to stand still for Syd, who was now in the chair with Cutter behind her, a gun to her head.

Montenegro had tried to enter at first, but Cutter placed the gun to Syd's temple and ordered him to leave. In the last two hours, Montenegro and Lasek had tried to negotiate with Cutter from behind the one-way glass enclosure. "Let Syd leave," Montenegro spoke through a microphone. "Then I'll come in - unarmed - so we can talk."

Cutter glanced down at her. "Hell no! She's my leverage. It's not my fault you decided to send a green chick with a gun in a room to interrogate me. That's on you."

Syd slid her tongue along the roof of her mouth but couldn't generate any moisture. Her mouth had gone dry seconds after Cutter had stolen her firearm. She coughed and gagged.

"I think this pretty lady needs a drink, and so do I," said Cutter. "It's damn hot in here."

Syd remembered hearing about this tactic in training.

They must have turned up the heat in the room from 72 to 80 degrees.

"I need two cans of soda right now," said Cutter. "And don't even think about bringing any of that diet shit in here.

"What'll you have, little lady?"

"Water, please. With half a lemon."

Cutter was now grinning, his eyes wide and alert. "If this high-society chick wants a lemon, then someone better bring her one. It might be her last request."

Pratt held a towel on his forehand to absorb perspiration. "I can't understand how this happened. But we'll deal with those details later."

He looked toward Montenegro, who had emerged from a back room with two colas and a bottle of water. "Can you sneak a gun in and disable him? Without anyone getting hurt?"

"Not going to be easy," said Montenegro. "If Cutter pats me down, the gig's up. He may turn his rage toward Syd." He placed the drinks on the table. "I'm waiting for someone to cut a lemon and bring it to me. It might be a few minutes."

Several detectives had slipped into the room after the standoff began, including Mitsoff. "Seriously?" he said. "Maybe you should ask Syd if she needs a pillow and a mint, too."

"It's the Mojave Desert in here," shouted Cutter. "And I'm running out of patience."

Pratt stared at Cutter through the glass. "The situation's deteriorating. Montenegro, bring in the drinks and forget about that damn lemon."

Montenegro looked at Syd. Her eyes were closed as she took slow breaths. "I think we should give her exactly what she asked for, chief."

Pratt considered. "We've waited over four hours. I guess we'll wait for the lemon."

Cutter, sweating profusely, scooted closer to Syd. The room reeked of perspiration when Syd first walked in.

Now, she discerned an additional tang of adrenaline and cortisol.

She noticed Cutter fumbling with her beloved 9mm Glock. How could she have been so careless? The thought about dying by her own weapon made her even more sick.

"Where the hell is that drink?" Cutter barked, "I know you're all watching. If someone doesn't bring me something to drink in about 30 seconds, pretty little blondie is going to take one in the knee."

A voice came over the microphone. It was Pratt's. "We're working on it, Cutter. We're slicing Detective Livingstone's lemon right now."

"We're dying of thirst and you're asking for a bitchin' lemon," said Cutter. "Just like a woman."

There was a knock, and the door opened slowly. Montenegro appeared with a strained smile. "I come bearing refreshments. Nothing like a cool drink to go with some nice conversation."

Cutter pressed the gun against Syd's temple. "Put the shit down and get out, Sergeant Montezuma, or whatever the hell your name is. I'm working with Miss Pretty here to come up with a list of demands. You guys ain't pinning a murder rap on me."

After Montenegro vacated the room, Cutter moved the pistol. "I need you to take some mental notes. We're busting out together."

"Okay," said Syd evenly. "But while we're drinking, tell

me about what happened in that amusement park. McBride is solid as a rock. I know you couldn't have beaten him up."

Cutter stared at Syd. "I ain't no wuss, missy. I can hold my own, but there's no way I killed that guy. I told ya - somethin' ain't right."

Cutter closed his eyes, still clutching the firearm tightly. When he opened them, Syd noticed tears. He swayed in his chair. For the first time, he appeared vulnerable - even frail. He looked like he might melt into the floor.

"I've been in hundreds of fights. Won most, lost a few. But this one could send me down. I don't know what happened."

"You never meant to hurt McBride," said Syd, watching his trembling hand clutch her gun. "And I don't think you want to hurt me or anyone else."

Cutter opened the first can of cola with his free hand and downed it in three gulps. He let out a burp that reverberated throughout the room. "I thought there was a real chance I'd get my ass kicked. But the guy crumbled like a sandcastle."

Syd liked the fact that he was opening up, but felt he could turn at any moment. "Rex, I'll help you. You're not going down because you got into a fight."

Cutter sat high in his chair. He placed the gun on the right side of the table, away from both of them.

Syd unscrewed her water bottle. She palmed the cut lemon and held up her hand toward the two-way glass. On the other side, Montenegro's eyes grew wide.

The last thing Cutter remembered before losing consciousness was a stinging sensation to his eyes, a powerful blow to his face, and a rather pleasant fragrance of citrus.

CHAPTER 8

The name 'Enforcer' sounded cold and unsympathetic. But members of the RealVigilante site on the dark web are tough and judgmental. Appear weak and you're inviting scorn and ridicule. And no one will share their information.

The moniker 'The Enforcer' seemed to resonate. Some even began referring to The Enforcer as 'Big E'. And The Enforcer never revealed their gender, but most seemed to assume a guy was behind the posts. And that was fine.

Next to a cup of tea to fuel the creative juices, The Enforcer began to type.

```
Babson perished face-down…his brains
mixing with bath water. I know because
I was there. He made a crucial mistake
- not locking the door to his own
house. Criminals are a stupid bunch.
    Someone who's not gone is the
reprehensible Frank McBride - although
```

reports about his condition indicate he won't be alive for long. I spent hours following him in that park, waiting to strike. Whether I performed my job well remains to be seen. Depends on if he lives or dies.

I thought terminating someone who committed such a heinous crime would be satisfying, but it wasn't enough. I'm not a killer by nature, but someone's gotta bring justice.

This is what happens when people skirt the rules of our unjust system. As long as I'm alive, they will receive their deserved punishment. Maybe someone reading these lines will take my place when I'm no longer here. Could it be you? For now, just watch and learn. After all, there is MORE 2 COME.

CHAPTER 9

Syd even calculated the math in seconds - 1,209,600 of them.

The uncompensated suspension levied by Pratt, Lasek, and a reluctant Griffith was meant to serve both as a penalty as well as a time of self-reflection. Was she cut out to be a cop? Is this how she wanted to spend the next two decades of her life?

Going into the meeting with her higher-ups, Syd felt like a criminal facing the sharp blades of a guillotine. But at the conclusion, she felt more like someone who had just had an arm amputated - without anesthesia. They had all agreed that Syd should serve a 14-day suspension for conduct that "endangered her life, as well as the lives of her fellow officers."

Lasek's words reverberated in her brain. "You put yourself - and this entire department - in great danger. But your decisive action defused the situation. You have the potential to be a good cop, but another mistake like that will cause you to be terminated."

At a coffee shop a few hours after the meeting, Montenegro insisted, "You're going to land on your feet. You'll be back at work before you know it, and you can put this entire thing behind you."

But the suspension would be a part of the public record and there certainly would be a newspaper story about it.

When she told him about the situation on the phone, Syd's fiancé Enzo Martin cut short his participation in a tennis tournament to fly in. Walking in the door to her apartment, he put his arms around her, and she buried her face in his shoulder. "Not only did I disgrace myself, and the department, I cost you thousands in prize money," she wept. He spent three days with her before flying out, during which she poured out her soul and wallowed in self-pity.

After Enzo's departure, Syd decided she needed to stay active for the sake of her mental health.

She wouldn't have to worry about the perils of unemployment…at least for the time being. And she had a project from Pratt, who remained rigid in the presence of Lasek but had pulled her aside after the meeting. "You made a rookie mistake," he'd said. "But, off the record, we may have exposed you to a dangerous situation too early. Take this time off to recover and gather your thoughts. I'm confident you'll come back strong."

Syd was surprised to find him so understanding. But perhaps he was better at relating to women than Lasek. Closing the door to his office, he had said, "Since you're going to have some time on your hands, I'm going to give you something to keep you from going stir crazy."

Pratt handed Syd an envelope. "We'll categorize this as

volunteer work, performed off-the-record. My hunch is you won't find anything, but I'd like you to check it out."

"What is this?"

"Dark web chatter," he said. "I've included some sites that mentioned our precinct. Probably bullshit, but it's worth checking if you have time. Nothing mandatory."

"Why is this important?"

Pratt lowered his voice. "Some things have come out in the media that were internal to the department. If someone is leaking information, I'd like to know who. The info was leaked prior to you starting here, so I know I can trust you. But again, totally voluntary."

Syd stuffed the envelope in her coat pocket. "I'll see what I can do."

She nodded and turned for the exit.

"One more thing," said Pratt. "Lasek wants you to work under Mitsoff when you return. It's mostly administrative, but I need you to perform well. At least for the time being, you're going to be under a microscope."

With Enzo home for the first three days of her suspension, Syd had little time for anything except focusing on their suddenly troubled relationship. While no date had been set, they'd planned to marry next year. During this visit, most conversations turned into a debate, which often escalated into a fight.

Their relationship had survived a major crisis several years ago when Syd had been stalked by a maniacal killer during her final year on the pro tennis tour. Barely emerging with her life, Syd felt closer to Enzo than she had to anyone. With their financial struggles now behind them, they had envisioned a lifetime together. Once he retired from competition, they would start a family, and Syd would settle into a secure position in law enforcement, hopefully rising to the ranks of lead investigator or even police chief.

After Enzo had rushed home to be with her, Syd sensed that something had changed. Before he left, they agreed that a cooling-off period would be best. With Syd home on suspension, Enzo could focus on the next tournament without fearing for her safety. She would consider if she wanted to remain a police officer. If she decided to stay, Syd knew she'd have to determine whether their relationship was salvageable.

Now, as she sat on the couch nursing her third glass of wine, Syd watched a police press conference on the television. Lasek stood in front of a podium in a tiny side room inside the Walsh County Courthouse. By the look of the room—dusty tables stashed in a corner, dirty scuff-marked floors, and a portable chalkboard with writing from a past day—it had been hastily thrown together. Behind Lasek stood Pratt and Griffith.

The first question came from Canton Tribune reporter Anisette Morgan: "Is it true, Commissioner Lasek, there's a vigilante killer in our community?"

Lasek held up his hands as if trying to create some distance from the question. Before he had time to answer, another voice jumped in. "Have you arrested a suspect yet?" Then the floodgates opened.

"Is Rex Cutter responsible?"

"Is Gabriel Babson's killer really a woman?"

"Is it true the killer left a message?"

Lasek cleared his throat loudly, his face stern. "Everyone, please sit down NOW." The room quieted. "Ladies and gentlemen, we've called this conference to address the rumors circulating between the public and the press about a so-called vigilante killer."

Syd saw Lasek squint as cameras clicked and flashed. He continued. "While the death of Gabriel Babson was tragic - as was the attack on Frank McBride - those attacks were totally separate occurrences. In other words, we have no reason to believe they were performed by a vigilante or serial killer."

Craig Todd, a young reporter at a local CBS affiliate, rose. "We've heard there was a message at the scene, tying the two attacks together. What exactly did the message say?"

Syd leaned forward. She knew everyone on the Babson scene was under orders to keep the message from the public. Someone had leaked it. Pratt had been right.

"I have no details on any message left by a suspect," Lasek said. "At this point, that is purely speculation."

Morgan stood again, a recorder in hand. "Is it purely speculation that two murder suspects who somehow 'beat the rap' were viciously attacked within the same week?"

"The incident with Mr. McBride was a spontaneous occurrence, not much different from a bar fight. It was simply a physical altercation between two men. And that event is totally unrelated to the apparent murder of Gabriel Babson, which we're still investigating. Any attempt to tie these two events together at this time would be speculative."

Groans erupted from the media. Another reporter called out. "What are you going to say when there's another attack of someone notorious? Will that also be a separate event?"

"Okay, that's all we have at this time," said Lasek. "Nobody can predict the future. We will update you immediately when we have more information on Gabriel Babson."

Lasek left the podium and headed toward the exit, with Pratt and Griffith following, ignoring additional questions.

Syd rose from the couch, turned off the television, and carried her wine glass to the kitchen table. She began to shuffle through the paperwork she sorted into stacks. Near the bottom of the second pile, she found what she was looking for—the envelope Pratt had given her.

She paused. Opening the envelope came with expectations - and meant breaking protocol. She was flattered that Pratt trusted her. She sensed that he respected her as a former world-class athlete. He once told her he saw something special in the way she conducted herself among her peers. He didn't view her as simply a beat cop. He had higher aspirations for her career.

Syd took another sip of her wine, still staring at the envelope. When she got back, she could return it, unopened. He said there was no obligation. Giving it back meant never knowing what he had in mind. But he might interpret that as betraying the trust he'd placed in her. He seemed like an ally - someone who could take her to the next level in the department.

Syd couldn't deny that the idea of taking matters into her own hands was enticing. She was a fighter, and she needed a win after the interrogation disaster. But she understood that acting outside of the law contained serious consequences.

No more thinking. Just do it.

She opened the envelope and removed its contents. No going back now.

Pratt had made it easy to know where to begin. A printed list of instructions was headlined with "Start Here" in large, bold type. She was told to access the dark web using a TOR browser, which stood for "The Onion Router." Three antivirus software programs were listed, asking her to choose one. She was asked to purchase a Virtual Private Network (VPN) to provide an even increased level of anonymity. There were also directions on how to select a dark web search engine such as "Torch" or "DarkSearch."

One final instruction on the sheet read as follows: "Cover your webcam with tape when the computer is not in use, in case a RAT device gets installed."

And then one PS: "Don't download from any websites."

CHAPTER 10

The Enforcer's email account was a mess. More than 9,999 unopened, but then, the 'Big E' - a nickname from other RealVigilante forum members - seldom opened unsolicited emails.

Cleanup would have to wait for another day. Today, The Enforcer had a different annoying weekly task. Might as well get it over with.

It was an outdated but reliable espionage trick. First, log on to your collaborator's email. Then go to the unsent drafts folder and read what you find there. That way, two parties can communicate without actually sending the message, which was less traceable if the shit ended up hitting the fan.

It was a complete waste of time, but they had agreed to do it. The first look, however, proved that today was different. The subject line read, "READ IMMEDIATELY!" The Big E nearly knocked over a cup of steaming coffee.

The sender got directly to the point with no salutation.

We agreed we're doing the right thing. But now I'm not sure. Someone's onto me. They know what I've done, which could lead them to you. I may have to go public, but I'll do everything in my power to leave you out of it. We need to meet soon.

Major buzzkill. Things had been progressing so well.

The Enforcer needed to buy time and responded with fast keystrokes.

Coffee at Starbuck's in a couple of days. Keep your mouth shut and ears open. Everything will be okay. Stay calm. Be patient.

That done, The Enforcer could dive back into the great escape of RealVigilante. Playing the role of Big E was stimulating, bordering on orgasmic. The forum wasn't replete with leaders, but there were plenty of followers.

A few familiar names on the chat were CreepBuster, JusticeFinder, and BoredChairman.

And a few unfamiliar ones…DipStick and RetroDude.

The Enforcer began typing.

First, an apology to Walsh County's finest for leaving a mess behind. You shouldn't be cleaning up carnage created by judges, juries, and lawyers who play a dangerous game of catch-and-release.

Second, kudos to everyone taking part in eliminating vermin in their parts of the country. We're all working for the common good.

In my backyard, a murderer is dead, another is dying. And there are More 2 Come.

The Enforcer

Not the best message ever, but not bad in a pinch.

The Big E resumed an internet search.

First, Morris Craybill. He lived with the body of his dead mother for two years, collecting and cashing her Social Security checks. Neighbors reported frequent arguing when she was alive. Tests on the remains couldn't determine if a homicide occurred, but the woman's friends were convinced. Craybill was convicted of fraud and abuse of a corpse, but not murder. His incarceration lasted only two years.

The Enforcer had a scale for each criminal, The "Wow Factor," based on accessibility, outrageousness of crime, and community impact. This one had a Wow Factor of 3 out of 10.

Next, Chloe Maynard, who had recently been granted a new trial after spending four years in prison for the murder of her husband, Rafael. He had been shot in the back of his head while sleeping, and she testified that she hadn't heard the intruder enter the bedroom due to a prescription sleeping aid. Several of Rafael's friends said that he planned to demand a divorce that same night. A judge approved the request for the new trial after determining a juror reviewed evidence not presented at the trial.

Wow Factor: 6/10.

Now, Penny Cefalo. She had used a gudao - a Chinese meat cleaver - to nearly decapitate her boyfriend, Derek Stovall. Cefalo admitted killing Stovall but claimed self-defense. Her ex-husband had been preparing to testify that she attacked him with a kitchen knife on two occasions, but the presiding judge deemed her history of domestic violence inadmissible. The prosecution presented evidence from

Coroner Pennington that Cefalo continued to hack away at Stovall for several minutes after he was dead. After three weeks of deliberation, the jury returned hopelessly deadlocked. The prosecution considered retrying the case, but never proceeded. One year after the non-verdict, Cefalo opened an axe-throwing entertainment business in Walsh County, causing widespread controversy.

Wow Factor: 10/10.

CHAPTER 11

"What do you mean you're not worried?"

Pratt's voice boomed from Syd's cell phone as it lay on her kitchen table, set on speaker mode. He had just phoned Syd to inform her of breaking news: Rex Cutter had been released on bail, confined to his home with an ankle bracelet.

"Chief, with all due respect, I don't think Cutter's going to hunt me down," said Syd. "He never intended to kill me."

She could hear traffic in the background. He was obviously calling from his vehicle.

"I wouldn't have guessed that when he held a pistol to your head," said Pratt. "He seemed like one desperate dude."

Syd clicked her phone off speaker mode, sensing Pratt might have been uncomfortable speaking freely. "I was terrified at that point. He doesn't strike me as a stalker though, just a reactive type. How did he manage to get released?"

Pratt scoffed. "He hired a slick defense attorney who convinced the judge to lower his bail to $100K, meaning

Cutter had to come up with half that amount. Somehow, he did it. Lasek says the judge is a liberal POS.

"Anyway, I'm telling you this because we can provide limited protection. We'll have a car cruise by your place often, even parking outside for several hours a day."

Syd thought for a moment about Pratt's offer. She was scared - terrified in fact. But not at the thought of a vengeful Rex Cutter lurking in the shadows. She was frightened by what she'd uncovered on the dark web - vigilantes like The Enforcer and others, crazy enough to take the law into their own hands.

"I feel safe in my own home," she said. "Chief, don't think because I turned in my service weapon, I'm unarmed. Believe me, I'm well equipped to protect myself."

Momentary silence. Then Pratt spoke. "I recommend protection, but I won't force it. But speaking of optional things, have you conducted any research?"

Syd spent the next ten minutes describing some of the data she'd uncovered on the dark web. Most specifically, details about someone calling themselves "The Enforcer."

Pratt didn't seem surprised. "So, this whacko encourages people to kill unpunished criminals? Do you think The Enforcer's legit, or just some blowhard vying for attention?"

"Seems to know a lot," said Syd.

"Have you communicated with The Enforcer online?" asked Pratt.

"No, I'm still feeling out the dark web," said Syd. "Would you suggest that I do?"

Pratt cleared his throat. "Don't engage until we devise a plan after your suspension ... which is rapidly coming to an end."

Syd felt the conversation was progressing toward small

talk, an area where she didn't feel comfortable. Something was on her mind. She might as well say it. "Chief, you suspected there was a leak in our department all along. How did you know?"

"It was Lasek," said Pratt. "He called everyone into his office who was at the Babson murder scene - Detective Kevin Fosterno, Griffith, Coroner Pennington, and I believe four technicians. He takes out his whiteboard and lists everybody by name. And then he writes the message left by the presumed murderer. Are you aware of that?"

"No."

"Well, apparently, the killer carved a message with a knife on the big screen TV. It read: '2 Down, More 2 Come.' Ring any bells?"

"The Enforcer has referenced the 'More 2 Come' phrase," said Syd. "Maybe The Enforcer put it out there after the murder."

Syd could hear Pratt sigh. "That's the weird part. Lasek, Griffith, and I monitored the dark web before the attacks began, keeping an eye out for potential criminals. I never took the vigilante talk seriously. Then, a day after the Babson murder, I received a call from a reporter asking me about the phrase 'More 2 Come.' She refused to reveal her source."

Her mind now in overdrive, Syd tried to make sense of this new revelation. "So, you're saying between you, Lasek, Fosterno, Griffith, and the technicians, one of them is the leak?"

"Who else?" said Pratt.

"The murderer?" asked Syd. "Assuming it's not one of us?"

"A murderer is taking a big risk approaching a reporter," said Pratt. "And no one else would have known about that message. The girl Babson hooked up with at the bar never left her own apartment. Griffith confirmed that."

"I talked to Montenegro after the murder. Wasn't there someone who found the body?" asked Syd.

Five seconds of silence. "True, she was at the scene. But she claims she saw the deceased and got her ass out of there. Never mentioned seeing a message."

"But she could have," said Syd. "And maybe she blabbed to friends. Now it's out there."

"You have good instincts," said Pratt. "Here's another angle. Do you think it's possible that someone in that room told another cop? And maybe he or she talked about it to someone on the outside?"

Syd nodded. "That could've happened."

"Okay," said Pratt. "And since we're theorizing, which cop in our precinct is most likely to talk to someone on the outside - based on their character?"

After a noticeable pause, Syd responded. "I'd hate to guess."

"C'mon, Syd. This conversation is between us. It's only a theory. Who?"

"I won't mention anyone's name," said Syd. "But it's not a T-M player." She paused. "My gosh, did I just say 'T-M player'? I meant to say, 'team player.'"

Pratt smiled. "Exactly the person I was thinking of. Keep your eyes and ears open. Again, this is a long shot."

Syd promised to contact Pratt immediately with anything new. He'd praised her regarding her instincts. Perhaps she was on the way to regaining a measure of respectability as a law enforcement officer.

After her conversation with Pratt, Syd's first instinct was to inform Enzo about Cutter's release, but she didn't want to worsen his already compromised mindset. Two more glasses of wine later, Syd decided to tell Montenegro.

"I already knew about Cutter," said Montenegro. "There's not enough room in jail anymore to house all the crazies. Hopefully, he'll be content staying home with his ankle bracelet, watching reruns of Family Feud. Are you worried?"

"Not particularly," said Syd. "I declined Pratt's offer of protection."

"You can stay with Stacey and me," said Montenegro. "We have a spare room. I'll make sure you're comfortable."

Syd could hear the couple whispering in the background. It was an awkward 30 seconds. She regretted calling him.

"Stacey's fine with that," said Montenegro, returning to the phone. "I can pick you up and bring you here."

Syd attempted to be diplomatic in her refusal. "I'm already on suspension, Stuart. If I run to the safety of a fellow officer and place another family in jeopardy, it'll make things worse."

They debated for several minutes while Syd emptied the remainder of the bottle into her glass.

"I'll be fine here," she said. "Pratt's given me plenty to work on."

There. She had said it. Was it because of the wine, or did she subconsciously want Montenegro to know?

After a brief pause, Montenegro responded. "What are you talking about? Pratt can't give any work to you. You're on suspension."

Syd placed her left hand over her mouth, but it was too late. She scrambled for words. "It's nothing. A verbal agreement. Off the record."

She could hear Montenegro's footsteps. It seemed like he was walking the phone into another room. "What did he ask you to do? Does anyone else know?"

She could end the call now with a click of a button. If he called back, she could ignore it. But she would never do that to Stuart.

"He asked me to explore the dark web, looking for people discussing the vigilante case. Nobody else knows."

Montenegro groaned. "Pratt's taking a big risk. I guarantee Lasek knows. Pratt doesn't do anything without checking with him."

Her face flushed, Syd sensed the potential for a panic attack. "Stuart, you can't tell anyone else. I shouldn't have called you while drinking."

"None of this is going anywhere," he said. "But now you'll have to keep me posted about what you find."

"Have you ever been there before - on the dark web?" she asked.

"I'm familiar with it. Going on isn't illegal unless you break the law. Our own government originally created it to allow spies to communicate. But you shouldn't do what Pratt's asking. You've been through enough."

It was too late to go back now. She'd already rung that bell. "I'll be careful," she said. "And remember, we never talked about this."

Syd's heart pounded as she hung up with Montenegro. The weight of Pratt's request and the dangerous territory she was delving into on the dark web were starting to consume her. She took a deep breath, trying to regain control of her thoughts and ignore the lingering uneasiness. Their conversation confirmed there was much more at stake than she'd first thought. Pratt's involvement, Lasek's knowledge - they all pointed to a network of secrets and deceit that stretched beyond Cutter and the vigilante case. Navigating the dark web would be treacherous, but if she could break the case, her efforts and Pratt's faith would be justified. And her reputation as a law enforcement officer would be all but restored.

CHAPTER 12

After several days of navigating the dark web, Syd felt as though she wanted to throw up…or at least take a hot shower. At first, she discovered sites offering discounts on products such as designer tennis shoes and handbags. She stumbled upon self-help pages, providing details on everything from "Becoming More Organized" to "How to Cure Acne."

More disturbing were pages soliciting drugs, fake prescriptions, firearms, and stolen credit cards. A hired killer was advertising their services to terminate anyone—from private citizens to prominent politicians. It was the human trafficking and other demented sites, however, that damaged her soul.

A young girl pleaded for someone to kidnap her. Another person advertised a book on how to cook human flesh. Someone else provided information on how to dismember and consume various parts of a woman's body.

As a detective, she wanted to track each individual and incarcerate them. But becoming the chief whistle-blower on the dark web wasn't what Pratt had in mind. She needed to uncover specific sites discussing the Walsh County police and the vigilante killer. Pratt had suggested several websites to peruse, along with some general instructions on search engines.

Using the term "police departments - Ohio" in her search engine, Syd sought to uncover whatever information was available on Walsh County. Many on the dark web professed an interest in protecting society from authority figures, with cops at the top of the list. Some wanted to defund police departments in their cities, while others advocated for firing - or even killing - police officers. The anti-police narrative was disturbing, but Syd felt these weren't the individuals who would promote ridding society of unpunished lawbreakers.

Revising her search to include words that aggrandized vigilantism, she uncovered several sites that discussed the ongoing situation in Northeast Ohio. Judging by the dates of the posts, none occurred before the attacks had begun. The only page where someone claimed to be the person committing the attacks was 'RealVigilante.'

Syd had a few concerns about The Enforcer's post. For one, they mentioned Walsh County as if it were their own backyard. It seemed strange for an outsider to make such a claim. Second, the information they provided was precise and could only be known by either the culprit or someone who had conducted a thorough investigation. And the data was current and precise.

In her training, Syd had studied people who confessed to crimes they didn't commit. Some were coerced under duress during interrogation. Others wanted to achieve notoriety. Neither seemed applicable here. Perhaps this was a crackpot, but she didn't think so. Perhaps they yearned for a justice the law-and-order system was incapable of delivering.

Syd found another Enforcer post from weeks earlier. It mentioned both McBride and Babson by name. Even more peculiar, it listed details about Babson's death that were never released— like the bloody bathwater and his failure to lock his front door.

Against her better judgment, she found herself dialing Montenegro from her personal cell. He answered on the third ring.

"So, you've changed your mind and decided to move in with us?" joked Montenegro. "Or is this an inadvertent butt-call?"

Syd cleared her throat. "You better be careful, or I'll report you for harassment," she said. "I only make butt-calls to Enzo."

"Oh Geez, I'm glad my wife isn't hearing this conversation. She could get the wrong idea. What's up?"

Syd stared at her computer screen. She had just taken snapshots of The Enforcer's posts in case someone made them disappear. "Somebody's on the dark web calling themselves 'The Enforcer.' They may have personal knowledge about the vigilante crimes."

"How do you know it's not some loon?"

"They know facts about Babson's murder. Stuff potentially only the murderer or an accomplice would know. Or…"

"I know," said Montenegro. "A cop."

Montenegro sighed. "Have you shared what you found with Pratt?"

"Some of it," she said. "I'm convinced this person is the vigilante."

She detected another deep sigh. "Syd, you shouldn't be

going at this alone, either on the web or in person. You have no idea who you're dealing with. Why don't I get on the site with you next time?"

"I'll consider it," said Syd. "But now I understand why they call it the *dark* web. It casts a pall over your life, even when you're not on there."

"Turn your computer off for a few days," he said with a chuckle. "The dark web ain't going anywhere."

"I'll consider it," said Syd. "I wanted you to know in case this thing ends up going sideways."

Montenegro's voice raised. "Syd, it's not going anywhere as long as you don't get involved with the vigilante or this idiot on the dark web."

Syd grew silent for a moment, then found her voice again. "We could already be involved, Stuart. Lasek thinks there's a leak in the department."

"I've heard that talk in the office - don't know if I buy it," he said. "We should get on the dark web together. That way, when we see The Enforcer in action, we can cross each other off the list."

Silence.

"Syd, I hope you know I'm only kidding."

Syd's voice cracked. "I'm sorry. I trust you, Stuart. This dark web thing has knocked me off-balance."

"I'll make you a better offer," said Montenegro. "If you want to meet in person, I eat lunch on Wednesdays at that great little brewhouse in Minerva. I'll buy you a beer. And maybe we can put our heads together and come up with a plan."

After hanging up, Syd realized Montenegro had calmed her. He was a voice of reason in her now chaotic world. She longed to call Enzo, but she didn't want to disturb him during a tournament. She'd already cost him a sizable amount of money.

Only a week into her suspension, the walls were starting to close in. Perhaps she'd take a run and finish the day out with a trip to the gym. She needed to stay fit and strong in case someone like Cutter surprised her again.

With only three days left in her suspension, Syd hadn't grown any more accustomed to the dark web. She noticed The Enforcer on RealVigilante another time and - despite Pratt's and Montenegro's advice - attempted to interact, using the screen name "DarkMistress." The Enforcer either didn't notice her among the comments or simply refused to engage. She hoped she'd get another opportunity.

She found discussion boards on both McBride and Babson. While a few individuals proclaimed their innocence, the overwhelming majority claimed that they had both gotten away with murder. Many were thrilled that they both seemed to receive their comeuppance long after their trials had ended.

Penny Cefalo, however, was a different story. By the names of the people posting on the discussion boards, it appeared that a majority of the women supported her right to defend herself from an abusive boyfriend. On the flip side, most of the male-sounding names believed she should have been incarcerated for life.

Syd decided to perform additional research on Cefalo, who certainly fit the profile of a local celebrity the vigilante might target. An intriguing figure, she unapologetically opened up an axe-throwing entertainment business after the deadlocked jury couldn't render a verdict. She either had an incredibly warped sense of humor or she was openly flaunting the justice system. Was she a maniacal killer who took pleasure in decapitating her unfortunate boyfriend? Or maybe she found herself immersed in a kill-or-be-killed situation? Remembering there was an episode on the show "Timeline-24", Syd located the case on the network website.

After the two-hour episode, Syd understood how the jury had become deadlocked. She herself would have voted to acquit based on the evidence, although she had serious reservations about Cefalo's innocence. She understood why prosecutors were hesitant to refile the case. During one commercial break, the network offered viewers the opportunity to go online and watch her actual trial transcript. Syd was relieved to discover it was still available despite the dated broadcast. She fast-forwarded the video to Cefalo on the stand as she was interviewed by her attorney, David Wilcox.

The woman in the video, dressed in a conservative gray blazer and black slacks, seemed out of place. Her hair was wound tightly in a bun, and she was having trouble remaining still. It appeared as if she felt confined in the courtroom.

Her attorney was doing his best to portray her in a positive light.

Wilcox: Some people in this courtroom aren't going to understand how you caused the death of someone you truly loved. Can you help us understand?

Cefalo: It sounds crazy, but we were in love. If it

weren't for his jealousy and drinking, our relationship would have been almost perfect.

Wilcox: What happened that night?

Cefalo: We attended my niece's wedding. Derek was drinking Manhattans. He doesn't do well with hard liquor. But I didn't want to nag.

Wilcox: Were you drinking too?

Cefalo: Yes, but nothing hard. Maybe two or three beers.

Wilcox: So, tell us about your confrontation with Mr. Stovall that night.

Cefalo: It was a stupid argument. Derek was sloppy drunk. We danced to a couple of songs. While he was at the bar, another guy asked me to dance. I assumed he was a family member. We danced a few fast songs.

But then, I slow-danced with him. When I returned to the table, Derek was fuming.

Wilcox: Did he threaten you?

Cefalo: Not at that time. He called me a "whore" and a "slut." I knew we had to leave. I barely had time to wave at the bride on the way out.

Wilcox: So, you drove home in his car?

Cefalo: Yes. It was fifteen minutes of hell. When he wasn't cussing me out and threatening to kill himself, he was vomiting out an open window.

Wilcox: What happened when you arrived home?

Cefalo: He was sitting next to the toilet. For a moment, he'd passed out on the floor. I was okay with that because I could go to my room, lock the door, and sleep in my own bed. But then, he kicked open the bedroom door. I was standing by the bed with only panties on. He grabbed me by the hair and pulled me onto the bed. He said he was going to do the same thing with me that I wanted from that man.

In that instant, Syd felt a strong bond with Cefalo. She had been in a relationship with a possessive partner before. It never escalated to violence, but she knew the dangerous nature of jealousy.

Wilcox: What happened next?

Cefalo: He groped my breasts and tried to remove my panties. His grip was like steel. I crashed my elbow into his nose. He screamed and covered his face. That gave me time to jump up and run out of the bedroom.

Wilcox: Why didn't you run out of the house?

Cefalo: I ran into the kitchen. I tried to leave by the side door but pulled the door instead of unlocking it. He caught me before I could get out. He grabbed my shoulders, blood pouring from his nose, and dragged me into the kitchen. I knew I was going to die. I remembered the knife drawer. I reached in and grabbed one. I didn't want to use it, but I had no choice.

Syd paused the video. For a moment, she felt like she was in Penny's shoes, fighting for her life. People controlled by jealousy could seem capable of almost anything. Once she regained her composure, she resumed watching.

She was eager to see how Cefalo fared under the cross-examination of the prosecutor, Victor Fuentes, a middle-aged man whose fatherly appearance concealed his cunning and guile.

Fuentes: Ms. Cefalo, you had a tumultuous experience on the night in question.

Cefalo: That's the understatement of the year. It was beyond horrible.

Fuentes: Had Mr. Stovall ever threatened you before that night?

Cefalo: He had only threatened to leave me and trash my house.

Fuentes: Why did he threaten to kill you on that particular night?

Cefalo: Because I danced with that man.

Fuentes: Had he ever been jealous before while drinking?

Cefalo: You could say that. I'm not sure why he tried to kill me this time.

Fuentes: How much money did Mr. Stovall earn yearly?

Cefalo: I'm not totally sure. Maybe a couple hundred thousand.

Fuentes: I have Mr. Stovall's W-2 from last year. He made in excess of $1.3 million. If I called several people to the stand who claimed you bragged about Mr. Stovall's net worth, would they be lying?

Cefalo: It would depend on who they were. I don't remember.

Syd could understand why Fuentes' track record was exemplary. He proceeded in a smooth, controlled manner before finally backing the witness into a corner.

Fuentes: Is it reasonable to surmise that losing the affection of someone making $1.3 million might be stressful to someone in your circumstance? (Objection. Sustained.) I'll rephrase. Assuming that Mr. Stovall's wealth provided you with a nice lifestyle, wouldn't a breakup be painful?

Cefalo: I didn't care about his money. I loved Derek for who he was.

Fuentes: So, you harbored no ill will or anger toward Mr. Stovall.

Cefalo: No. I loved him.

Fuentes reached into his pocket and removed two photos.

Fuentes: These pictures were taken at the scene after the struggle. Mr. Stovall is nearly decapitated. You were angry when you did this, right?

Cefalo: No. He was going to kill me. It was self-preservation.

Syd was perplexed. Of course, she was angry with him, and the anger was justified. She wished Cefalo would've come clean instead of telling the jury what they wanted to hear.

Fuentes: An expert testified he was defenseless long before his head was nearly severed. The knife you grabbed. Did you have time to pick it out?

Cefalo: No. I opened the drawer and grabbed the first one I felt.

Fuentes: There were eight knives in that drawer.

You just happened to select the one designed to cut through animal bone?

Cefalo: That's the one I grabbed.

Syd paused the video. She wanted to believe Penny, who refused to be intimidated by the prosecutor's questions. Cefalo was tough and confident, but was she using her strong personality to sell a false narrative to the jury? Syd was glad she hadn't been a juror. She understood why they were deadlocked.

CHAPTER 13

"They put you under the direction of who?" asked Montenegro shortly after Syd had entered his cubicle on her first day back to work.

"I know," Syd said, shaking her head. "As if getting suspended wasn't punishment enough."

"Lasek's crazy," said Montenegro, a vein protruding from his forehead as he paced the floor. "I wouldn't put Mitsoff in charge of feeding my goldfish. Lasek hasn't been around here long enough to understand our team chemistry."

"Pratt and Griffith were obviously in concurrence," said Syd. "Hopefully, it's for a short time. I need to be on my best behavior."

"That won't be easy, answering to a dickweed like Mitsoff. He wasn't born with the tact gene."

"Maybe you could check in and keep me on the straight-and-narrow," said Syd. "If he makes another sarcastic comment, I might strangle him."

Montenegro peered over the cubicles. "Maybe Mitsoff

called in sick or overslept his alarm. This may be your lucky day."

"Afraid not," interrupted Griffth, peering over the makeshift wall. "He just pulled into the parking lot with a new ride. It's a Harley - one of those Fat Boy Models with a Milwaukee-Eight 114 engine. He's feeling pretty good about himself."

Montenegro closed his eyes for a moment before speaking. "Were you in on the decision to put Mitsoff in charge of Syd? I would've thought suspension was punishment enough."

"Pratt and Lasek put their heads together," said Griffith. "Nobody asked my opinion…not that it would've mattered."

Syd glanced at Montenegro, wondering if he also heard tension in Griffith's voice. "It's really okay, Captain Griffith. I screwed up."

Griffith smiled slightly and nodded. "Livingstone, I appreciate your candor. But remember, we're alike in a lot of ways. We work in a small town dominated by good ol' boys."

Syd took a deep breath. "I created this mess."

"True, you could've been more careful," said Griffith. "But I wonder how Lasek and Pratt would react if Cutter disarmed a male officer. There's one thing I'm sure of. Any respect will have to be earned. And as a woman - especially a young, attractive one - you're going to have to work twice as hard."

Montenegro nodded. "It's gotten better, but it's far from perfect. This is backwoods territory, and not everyone has changed. But I've got your back, Syd - along with Captain Griffith."

Syd smiled. "Thanks, Stu. At least I neutralized the Cutter situation before anyone got killed."

Griffith laughed aloud. "Neutralized? Your punch

practically awakened that man's ancestors. I didn't know tennis players packed such a wallop!"

Syd rubbed the knuckles of her right hand. "I'm still feeling it. I hated striking Cutter because I think there's a decent person inside that bravado. He needs counseling."

Griffith glanced at Montenegro. "Livingstone, may I give you a little advice? Start worrying about your own welfare for the time being. A big heart sometimes gets into a tight spot."

If the suspension had seemed long, what came next seemed like an eternity. Syd was relegated to the evidence room, tasked with destroying anything deemed obsolete.

"This is a great time for you to experience the inner workings of the department," Lasek had said. "In retrospect, we may have thrown you into the fire too soon."

Syd had attempted to maintain a straight face during Lasek's lecture. Her most important assignment before interviewing Cutter had been investigating beer-stealing teenagers.

Enzo had phoned Syd for the first time in several days the night before. He'd expressed concern about her safety and mental health.

Syd wanted to cry on Enzo's shoulder about everything: how she was lucky to be alive after having a loaded gun against her temple…the indignity of being suspended…and the frustration of having to work under a Neanderthal. But something in Enzo's voice - something distant or unresolved - forced her to remain silent. The pain was an echo of past heartbreaks: her father's abandonment, an auto accident that claimed her brother as a young boy, and the suicide of her best friend. To her chagrin, they never discussed their engagement or upcoming wedding.

Despite Walsh County being small, its evidence room burst at the seams. Cluttered cages were stuffed with boxes containing data from past cases. Cleaning people weren't allowed in the area due to the sensitivity of the material, leaving the surroundings dusty and cobweb- filled. Detectives were told to keep the room clean and organized, but that directive was basically ignored.

As she was removing a box from the back of one of the cages, a voice caught Syd off-guard.

"This place is a dump," said Mitsoff, wiping dust bunnies off his sleeve. "When you're finished clearing out some of this evidence, I'll put you in charge of organizing a detective clean-up crew. You might not be the most popular person in the precinct, but at least it'll be clean in here."

Syd peered at him from behind a row of crates. "The material in these three boxes goes to the shredder," she said. "Two suspects pleaded guilty. The other died before she could go to trial." She hefted the first of the 70 lb. cartons. Mitsoff offered no help.

"I'd like to have this section cleared before the end of the day," he said. "More cases are coming, and the department needs the room."

"I'll knock myself out," said Syd, looking at the large clock displayed on the wall. "It's 3:30 now. That's a lot of data to dispose of before 5."

Mitsoff shook his head and smiled. "I have the utmost faith in you, Livingstone. And if circumstances require, I'm sure you'll put in extra hours to finish the job."

How much time would I get for kicking the crap out of this weasel? Six months? Nine?

Syd was jolted out of her daydream when she felt a hand on her head. She flinched, surprised by how close Mitsoff was to her.

"Hold still, there's a web I need to remove," he said. "The last thing you need in your life is a spider bite, especially after what you've been through."

Little prick.

"I've got it!" he said, holding a disintegrating web up to her face. "Feel free to thank me any way you like."

A good shot to Mitsoff's solar plexus seemed appropriate.

"The only way I can thank you is to complete the task," said Syd. "And I work more efficiently alone. So, if there isn't anything else…"

"Nope, that's it," said Mitsoff. "I can take a hint. But don't forget to arrive early tomorrow. I have a big day planned."

Syd gritted her teeth as Mitsoff sauntered away, his smugness hanging in the air like a foul stench. She couldn't let him get to her. A project loomed at home, one far more important than anything Mitsoff could concoct.

CHAPTER 14

Syd was in the process of carrying two boxes of shredded files out of the building when the double doors of the Walsh County police station swung open. Penny Cefalo strode in as if everyone was expecting her arrival. Syd recognized Cefalo thanks to the episode of Timeline-24, but the woman had an even larger presence in person. Black spiked mohawk hair momentarily diverted attention away from her heavily made-up face and bright red lipstick. A black tank top, tight-fitting leopard leggings, and matching low-rise leather boots screamed both defiance and confidence. She marched past the precinct's reception desk, ignoring the desk sergeant, Peter Musselman.

"Ma'am, wait," said Musselman. "You can't just…"

"On my way to Lasek's office," said Cefalo without looking back. "Is it down the hall and to the left?"

"No, on the right. But you need an appointment."

"Got one," said Cefalo. "You can return to your duties."

"Hold on," said Musselman. "This is a police station, and you can't…"

Getting wind of the commotion, Lasek leaned out of his office and spotted Cefalo. "It's okay, Musselman. I can take it from here.

"Nice to meet you, Ms. Cefalo. You mentioned you had something urgent."

Not missing a beat, Cefalo held up a plastic grocery bag. It shocked Syd to see the woman shivering visibly.

"You know exactly what's going on. Why don't you come clean?"

Syd observed Lasek peer over Cefalo's shoulder and noticed her in the hall. To her surprise, he waved her in.

"Ms. Cefalo, I'd like you to meet someone," he said. "This is Detective Sydney Livingstone. Would you mind if she sat in?"

Cefalo glanced at Syd, who was straining under the weight of the boxes. "It's all right by me," she said. "Do you always make your female officers lug cartons around?"

Syd did her best to suppress a smile. "I'm working on a project. It's no big deal."

"Then by all means, cop a squat," said Cefalo, who threw her own jacket over a chair and sat down. "No pun intended. And please, put down those damn boxes."

Syd placed them in a corner of Lasek's office. She took a seat in a chair across from Cefalo.

"Back to what I was saying," said Cefalo, now focused on Lasek. "What are you guys trying to pull?"

"Don't know what you mean," said Lasek. "Elaborate, please."

"All right, I'll play along," said Cefalo, shifting in her seat. "Somebody in Walsh County - either in this department or the prosecutor's office - is screwing around with me. And I want to know why."

Lasek shrugged, palms upward.

"You don't know?" she said. "Then I suppose I'll tell you."

She shook the plastic bag over Lasek's desk. Out fell a cut square piece of denim and a typed letter. The denim was covered with rusty brown patches.

"The boyfriend I was accused of murdering. These are part of his jeans. They were displayed as trial evidence. How do you suppose this got mailed to me?"

Picking up the note, Lasek perused its contents, then passed the note to Syd.

```
If you think you've gotten away with
it, you're wrong. It's not over.
There's MORE 2 COME.
```

Lasek glanced briefly at Cefalo and then picked up his desk phone. "Pratt, I need you to come to my office…right now."

"Excuse me," said Cefalo. "I thought you were the top dog. Who did you call?"

"I am the top… I mean, I'm in charge. I'm the police commissioner. Pratt is the police chief."

Cefalo nodded. "Well, maybe this Pratt is the one behind it. Has to be someone with pull."

Pratt walked in and glanced down at Cefalo and Syd. "Why, Ms. Cefalo. I didn't expect to see you here."

"I didn't expect to be here until I received this special delivery. I remember you from my trial. Have you been trying to intimidate me?"

Pratt glanced at Lasek, head tilted to one side. Syd handed him the note while Lasek gestured to the denim.

"Ms. Cefalo claims this was mailed to her home," said

Lasek. "She believes it's a patch of her boyfriend's bloody jeans and that someone in Walsh County is harassing her."

Pratt read over the note again. "When did you receive this?"

"Yesterday."

"Where's the envelope?" asked Pratt.

"It went out with yesterday's trash. I guess I wasn't thinking."

Lasek interrupted. "What makes you think this delivery is from Walsh County?"

"The bloody jeans were used as evidence in the trial. Where does it go after a trial?"

Syd watched her superiors exchange a glance. "We have an evidence room," Lasek allowed. "But items are stored till they are deemed obsolete. We wouldn't have thrown anything out from your case."

Cefalo chuckled. "Yes, especially because you may want to refile someday. Or to harass me until I confess to a murder that was self-defense?"

"I can't imagine this came from our office," said Pratt. "We'll check on it. In the meantime, I'd ask you to be careful."

"Why?" smirked Cefalo. "Is one of you hunting me down? I've heard there have been others."

"We don't know," said Lasek. "It's probably a loser who cut up a pair of jeans and doused it with ketchup. But leave everything here. We'll run tests."

Cefalo's smug expression changed. "If it's not one of you, then someone else is stalking me."

Pratt spoke up. "We'll send a car to check your place several times a day," he said. "Lock your doors and activate your alarm system if you have one. I've got a feeling you know how to protect yourself." Syd remembered the evidence photos of Stovall.

"You make a good point, Commissioner," said Cefalo, rising from her seat. "The last guy who attacked me didn't fare so well."

CHAPTER 15

They watched Penny Cefalo make her way out of Lasek's office, then Pratt took a seat. Everyone was quiet for a moment, then he turned to Lasek. "Why is Detective Livingstone here? No disrespect, Syd."

"She was walking by when Cefalo arrived. I wanted another officer present, just in case."

"What do you think we're going to find in the evidence room?" asked Pratt.

Lasek took a gulp of coffee and shook his head. "I think the question of the day is: What *aren't* we going to find in the evidence room?"

"Your expression tells me you think that piece of fabric is authentic. I have doubts."

Lasek looked toward Syd. "Is Mitsoff in?"

"He was earlier," said Syd. "Not sure now."

"Hang tight," said Pratt, sticking his head out the door and looking down the hall, "Mitsoff's here. Let's ask him to give us a tour of the area. If he's organized, he should have no trouble finding the Cefalo data."

Syd stood, unsure whether she should tag along. The boxes remained in the corner.

"Come with us," said Lasek. "You're working with Mitsoff anyway." She trailed Pratt and Lasek as they approached Mitsoff's cubicle. The video on his computer monitor didn't appear work-related. Syd caught a glimpse of a dog sledding down a mountain. Once Mitsoff noticed their presence, he tapped several keys, causing the screen to go black.

"Gentlemen and uh- lady," he said. "What can I do for you?"

Lasek spoke. "How's the evidence room project progressing?"

"Not much has changed since we spoke last week," said Mitsoff. "There's still work to be done, but it's moving in the right direction."

"We'd like to see for ourselves," said Pratt. "Can you take us through?"

Mitsoff hurried to his feet. "No problem. Again, I haven't been working on it for very long."

"That's okay," said Pratt. "We're just curious."

Reaching into the top drawer of his desk, Mitsoff removed a set of keys. "Follow me. It's a work in progress, but I'll show you what I've accomplished." Syd resisted the urge to roll her eyes.

He led them into the evidence deposit room, a temporary location where evidence is initially stored. Along the wall were a series of pass-through lockers, which allowed materials to be deposited into the evidence storage room. He removed the keys from his pocket and opened the door to the room.

As the door shut behind them, Pratt glared at Mitsoff. "Something's not right," said Pratt. "This ain't the way the operation is supposed to work."

Mitsoff looked at Lasek and then back at Pratt. "I haven't explained my plan yet. Let me show you…"

"I don't care about your damn organizational procedure," said Pratt. "I'm talking about the way you let us in here. You're not the property officer. The only way into this room is through her. Do you know who our property officer is?"

"Yeah," said Mitsoff. "Detective Arledge. "We're friends."

"Where the hell is she now?" asked Pratt. "She monitors all access."

"She had to step out," said Mitsoff.

"How do you enter the evidence room, Detective Livingstone?" asked Pratt.

Syd's eyes met Mitsoff's before he answered. "I go through Arledge," she said. "I was told that's protocol."

Pratt continued to stare at Mitsoff but didn't speak. Lasek interrupted. "She's absolutely right. Protocol is to go through Arledge. She's in charge of maintaining the keys. So, Mitsoff, why were they in your drawer?"

Mitsoff smiled and nodded. "Arledge gives them to me when she steps out."

"Against protocol," said Pratt. "What happens to the keys when you use the bathroom? I guarantee you don't take them with you."

Mitsoff started to speak but stopped. He stared at the floor.

"Anyone paying attention could have removed those keys," said Pratt. "But we'll set that aside for the moment. Take us to the Cefalo evidence - the stuff presented at trial."

Clearing his throat, Mitsoff spoke. "You don't want to talk about my long term plans for this area?"

"No detective. The Cefalo materials," said Lasek.

Mitsoff hesitated for a moment before nodding. He led

Pratt and Lasek past rows of shelves filled with boxes and bags, each labeled with case numbers and dates. The room was dimly lit, with about a third of the fluorescent lights either flickering or out. He stopped in front of a locked cabinet, his hands unsteady as he fumbled with the keyring. After a few failed attempts, he managed to find the right key and opened the cabinet door. Inside were neatly organized files containing evidence from various cases. At the bottom, was a white box tagged, "Cefalo, Penny."

Pratt leaned in toward the box, but Lasek picked it up with both hands and removed it. It hit the ground with a thud.

"The moment of truth," said Lasek. "Anybody want to make a bet?"

Syd felt sick. If the evidence room had been compromised, she would again be in the midst of controversy. After returning from suspension, she had hoped to fly under the radar.

Mitsoff squinted. "What do you mean?"

"Shall I ask Mitsoff to leave?" asked Pratt.

Lasek shook his head. "No. We're in this together. Mitsoff, do you have a box cutter so we can open this?"

Mitsoff pulled a Smith & Wesson extreme ops folding knife from a pocket. He sliced the tape, stepping back to allow his bosses access.

The box was full of plastic bags. The knife used in the killing was not inside, as the evidence storage area uses a separate room for weapons; however, there were plenty of other items. On top, in a bag of its own, was a heart-shaped necklace with a broken chain - presumably worn by Cefalo during the struggle. A bag containing human hair was below it. By the color and length, it was presumably Penny's. Underneath a pair of mangled men's spectacles was an empty, fractured bourbon bottle.

Lasek continued pulling items until he found what he was looking for - bags containing clothing from the crime scene. "Here we go," he said, holding up a bag of what appeared to be men's clothes.

"I don't understand," said Mitsoff.

"The victim was wearing a pair of denim jeans. And here they are."

Lasek moved to a nearby table, where he placed the bag. Lasek and Mitsoff followed. Syd peered over their shoulders. The jeans were folded several times, and Lasek began to spread them out.

"For the record, I predict we'll find nothing," said Pratt. "There's no way…" He stopped in mid-sentence.

Lasek held the fabric at eye level. About a foot above the knee on the right leg was a missing section, cut into a square.

"Sonofabitch," gasped Lasek. "Cefalo was telling the truth."

"What truth?" asked Mitsoff. "I still don't know…"

"Someone removed a patch from Stovall's jeans," said Pratt. "They sent it to Penny Cefalo as some kind of warning."

"But they were intact when we got them," said Mitsoff.

"Detective Livingstone, you've been working in the evidence room. Do you have any explanation for this?" asked Lasek.

"I don't," said Syd.

"Normally, I don't go out on a limb," said Lasek. "But I think it's reasonable to assume whoever gained access to those keys is probably our vigilante."

CHAPTER 16

Syd wanted to remain inside her steaming shower. The sizzling water soothed her body, as it flowed down the back of her neck, over the length of her back and buttocks. Her knees, thighs, and ankles were the happiest of all, inflamed and tight after another day of moving and stacking boxes, sorting files, and rearranging crates on the concrete floor of the evidence room.

She wrapped a beige terry bath sheet around her torso upon exiting the double-glass doors. Using both hands, she squeezed her long blonde hair into a bun and covered it in a towel.

She yearned for a tall glass of wine to put the day's stress behind her, but she had somewhere to be. A litany of Mitsoff quotes echoed through her mind.

"If we can't find it, then it doesn't exist."

"Nothing's better than experiencing the 'Big O' - organization."

"There's no denial if we can't locate the file."

"Data can't be explored unless it's properly stored."

Did he really take the time to make up this shit?

She caught a glimpse of her face in the mirror and didn't like the expression that glared back. The discovery in the evidence room had left her feeling drained. It was not impossible to believe that the vigilante was a Walsh County employee. This meant every conversation at work could potentially be with a killer. Mitsoff was a constant thorn in her side, but did he really fit the profile of a killer? She couldn't say for sure. And Fosterno had been acting strangely for the past week. Despite his charm and charisma, he was also physically strong and powerful. Was he capable of murder? Other officers and technicians were also present at the crime scene, along with Coroner Pennington. Her mind was racing with possibilities.

She couldn't help but wonder if it could be someone she trusted, like Montenegro or Griffith. After all, she had been betrayed by people she trusted before. And what about Lasek and Pratt? Would they risk their lucrative careers to seek out criminals who had evaded justice? It didn't seem logical, but cases like this rarely did.

Equally unsettling was her relationship with Enzo. They'd swapped cursory texts over the past few days, but nothing substantial. She wondered if they were still engaged. Perhaps he'd met someone else on the tour, either another player or an infatuated groupie.

Enzo's not like that.

Her friendship with Montenegro remained strong. He'd made several forays to the evidence room, each after Mitsoff had left.

"Just say the word, and I'll make him disappear," Montenegro had said during one of his visits. He formed his thumb and forefinger into the shape of a gun and pulled the trigger - all while smiling. But then his face turned serious.

"Let me know if that guy ever touches you or does anything inappropriate," he'd said. "I'll roast his ass."

Mitsoff had straddled that line, but she didn't want to go there. Not now.

"You're a good friend, Stuart."

Montenegro smiled. "When Enzo gets back, we all need to go out," he said. "I've told my wife all about you. I feel like I already know Enzo. When do you expect him?"

For a few seconds, there was an awkward silence. "Not quite sure," she mumbled, hoping he hadn't noticed the pause. "You never know with tournaments. You're in one day, out the next."

A cell phone alarm interrupted her thoughts. The Majestic Nightclub was the setting for tonight's city hall sponsored event, honoring Walsh County officers. It included dinner and drinks. Most employees involved with law enforcement were invited, including the police department and personnel from the prosecutor's and medical examiner's offices.

Unlike most of her colleagues, Syd would be attending alone. Mitsoff had joked about giving her the number of an escort service. "I've used them before," he said with a grin. "Not a bad deal for $150. The best ones act nice in public and get nasty in private. But that was long before I met Michelle."

Syd couldn't think of many positives about attending, but the opportunity to meet Michelle intrigued her. What kind of woman would choose to share her life with an insecure, condescending man? Did he fool her? How would she react when she discovered his true character?

And then there was Montenegro. Still practically a

newlywed after two years of marriage, she wondered about his wife. What was her name? Tracy? No, it was Stacey. She was excited to meet her.

Griffith was outspoken on everything except her personal life. Perhaps she'd be accompanied by her significant other, Jasmine Harris.

Lasek kept a picture of wife Eileen above his desk, but no evidence of children. Pratt frequently spoke about family - an adult daughter and a teenage son. Fosterno was married and divorced three times. He could wind up bringing just about anyone.

Syd's eyes welled up as she thought about Enzo. It would be so much fun if he were here. They would have made love in the shower while sipping champagne. His athletic body cleaned up nicely in a suit jacket and pants, which he always accentuated with a novel tie selection. She pulled her cell phone from her jacket pocket and sent a quick text:

> Heading 2 police awards ceremony. Wish u
> were here. Good luck in your match
> 2morrow.

Syd placed her cell phone on the kitchen table next to her laptop. As she was about to leave, it dinged. Enzo responded with a double-heart emoji. No words.

She couldn't help but steal a quick look at her laptop. She hadn't checked the dark web all day. If she left now, she'd be fashionably early for the event. But there was something about The Enforcer that drew her to the computer. Why not check the RealVigilante website? If The Enforcer hadn't posted anything, she'd be out of there in two minutes. If The Enforcer submitted something, she'd still make it there on time since she knew where the speed traps were located.

The Enforcer had promised a purge of the local criminal element. After that post, McBride was attacked and Babson murdered. What if they posted something today that she could share with Pratt and Montenegro while at the event? She decided to check.

To her relief, she saw nothing. Then, almost on cue, a post appeared.

```
One fish slipped out of the net. But
the frying pan still awaits. MORE 2
COME.
```

Who was The Enforcer referring to? Syd hadn't heard about any recent crimes. Was there a context or secret code she didn't understand? Using her cell, she snapped a picture of the post.

As she stepped outside, ready to start her journey to The Majestic Nightclub, Syd's heart raced. Who was the "fish" that slipped out of the net? And what did the frying pan symbolize? She texted Montenegro and Pratt the image, hoping they could provide some insight.

If only she had known, Syd could have planned to ask her questions in person. The Enforcer was also going to be there.

CHAPTER 17

With a light mist falling and the temperature dipping into the mid-forties, the entrance to The Majestic Nightclub was a welcoming sight. Syd ducked under the checkerboard canopy. She handed her jacket to a coat-check employee, a goth-looking girl who resembled Billie Elish, then proceeded down a lighted passage and into a large reception hall, which housed at least two dozen dining tables. At the front of the room was a wooden podium, equipped with a microphone and two large speakers.

Squinting in the dim lighting, Syd scanned the area before spotting a waving Montenegro. Seated next to him at a table to the right of the podium was Stacey, in a beige strapless dress, her brown hair in a coil at the top of her head. Syd could tell that Stacey had spent a considerable amount of time in the workout room.

Montenegro stood to greet Syd, who offered her hand. He pulled her into a tight hug instead, then turned and introduced Syd to his tall, lean wife.

Stacey stood and smiled gently. She extended her own

arms to embrace Syd. "Now I have a face to go with the name. And it's a stunning face!" She playfully smacked Stuart on the left shoulder.

Stuart resumed his seat. "You're both beautiful people. I'm lucky to have one as my wife and the other as my partner."

"How lucky can one guy *get?*" interrupted Mitsoff, flopping into a chair across the table.

Syd watched Michelle thrust her right elbow into Mitsoff's side.

"I was joking! Quit taking life so seriously. And speaking of serious, here comes the brass," said Mitsoff as Lasek and Pratt approached the table. "Let's pretend we're one big, happy family."

They were serving salads when Mitsoff returned from the bar with a pair of beers. "I wonder when Fosterno will show up. I can't wait to meet his 'woman of the month'."

Pratt broke in. "Fosterno's running a few minutes late. Hope he doesn't miss dinner."

Syd felt Montenegro tap her after she began digging into her salad. "Fosterno's on a new assignment," he murmured. "It's Lasek's and Pratt's brainchild. He's providing protective custody to none other than Penny Cefalo. Strange bedfellows, aren't they?"

"Let's hope they're not," said Syd. "What prompted that?"

"Last night, the back of her car window was shot out. A drive-by. She was too shaken to provide any details."

Syd remembered The Enforcer's words: "One fish slipped out of the net."

"The post I sent you tonight suddenly makes more sense," said Syd. "This shit is getting serious."

Montenegro looked toward Pratt and Lasek, who were in

conversation with their spouses. "Have you spoken with Pratt about your unofficial project?"

"He wants to meet in a couple of days," said Syd. "Now that I'm back to work, it's not so unofficial."

As the main course arrived, Fosterno stumbled in, pulling on his suit jacket and straightening his tie. "Didn't mean to be late," he said. "Time got away."

Syd noticed Lasek and Pratt stealing a glance at each other.

"Looks like I'm in time for the main meal," said Fosterno. "I'm a meat-and-potatoes guy, anyway. Don't care much for grazing food."

To Syd, Fosterno seemed preoccupied as he ate, checking his phone every few minutes. Mitsoff slid a beer bottle in his direction. "Slow down, big guy. We're here for the entire evening."

Fosterno swished the beer in his mouth. "First time you ever gave me anything, Mitsoff."

After most had left the table for the bar, dance floor, or restroom, Montenegro used the opportunity to speak with Fosterno in Syd's presence.

"Are you all right, Kevin? You seem a bit unsettled."

Fosterno exhaled. "I wish I could say everything's fine, but there's something about this Penny Cefalo assignment that doesn't sit right with me."

Syd exchanged glances with Montenegro, who leaned in, his voice low. "Are you suggesting that she might not be as innocent as she claims? Are you in danger?"

"No, not from Penny," said Fosterno. "At first, she didn't trust me. Can you imagine? But we're past that now. She's really needy. She's texted four times since I left her place."

Syd furrowed her brow. "What does she want?"

"She's convinced someone's trying to kill her," he said. "And I'd have to agree. But she's leaning on me hard. In ways the department might not approve."

Montenegro snorted. "You guys haven't been nasty together, have you?"

"Hell no!" said Fosterno. "Well, at least not yet. I will tell you this though. She's one attractive woman."

"Don't go there," said Syd. "You'll end up in trouble...or worse."

"I'm texting her one more time and then turning off my phone," said Fosterno. "I'm supposed to give a speech tonight. I haven't penned a word."

Montenegro leaned in closer. "Have you spoken to Lasek or Pratt about your concerns?"

Fosterno shook his head, frustration evident in his expression. "I've been so caught up with Penny I haven't had a moment to breathe."

Syd accompanied Stuart and Stacey to the bar for an after-dinner drink. Two young bartenders - one male and one female - appeared frazzled, doing their best to diminish the growing line. At the front of the line, she heard Fosterno finishing a story.

"And I said, 'Neither did I until you shined the light in here!'"

Mitsoff and his girlfriend joined the line. He looked at Syd and Montenegro. "Why would Lasek and Pratt assign a guy who pole-vaults through life to protect a sexy, notorious woman?"

Syd shrugged. "Leave me alone, Tom. I'm flying below the radar tonight."

Mitsoff seemed oblivious. "Lasek's new, so I guess he could claim ignorance about Fosterno. But what the hell was Pratt thinking?"

Syd glanced at the Montenegros. "I'm going back to the table."

By the time the awards ceremony commenced, most of Walsh's County's employees were well into their second or third cocktails. The mood of the gathering turned significantly more festive. A group of patrol officers and firefighters - who battled against each other annually for softball supremacy - were the biggest culprits. Syd hoped they would kick off the awards ceremony before the situation got too far out of hand.

She had declined the luscious-looking dessert choices, key lime cheesecake, and tiramisu layer cake. The main course had been delicious, but the arborio rice had already compromised her low-carb diet. She continued to sip her Diet Coke. Tonight, she would leave the real partying to the veterans of the police force.

Everyone was now at the table: Fosterno, Mitsoff and Michelle, the Laseks, the Pratts, Coroner Pennington and her husband David, and Griffith and Jasmine.

Pratt left the table to take a call. A few minutes later, he returned, tension in his face. He put down his phone and cleared his throat. "I just received a call from the hospital. Frank McBride has awakened from his coma."

Syd's thoughts turned to Rex Cutter. He'd have been free and clear by now if he hadn't attacked her in the interrogation room.

"Looks like McBride beats the odds again," said Griffith.

"He's acquitted by a whacked-out jury, and then survives a lethal dose of insulin and an ass-kickin' from Cutter."

Melissa Pennington squirmed in her seat. "I spoke to one of McBride's physicians," she said. "They didn't expect him to pull through."

Well into his fourth cocktail, Mitsoff piped up. "Hey, Melissa…I mean Coroner Pennington. How was it that your office couldn't tie McBride to his wife's murder? I mean, we all know the guy couldn't have been very careful."

The table went quiet.

Melissa stared at him while everyone else looked on. "Detective Mitsoff, I wasn't aware you were an expert in taphonomy. Where did you study?"

Mitsoff hesitated. "I probably never studied it since I don't know the meaning of the word. Does anyone have a dictionary app on their phone?"

"I can save you time," said Melissa. "Taphonomy is the study of organic remains from the time of death until discovery. The method in which a body decomposes is a complicated process, especially when affected by insects and the environment. You do understand her body was abandoned outside in a makeshift grave for a long period, right?"

Syd wondered whether Mitsoff was clear-headed enough to wish he hadn't broached the subject.

Melissa continued. "If you would've been kind enough to direct us to her body within the first couple of weeks, or even months, we probably would have extracted viable evidence. But since we never heard from you, Detective Mitsoff, we acquired the body far too late to make any definitive conclusions - except that she perished as a result of homicide."

Mitsoff cleared his throat. "You'd think there would've been a fiber, hair or something," he muttered.

Lasek glared across the table. "Mitsoff, we'll discuss your drunken theories another time. Everything's about to start now."

The room grew quiet as a speaker approached the podium. The emcee for the ceremony was County Commissioner Bobbi Fair. "I'd like to thank the wonderful employees of Walsh County for being with us."

Polite applause.

"Tonight is reserved for honoring individuals who have made Walsh County one of the safest places to reside in Ohio. So, let's begin with our fine police department. I'd like to introduce Commissioner Ed Lasek."

Hoots and hollers. A standing ovation.

For the next 30 minutes, Lasek gave a presentation on the awards for community service, which went to Montenegro and Mitsoff for their work with the D.A.R.E. program. As Lasek talked, word circulated quickly through the room that McBride had awakened from his coma. The Enforcer had trouble dealing with the news. The amount of insulin in that syringe was enough to kill at least two people, even without that minor-league beatdown. How had McBride survived? Superior conditioning? Or maybe some of the insulin seeped out before the needle penetrated - a definite possibility. Or maybe it was plain dumb luck.

The Enforcer had known many good people who were victims of incurable diseases, car crashes, murder, and other forms of mayhem - some enduring several tragedies in a short time. McBride was on the other end of the spectrum. He retained his job. Worse, he collected his wife's life insurance and married his mistress. Not to mention keeping custody of his kid.

Would he remember the person who snuck up on him at the park and injected him with that needle? Would he be able to identify The Enforcer in a lineup? Shit. McBride was a dangling participle…a hanging chad…the last leaf in an otherwise pristine yard. Worst of all, he was a danger to The Enforcer's bigger plan…which couldn't afford to fail.

CHAPTER 18

Sitting across the table from Fosterno, Syd noticed that he couldn't seem to sit still. At first, he denied that anything was amiss. But after Syd persisted, he motioned for her to lean in.

"This is going to sound crazy, but someone's following me right in here. Tonight."

Syd resisted the urge to scan the room. "What are you talking about?" she asked. "There are fifty cops in here, most of them armed to the teeth. Are you sure?"

Fosterno nodded, almost imperceptibly. "I've had more than twenty years' experience as a cop and PI. I know my surroundings. And this isn't the first time."

No one at the table seemed to notice their private conversation. Mitsoff and Michelle were laughing at a video on his cell while the Montenegros were busy sampling each other's drinks. Melissa Pennington and her husband were out of earshot at the end of the table.

"Can you see the main bar area over my right shoulder?"

he asked. "Not the cash bar, but where the regular customers are."

"Yeah, pretty well," said Syd.

"Do you see a guy sitting there? He should be alone. And don't stare."

Syd squinted. "There are several people hanging around. Is the guy you're talking about wearing a hat?"

"That's him," said Fosterno. "Every time I turn to get a glimpse, he moves away - like a shadow. Is he still looking this way?"

"It's kind of hard to tell from this distance, but I think so."

"I need you to act natural," said Fosterno. "Pretend we're having a normal conversation, like about the weather or something."

The intensity in Fosterno's eyes made her feel the danger was real. She wanted to mimic a normal conversation but was at a loss for words. Then, an Idea came to mind, and she started talking again.

"Peas and carrots. Watermelon. Peas and carrots."

Fosterno looked quizzically at Syd.

"I've got you covered," she said. "Peas and carrots. Watermelon. Peas and carrots."

"Okay, you're beginning to freak me out more than *that* guy."

Syd sighed. "I'm saying things that background actors say when they're pretending to carry on a conversation. There's something about saying 'peas and carrots' and 'watermelon' that makes conversation appear natural."

"Where the hell did you hear that?" asked Fosterno.

"I don't know. I read it somewhere. Or maybe someone told me."

"Is he still alone?" asked Fosterno.

"Yep."

"I'm not going to turn around," said Fosterno. "Do you have time to snap a picture without being too obvious?"

Pratt's voice over the PA interrupted Fosterno's response. As they both turned to face the podium, the stranger got up from the bar and disappeared from view. Pratt's presentation focused on Griffith and her efforts to shut down a human trafficking ring in the county.

Syd liked Griffith. As scruffy and obstinate as the woman could be, Syd usually found herself smiling and in good spirits while in her presence. She liked blunt people who spoke the truth, sometimes even to their own detriment. Listening to the applause, she wasn't the only one who admired Griffith.

"Do I have a great partner or what?" Fosterno grinned at Syd as they both clapped. "When she's not working with me in the field, she's pretending to be someone else - usually somebody pretty bad."

"Listen, I think I prematurely sounded the alarm," he went on. "That guy probably isn't following me. It's paranoia. Maybe PTSD."

After receiving her award, Griffith remained at the podium to announce the evening's final recipient: Fosterno himself.

"Moving along to our last award of the evening," she said. "Sometimes I feel blessed. And other times I feel cursed. And I'm talking about my partner, our legendary detective, Kevin Fosterno."

Fosterno smiled sheepishly and waved as he rose from his seat to approach the podium.

"Working with Kevin is like being surrounded by many

different types of bread," she continued. "White bread is the first that comes to mind."

Laughter throughout the room.

"He used to remind me of flatbread in his younger years, but his liking for fine food and dark beer has certainly changed that," she said while making a rounded-arc motion by her midsection.

"Sometimes I think of him as more of a baguette, because every time I ask him to work late with me on an investigation, he says something like 'Why don't we just baguette for the evening'"?

Additional chortling and howling.

"As you are aware, Detective Fosterno has been married a few times. When he's in church and sees the priest, sometimes he accidentally says, 'I do.' Plus, he's been active in the dating scene. So that's where 'banana bread' certainly applies." She paused for the laughter to die down.

"But in the end, I would say the one type of bread that best describes Detective Fosterno is 'Pita'," she said. "And what 'PITA' stands for is 'pain in the ass.'"

Everyone in the crowd was now standing and applauding. As abrasive as Fosterno could be, it was obvious to Syd he was well-liked.

"Put a crown on him because he's a royal pain in the ass," shouted Mitsoff while Michelle frowned at him.

Griffith glanced at Mitsoff but continued. "So, without further ado, I'd like to ask Detective Fosterno to *loaf* his way up here," said Griffith.

Lasek arrived at the podium seconds before Fosterno got there. When Fosterno met him, Lasek placed his arm around his shoulders.

"Captain Wilma Griffith, that was one *crummy* way of

introducing one of our biggest award-winners of the evening," said Lasek.

Groans and boos cascaded from the audience.

Watching Fosterno next to Lasek at the podium, Syd felt he looked out of place. He was taller and significantly broader than Lasek but looked preoccupied. Syd noticed that he kept sneaking glances at the public bar area.

She longed to check out the situation, but disrupting Lasek's speech probably wasn't a good idea. Flying below the radar was a better alternative.

But still, was the man bothering Fosterno again? She kept her eyes on Fosterno as Lasek said, "And despite Detective Fosterno's sometimes unconventional methods - as Captain Griffith alluded to - he exemplifies the courage and work ethic that make Walsh County Police Department the envy of Northeast Ohio."

Fosterno acknowledged the audience's applause - while stealing another glance.

Lasek went on. "As you all know, the scope of a police officer's duties is not determined by a clock. An officer may be called to action when they least expect it. In the case of Detective Fosterno, the situation occurred on a Sunday night while he was enjoying a night on the town.

"He recognized the model and license plate of a car driven by two fugitives wanted by the FBI. He followed the suspects for nearly 20 minutes, even though his cell phone had powered down."

Syd had heard about this around the precinct, but she didn't know the details of the story. She began to pay more attention.

"The pursuit continued all the way onto rural Pfeiffer Road, where the suspects' vehicle spun out and crashed into a field," said Lasek. "Without the use of a phone, Detective Fosterno encountered gunfire from both suspects. Despite being outnumbered and with no backup, Detective Fosterno returned fire and fatally wounded the individuals.

"Although we never celebrate the death of anyone, the bravery and fast thinking of Detective Fosterno no doubt saved innocent lives. The suspects were members of a drug syndicate that had murdered at least seven people and assaulted many more here in Walsh County. And he performed this heroic action while he was technically 'off-the-clock.'"

Pratt held a large plaque. Lasek took the plaque from Pratt and smiled at Fosterno. "And while there are plenty of deserving officers among us, Kevin Fosterno's heroic effort in the face of imminent danger is the deciding factor in naming him 'Walsh County Officer of the Year'."

With Fosterno now standing alone in front of the podium, he raised the plaque high above his head as everyone in the audience stood and applauded.

Syd was happy for Fosterno. Despite his propensity to be boisterous, he had won her over with his honesty and decisiveness. He seemed like a big brother, a gentle giant you'd want to have in your corner.

Stuart bent forward and spoke to Syd. "Everything Griffith said is true. He's a blue collar dude who never learned the art of bullshitting."

At the end, many cops vacated their seats to congratulate Fosterno, including Syd and Montenegro. They waited their turn as a crowd gathered around him. Holding the huge silver plate, he collected hugs, backslaps, and more embraces. But Syd could see him looking past the people surrounding him. She followed his gaze.

The man was back in the bar area, staring without expression. He wore a long, tan coat and brown fedora. She saw him meet Fosterno's eyes, get up, and head for the exit. Fosterno handed his award to Griffith, calling out, "I'll be right back. I gotta hit the john."

As he walked toward the door, Syd noticed him reaching into his jacket. It was a familiar movement of a cop, going for the revolver in his shoulder holster. Unsure of what she would find outside, Syd followed Fosterno to the exit door, stopping at the table to extract her own revolver from her purse.

The cool night air hit Syd as she stepped out of the bar. She scanned the dimly lit alley behind the building. There was a sound of footsteps; someone was chasing someone. She turned the corner of the brick building and saw Fosterno holding a man in a rear chokehold with his gun pressed against the man's head. He was shaking, his finger hovering over the trigger of his weapon. Her gun raised, Syd peered at the other guy, who was gasping for air. She saw he didn't match the description of the stalker. In fact, he looked strangely familiar.

"Kevin, put your gun down," she screamed. "He's not who you think he is."

The man attempted to speak, but only gurgled.

Syd shifted her aim to Fosterno. "Kevin, I'm not fucking around. Put the gun down and release your grip." She cocked her gun. "Do it NOW."

Syd heard someone approaching, and then Montenegro was at her side, his own gun drawn.

Fosterno allowed his gun to drop to the sidewalk and released his grip on the man's neck. As she and Montenegro drew close, Syd recognized Detective Oscar Cataldi, a three-year veteran of the force. Cataldi placed his right hand over his neck and dropped to his knees, panting. Montenegro stepped forward. "Fosterno, what the hell? Why were you holding a gun to Cataldi's head?" Fosterno stood, his hands raised in surrender before his shoulders slumped.

Syd knelt, holstered her weapon and exhaled. "Are you okay, Cataldi?"

Cataldi coughed and attempted to clear his throat. "Considering where I was 20 seconds ago, I'd say I'm much better," said Cataldi.

"Why were you outside?" asked Montenegro.

"I needed a vape," Cataldi said, pointing to the pen which lay broken on the ground. "I know the department frowns on that, but isn't this kind of an overreaction?"

"I thought he was the guy following me," Fosterno said. "I didn't mean to—" He broke off, then gulped.

"Please don't report this. They'll send me to be evaluated or something. I made a mistake. I'm sorry, Cataldi."

Cataldi got to his feet and stepped in front of Fosterno. "I won't press charges," he said, "Let's pretend this was a little disagreement between friends. No one needs to find out."

"Thanks, Cataldi, I'll take it from here," said Syd, as she held open the door for Fosterno to re-enter. "No promises, Kevin. Go back inside. They're not done honoring you."

As they made their way through the crowded room, Syd hissed to Montenegro. "Is the responsibility for protecting Cefalo too much for him, or is there something else going on?"

"Here's a disturbing thought," he whispered back. "As crazy as Fosterno's acting, do you think it's possible that he's The Enforcer?"

She glanced at Fosterno, who was now surrounded by well-wishers. He was smiling, looking every bit the charismatic detective. You would never know this was the same fearful and paranoid guy from a few minutes before.

"Fosterno's acting strange," said Montenegro. "As crazy as it sounds, I'm starting to wonder if he could be the guy we're looking for."

"The Enforcer flies under the radar, striking surreptitiously. You think his attack on Cataldi fits that pattern?" she asked.

Montenegro paused. "Probably not. But he's acting erratically. We need a background check on Cataldi, just in case. Is it possible he escaped justice sometime in his past?"

Syd smiled. "So, you're saying I may have prevented The Enforcer from chalking up another victim?"

"Again, it's a long shot," said Montenegro. "My mind is exploring every possibility."

"I think we need to talk to Fosterno when everyone's done with him," she said. "Maybe he knows something he isn't telling."

Montenegro nodded. "Syd, I think it would be better if you approached him alone. Fosterno and I are cordial, but we've had a few run-ins. Typical guy stuff. I think he'll open up to you."

Once the crowd around him had dissipated, Syd caught Fosterno's eye and motioned for him to join her at a quieter corner of the room. He followed, a hint of apprehension in his eyes. "Kevin, what's going on with you?"

Fosterno took a brief look around to make sure no one else was in earshot. "Sorry I put you through this. This is the best and worst day of my life, all rolled into one."

"I need to know something. If I hadn't been there, would you have shot Cataldi?"

"Hell no!" said Fosterno. "I would've realized it was him."

Syd studied Fosterno's face. He may have been acting, but she didn't think so.

"Kevin, this goes beyond mistaking Cataldi for someone else. Talk to me," she urged, her voice soft but firm.

Fosterno hesitated, his jaw tightening. After a moment of silence, he spoke. "The guy I saw in the bar earlier - the one I mistook for Cataldi - has been following me for several weeks now. Maybe months. He's appeared when I'm at the diner, bowling, and even walking my dog in the park. But lately, it's gotten worse. I've seen him around Penny's house. Sometimes, he drives by slowly, like he's taunting me."

"Have you confronted him?"

"I've wanted to. But then, he vanishes."

"Are you sure it's the same person every time?" asked Syd. "Stress can play tricks on our minds."

Fosterno shook his head. "I know it looks that way because of the Cataldi incident tonight, but it's the same guy. And now I have physical proof."

Syd waited for him to elaborate.

Fosterno reached into his pocket and pulled out a crumpled envelope. He removed a wrinkled bar napkin with writing on it.

"Do you know Sully?" he asked, pointing to a large man in his mid-50s behind the bar.

"Can't say I do," she said. "Did he write this note?"

"No, but he gave it to me. He said while I was giving my acceptance speech, the guy asked him to give it to me. Sully assumed it was a congratulatory note."

Fosterno handed the napkin to her.

It bore a single sentence scrawled in messy handwriting: "You can run, but you can't hide forever."

Syd felt a chill. Maybe Fosterno wasn't The Enforcer, but a

future target. Now, she scanned the room, looking for signs of the stranger. "Do you know who might be behind this? Any enemies or someone with a grudge?"

"I'm a cop," said Fosterno. "I make enemies on a weekly basis."

"I'm not talking about breaking up fights or writing speeding tickets," she said. "What about someone associated with those two guys you killed?"

Shaking his head, Fosterno muttered, "I never thought it would come back to haunt me. It was kill-or-be-killed that night. In hindsight, I should have let their car drive by. I was off-duty. Now I've ruined my life and possibly Penny's."

Syd remembered that Cefalo's back window had been shot out by a fleeing assailant. It wasn't a big stretch to connect Fosterno's stalker to her.

"I have to ask you a strange question," said Syd. "Have you ever skirted the law or gotten away with a crime you should've been punished for?"

Fosterno shook his head. "Other than taking my neighbor's car when I was sixteen for a joy ride, I would say no. Certainly nothing to catch anyone's attention."

"Like The Enforcer?" asked Syd.

"No way. The Enforcer is a weird kind of equalizer who thinks they're righting the wrongs of society. I don't fall into that category."

"I would say Penny Cefalo does," said Syd.

"I've thought about that," said Fosterno. "But this guy's been following me long before I was assigned to Penny."

"So, then we go back to that shooting - the incident that led to you receiving tonight's award," said Syd.

"That's it," said Fosterno. "I've received other notes as well - texts from burner phones and anonymous emails. They want revenge for those gang members. They're going to kill me, Syd. And probably Penny, too."

Bringing the note back up to her face, Syd read it again. Fosterno attempted to snatch it, but she pulled it away and placed it in her pocket.

"Don't tell anyone about this," he said. "I'm confiding in you, Syd."

"I'm sorry, but I have to give the note to Lasek," said Syd. "You can't deal with this by yourself. As far as what happened with Cataldi, I won't say a word. Hopefully, no one else will."

She quickly scanned the room, but everything seemed normal. Guests were beginning to head for the exit. "I would suggest you take some time off, Kevin. Maybe head south for two or three weeks and let things blow over."

"Someone's already tried to kill Penny once," he said. "She's not the evil woman portrayed in the media. There's a soft side to her. If I go away now, something terrible will happen."

Syd sensed the weight of responsibility that Fosterno carried. His determination to protect Cefalo was unwavering despite the looming dangers. As she looked into his eyes, she saw a mix of fear and fierce determination.

"You can't do this alone, Kevin," Syd said. "We need to approach this strategically. We'll gather all the evidence, increase security around Penny, and track down any leads on this stalker."

"The department's got enough to do hunting down a crazy vigilante," he said. "What's happening to me is separate, and I need to handle it myself. I'm emotionally attached to Penny, and that's on me. I'm a little stressed now, but I can handle it." He began to walk away from Syd before looking back. "I've got to leave," he said. "Penny's alone, and that's making me even more nervous."

In less than a minute, he was out the door, carrying his award with him.

Before Syd could get back to the table, Montenegro approached. "What did Fosterno tell you?"

Stuart's eyes were intense, like he was ready to jump out of his skin. "That car chase we heard about tonight…the one where Fosterno killed those gang members," she said. "There are others that now want him dead. He believes the guy following him is one of them."

"A possible revenge plot here?" he asked, running a hand through his hair.

"He feels his past actions have caught up with him, and Penny may be in danger, too," said Syd. "Somebody already shot at her car."

Montenegro stepped back, looking puzzled. "It makes sense that the vigilante shot at Cefalo. She butchered her boyfriend and thumbed her nose at our justice system. But someone after him? I don't know. For now, we should protect both him and his crazy girlfriend."

Syd shook her head, a sense of unease in her stomach. "He doesn't want to involve the department. He believes he can handle it himself."

Montenegro sighed. "We're going to have to work around him," he said. "You know, help him without letting him know. Stubborn bastard."

CHAPTER 19

On her drive home from the evening's festivities, Syd's mind wouldn't let her relax. She felt the prick of little needles running up her arms and legs, making her shiver. She'd experienced this sensation before - on the tennis court when a match teetered in the balance. Syd's intuition was on high alert. Something wasn't sitting right.

Griffith openly received an award for her great undercover work. Did that make sense? Did they just blow her cover?

Why was Mitsoff questioning Coroner Pennington's expertise concerning the body of McBride's ex-wife, which hadn't been found for months? That was easy to decipher... simply an asshole being an asshole.

Why would Lasek and Pratt choose a known womanizer to protect a vivacious and dangerous woman like Cefalo? Maybe they figured Fosterno was the only person on the force tough enough to deal with her explosive personality.

Was there really someone following Fosterno? The note seemed to confirm it. Unless he made up the story about the bartender giving the note to him. No, that was a crazy thought. It's definitely legit.

Who was the fish that had escaped the net? Cataldi? No, Fosterno's attack on him occurred after she had already read the post. The answer could very well be Cefalo. Did The Enforcer assume that she was dead after shooting out her back window? Even Fosterno would agree that made sense.

McBride was now out of his coma. Would he retain any memory about what happened? She wouldn't wager her pension, but it was certainly worth checking. And would The Enforcer return to finish the job? Or was the original attack on McBride intended to throw everyone off?

As her Ford F-150 cruised in the right lane of City Highway 55, Syd knew she desperately needed either one of two things: a long-distance run or a stiff drink. Considering the time, she decided she'd settle for the high ball once she returned home. She hadn't imbibed like her colleagues because she didn't want to let her guard down mere days after her suspension had been lifted.

A small light glowed in the dark light in her truck cab. It was a text from Enzo.

> Knocked out of the tournament in Belgium.
> Made it to the third round, but the knee
> injury reduced practice time. Lost in three
> sets. A little down because I lost, but even
> more depressed because I miss you. Let's
> talk in the morning.

In the morning, not tonight? Interesting.

Pulling into her driveway, Syd's phone lit up again. Montenegro was calling. His voice sounded stressed, almost out of breath.

"Something's going on below the surface," he said.

"Fosterno acted like a scared little boy. There's something about Cefalo that's knocked him off balance."

Syd put the truck in park. "Whoever was tailing him left a note behind."

She could hear Montenegro turn off his engine and walk toward his front door, Stacey talking softly in the background.

"He probably believes his life is in danger," said Stuart. "Maybe this Enforcer is threatening him because he's protecting Cefalo. But that doesn't sit right."

"How so?" asked Syd.

"Because I get the feeling Cefalo doesn't need protection."

Syd took a breath, understanding where Montenegro was going. "But she fits the profile of someone the vigilante might target. And somebody already shot out her window."

Syd heard a thump and a muffled, "Night, babe. I'm going into the kitchen to talk to Syd," as Montenegro addressed his wife. Then he came back on the line.

"Syd, do you know there wasn't a single witness to that window shooting? What does that tell you?"

"The shooter acted while no one was around?"

"Possibly," said Montenegro. "But that's not what I think. Maybe she staged the entire thing. Maybe she's the damn vigilante, attempting to divert attention from herself."

"Why would she do that?"

"Maybe now - just maybe - she wants to portray herself as a victim. She might feel the DA's office would be hesitant to refile charges against someone who was being openly stalked."

"Interesting theory," said Syd. "You know about that missing piece of fabric, right?"

Montenegro laughed. "Yeah. I haven't figured that part out yet. It's possible she's working with someone on the inside."

"And the note on the napkin?" asked Syd.

"We need to find out who wrote it," said Montenegro. "Maybe Cefalo knows something."

Lying in bed, she couldn't stop thinking about Montenegro's words. It was terrifying to think that the perpetrator was someone they knew and within their reach. And with more victims on the horizon, time was running out.

In another part of town, The Enforcer lay in bed, staring at a clock that displayed 12:49. Trying to shake the winter doldrums wasn't easy, especially in rainy weather. The ceremony was certainly interesting, with a lot of unexpected events.

Sitting up, The Enforcer fumbled for the laptop computer that had somehow found its way underneath the covers. News of acquitted or unpunished villains being attacked had now hit the national media.

One article caught The Enforcer's attention:

POLICE STILL DO NOT ACKNOWLEDGE VIGILANTE ATTACKS

By Mike Hosier, Canton News

Rumors of a vigilante killer in Northeast Ohio have continued to swirl.

Yesterday, Penny Cefalo, whose case was featured on crime show Timeline-24, reported to police that a fleeing assailant shot out the back window of her sedan. No one was injured in the shooting. Cefalo's trial ended in a hung jury.

Earlier last month in Walsh County, a neighbor discovered Gabriel Babson in his home, an apparent victim of murder. Babson had been found not guilty in the death of his wife, Bridget, who drowned under questionable circumstances during the couple's rafting trip. Police refused to substantiate rumors pertaining to a message left at the crime scene.

In another development, Frank McBride, who won an acquittal after being charged with his wife's homicide, is still hospitalized after police say someone attempted to kill him with an overdose of insulin at a local theme park.

Despite the similarity of these attacks, police have been hesitant to acknowledge a pattern.

"There have been strange events surrounding these assaults," said Police Chief Delvin Pratt. "But sometimes incidents are not related, despite the media wanting them to be. Right now, we're investigating every lead. If we feel that a pattern exists, we will report that."

Online crime reporter Cynthia Jacobson claimed a framework to the attacks.

"Two times is a coincidence," said Jacobson on her YouTube site 'Crime Carnival'. "But three inside Walsh County indicates a pattern. We owe it to the public to inform them about what is going on."

The Big E clicked the 'X' in the right corner of the computer screen, making the article disappear.

Kudos to Cynthia Jacobson. She refused to ingest the shit sandwich foisted onto the public by the police chief. If a pattern wasn't obvious enough by now, it soon would be.

CHAPTER 20

The invitation from Wilma Griffith to have lunch was a welcome distraction. The calendar seemed to be stuck in late November, with Christmas reluctant to arrive. Working in the dim and dusty evidence room was already bleak, but Syd's mood was further dampened by having to take orders from Mitsoff. So, when Griffith invited her to lunch at a nearby diner, she eagerly accepted.

On the drive, Syd's thoughts turned to the developments over the last few weeks. While she hadn't forgotten Fosterno's odd behavior at the end of the awards ceremony, the overall situation seemed to stabilize. He was back working the streets during the early part of the day and supposedly providing protection to Cefalo afterward. Whenever she brought up the subject of the note, he shut her down.

In the last few days, she noticed Montenegro spending a good deal of time in the offices of both Lasek and Pratt. He had also paid a visit to Cefalo, questioning her about the note. "Cefalo knows almost nothing about it," he said. "She claims Fosterno refuses to discuss it."

Pratt summoned Syd away from her evidence room duties several times to discuss what she'd uncovered on the dark web. She'd captured most of The Enforcer's posts and sent them to Pratt in a file.

"This isn't some whack-job trying to act important," said Pratt. "This person is either directly involved or getting information from the murderer." And then he dropped the bomb. "The trail leads to an employee of Walsh County."

Her visits to Pratt's office had not gone unnoticed. Mitsoff brought up the subject on several occasions. She'd deflected his questions, blaming her visits on finalizing paperwork pertaining to her suspension. She wasn't sure if Mitsoff was buying any of it.

"Mitsoff's probably not the guy," said Pratt at the conclusion of their last meeting. "But I wouldn't bet my life on it. Someone removed that piece of fabric from the evidence room, and he's the one with easy access. Be careful."

Syd pulled her car into the parking lot of the diner, her mind still swirling. She took a deep breath and shook herself; this was a chance to talk about something other than the case.

Inside, Syd scanned the room and spotted Griffith sitting in a booth by the window. Looking up from the menu, she acknowledged Syd with a hand wave. As they exchanged smiles and a brief embrace, Syd surreptitiously scanned the room for other Walsh County employees. As far as she could tell, they were the only ones. For a moment, her apprehension was gone. She hadn't known Griffith for very long but felt confident she wasn't in the presence of a vigilante and allowed herself to relax for the first time in days.

Griffith leaned forward to squeeze Syd's hands in hers. "You've barely been back a couple of weeks, and I can already see stress in your face. That's why I invited you here - to get your mojo back."

Syd let out a small chuckle. It was a welcome gesture. As she sipped her coffee, Syd felt a sense of calm. For the next hour, the subject of work was hardly discussed. They shared stories about family and growing up, and Griffith's experience in the theater.

"I've got two undercover gigs for December," said Griffith. "And neither has to do with work. I'm playing Santa in one play and Mrs. Claus in another. I've been rehearsing for weeks."

"Hard to believe we've only known each other a short time," said Syd. "When we're talking, out of the office, I feel like I'm in the presence of a long-lost friend."

Griffith nodded. "I suppose sometimes the universe brings people together for a reason, even in the most unexpected circumstances."

Syd smiled and took a deep breath. It had been good forgetting about work for a while, but now she needed to ask something. "Your partner. Do you feel he's someone we can trust?"

Griffith broke eye contact to stare off into space. "I love Kevin like a brother. You saw that at the awards. But something's been weighing him. I wish I knew."

"Have you asked him?"

"On several occasions, but he insists it's in my head. Sometimes, the truth has a way of surfacing on its own, whether we seek it or not."

"How do you feel about the Cefalo assignment?"

Griffith shook her head. "I have my reservations. It's a high-profile gig, and Kevin's eager to prove himself."

"Has he mentioned that note? The one he received at The Majestic?"

"He told me it was probably nothing, someone just pulling his chain. But as perplexing as the note is, I'm more upset with Lasek and Pratt for placing him in the company of a nutcase."

The diner was now buzzing with activity. Tables were being cleared as newcomers arrived. Syd made another scan of the room. "Do you think Kevin's life is in danger?"

"Considering he spends a good part of his day with a slicer and dicer, I'd say yes."

"But you said he was acting strangely before the Cefalo assignment."

"No doubt, but it's gotten worse. I'm afraid for him."

The stress that had disappeared so smoothly was now making another cameo.

"Have you talked to Lasek and Pratt about the situation?"

Griffith chuckled. "Those two tuned me out a long time ago. I'm not one of the good ol' boys. And Syd, neither are you."

"Do you trust them?" she asked. "Could one be behind this vigilante thing?"

Griffith's eyes settled on Syd. She remained silent for several seconds. "Not liking their management style and not trusting them are two different things. But I did a little spying. It's out there if you search for it."

Syd felt a tightness in her stomach. "Did you search the dark web?"

"Dark web, light web, anywhere I could get a hit," said Griffith. "I uncovered stuff they don't talk about in meetings."

"I've got fifteen minutes," said Syd. "I'd like to know more. Off the record."

Now, it was Griffith's turn to scan the room. "Syd, do you know county employee salaries are a part of the public record?"

"I never thought about it, but sure, I guess."

"Well, Pratt is pulling in a little north of $130 grand. You make half that. How much did you donate to charity last year?"

"Around a thousand."

"Would you like to guess how much Pratt donated? Not five, ten, or even twenty. He donated - now get this - $110,000. The charity is called the BLS Foundation - short for Bare Lymphocyte Syndrome. It's a rare disease that mostly affects young children.'

Syd tried to process what Griffith was saying. "That's a large amount, but he has a disabled son. Maybe he's committed to finding a cure."

"That's an exorbitant amount," said Griffith. "He also owns a $900,000 property on Indian Rocks Beach in Florida. And the home he resides in, well that's nearly a million."

"That's odd," said Syd. "But maybe his wife is super-successful, or one of them inherited money."

"His wife is a teaching golf pro. And his parents were blue-collar. But now that you mention it, I've never thought about researching *her* parents."

"Some people are born on third base," said Syd. "It happens. Is that all?"

"That would be all, unless you go back 17 years," said Griffith. "While Lasek was in Flagstaff, his wife was attacked by a stranger inside their residence. She gave a description, and the department came up with a suspect. Three weeks later, the guy was found dead in his apartment. The coroner listed the cause as 'Suicide/Undetermined'."

"Maybe the guy *did* take his own life."

"Or perhaps," said Griffith, "this guy was the vigilante's first victim."

"You're saying this vigilante shit goes back seventeen years?" asked Syd. "That's a long shot - at the buzzer from full court."

Griffith giggled. "Okay, I admit that's a reach. But Lasek was reprimanded on several occasions in Flagstaff. The last time was three years ago. He lost his temper and placed his hands around the throat of one of his detectives."

"I noticed he keeps a stress ball on his desk," said Syd. Thinking about Mitsoff, she added, "Maybe I should invest in one."

She hesitated before asking, "How do you feel about Mitsoff?"

Griffith leaned her head on the back on her chair. "I searched for him too. I haven't discovered anything yet, but we know that man is trouble. And from what I understand, buddying up to Lasek and Pratt won't benefit him anymore. He's on their shit list about that evidence room situation."

Syd glanced at the time on her cell phone. "Anything else?"

Griffith nodded. "I'm sure Montenegro told you about his meeting with the newly awakened McBride…the assignment given to him by Lasek?"

"What?" asked Syd. "No, he never mentioned anything."

"Well, I'll be damned," said Griffith. "I thought you two shared everything."

"Evidently not," said Syd.

Griffith checked the perimeter of the room again. "Don't

quote me, because I heard this second-hand. Montenegro claims McBride went mum on him at first. But later in their conversation, McBride asked him to come back next week, saying that his memory might be returning. I don't know about you, but that sounds like bullshit."

Syd shook her head. "If Stuart said that, I'm betting it's true. I wonder why he didn't tell me?"

"He's told others," said Griffith. "You may want to give him a call."

"Probably an oversight," said Syd, her mind buzzing.

As she left the diner, she couldn't shake the feeling that the precinct held more secrets than she had ever imagined. Why hadn't Montenegro shared information? She had always been forthcoming with him. And with Mitsoff on thin ice with the higher-ups, could he become even more dangerous? And what about the data Griffith provided about Pratt and Lasek? Was that all true? If so, did it have any relevance to the case?

As she turned on the exit for the highway, Syd dialed Montenegro's number. She was disappointed he hadn't confided in her, but perhaps there was a valid reason. He answered on the third ring.

"Miss Livingstone, I presume?"

"Heard a rumor you met with McBride after he came to. How did that go?"

Slight pause. "Yeah, I was going to tell you. Lasek sent me there."

"What were you trying to find out?"

"This is coming across as slightly abrupt, Syd. Am I being recorded?"

"I hope you're kidding."

Montenegro laughed. "Of course I am," he said. "I hope you're not upset. I was going to tell you."

"Stuart, I'm curious. But you don't *have* to tell me anything."

"Hang on a second," he said. She could hear the background volume on the television decrease. "I *do* owe you an explanation. McBride was evasive at first. But then we started talking about sports. He loved when the subject turned to UFC. By the end, he was opening up."

Syd was unsure where he was going. "Did he reveal anything important?"

"Not a damn thing," he said. "Except for how the fight with Cutter started. He doesn't remember anyone hanging around him, and certainly doesn't recall anybody jabbing him with a needle."

This wasn't jibing with Griffith's version, but Syd continued to listen.

"He was amenable to another meeting, mostly because I developed some rapport. So, as I'm driving home, I came up with an idea. Probably ill-conceived, but what the hell?"

"What idea?" she asked.

"I decided to tell a few of the chattier individuals at the precinct that McBride was beginning to get his memory back. I told them McBride was confident he could provide more information about his needle sticker sometime next week."

"Was that true?"

"Hell no," said Montenegro. "But there's some evidence that the vigilante might be associated with a Walsh County insider, right? That tidbit of information might be enough to cause this vigilante to slip up. If someone starts acting suspicious, that might give us a clue."

Syd paused. She had never known Montenegro to be this impulsive. "So does this call add me to your suspect list? Maybe you believe *I'm* panicking?"

Montenegro chuckled. "Honestly, you never entered my mind. We're friends and we trust each other. That's never going to change."

"Does anyone else know this is a little fib, or only me?"

"Just you," said Montenegro. "And please don't breathe a word. As stupid as it sounds, it may work."

Syd wondered if he had shared his plan with Stacey, but didn't ask. "Have you noticed anything? Anyone acting peculiar?"

"Well, that's the ill-conceived part of my plan. With everybody on edge, we're all acting a little weird. I could make a case for practically anyone. But I'm still in the early phase of observation."

When their talk ended, Syd wondered if Montenegro's idea might spur the vigilante into action. She also wondered if he had truly weighed the ramifications of his plan. Would McBride remain safe from someone who had a vested interest in keeping him quiet?

CHAPTER 21

Unlike most winters, late December had not yet brought a significant snowfall to the Northeast Ohio area. Only five days before Christmas, snow flurries danced in the sky like blithe fairies, completely unaware of the destiny that awaited them - a quick and complete disintegration on the dry ground.

This Saturday morning seemed like the unofficial kickoff to the holiday hiatus. Most businesses - except department stores and gift shops - were operating with skeleton crews. The ambiance at Walsh County was festive and carefree.

Lasek's digital wall clock displayed 10:34, reminding him he'd already put in three hours in the nearly deserted precinct. He promised Eileen he'd be home by noon. A matinee movie, a Christmas shopping excursion, and a take-home dinner of Thai food were on the itinerary.

Lasek's door remained wide open. Chances of being interrupted were low. He enjoyed the enhanced view the open door provided and the flowing of air and sounds, especially during this more casual time of year.

Down the hall sat patrolman Ray Bauer, a six-month newcomer to the force, one of three cops in the building. Bauer worked the main desk, serving as the first contact of any visitor entering the precinct. Veteran Walsh County employees had first dibs regarding the vacation schedule, and many had selected the holidays to enjoy time off with their families. The additional officers out on patrol weren't required to report back to the precinct during this time of year.

As Lasek was putting the finishing touches on a report - concerning a man on fentanyl who had somehow managed to gouge his own eye out - he noticed Bauer standing at the entrance of his office, waiting for eye contact.

"Damn, Bauer, you startled me," said Lasek. "I almost expected the two little girls in 'The Shining.'"

"Sorry, Commissioner," said Bauer. "But you have a visitor - a Ms. Watson. Were you expecting her?"

Lasek shook his head. "I wasn't expecting anyone. This is my day to get on top of reports. Ask her if she can come back after Christmas, if it's not too important."

Bauer stammered like he didn't want to upset Lasek. "She says it's pressing, sir. She requested you specifically. But I'll take her statement if you don't want to meet."

The matinee. What time did it start? Maybe 1:30.

"Okay," said Lasek. "Tell her I have ten minutes, but I'm working a tight schedule."

"I'll bring her back," said Bauer.

Already rehearsing an eloquent way to keep the meeting brief, Lasek found himself staring at a young, attractive woman in a long burgundy winter coat and a dusty pink beanie. She could've walked off the pages of a fashion magazine with a stylish short haircut. She appeared to have a fair amount of Asian ancestry. Something was familiar about her.

"Good morning, Commissioner Lasek," she said. "You probably don't remember me. I met you during the police awards at The Majestic Night Club."

Suddenly, it clicked.

"That's right!" said Lasek. "You're Monica. No, wait, Michelle."

"Yes, that's me," said the woman.

"My apologies," said Lasek. "I was told 'Ms. Watson' was waiting. I never knew your last name."

"You can call me Michelle. I'm sorry I didn't call for an appointment."

Lasek couldn't help but smile. Michelle was even more attractive away from the dimly lit Majestic.

"You're Tom Mitsoff's significant other," he said.

"Well, kinda," she said. "We broke up a couple of weeks ago."

"I'm sorry to hear that," said Lasek. "Mitsoff rarely discusses his private life."

"Oh, I would've expected him to talk about those things," said Michelle, removing the beanie. She smiled shyly and looked toward a seat in front of Lasek's desk. "If it's okay, may I?"

"Of course," said Lasek. "Please sit."

Lasek glanced at the Keurig coffee machine he'd installed a few months earlier.

"May I offer you some coffee?" he asked. "I also have bottled water."

"No, I'm good," said Michelle. "It's just that, well, I found something concerning. It may have some relevance to you."

Leaning back in his chair, Lasek waited for Michelle to continue.

"Tom told me that the Cefalo woman had received something by mail recently that was presented at her trial. I think I remember it as being some sort of fabric - maybe from a piece of clothing?"

"Close enough," acknowledged Lasek. "Go on."

"Well, whatever it was, he said there was a rumor it may have been taken from the evidence room - like by an actual member of the Walsh County Police Department?"

"We don't know," said Lasek. "We're still looking into it."

"Okay, well, I heard that story a while back, but I kind of forgot about it," she said.

"All right," said Lasek, glancing down at the clock on his cell phone. "So, what did you find?"

Michelle let out a deep sigh. She brought her fingers up to her lips as if trying to extract the right words. "It was during our final date. He'd finished pumping gas and headed into the store to buy a soft drink. I could tell he was planning to break up with me. In the minute I had by myself in his car, I did something I shouldn't have." She paused, staring down at the floor. "I hope I won't get into any trouble."

She looked like a shy teenager seeking approval.

"You're safe here," said Lasek. "Your story has my attention. Please continue."

Michelle left her seat and walked to the partially opened door. "Mind if I close this?"

"Not at all," said Lasek. "Please go on."

Michelle returned to her seat. "Everything had been going well, so I hadn't been expecting it, but I could see he was going to dump me. All I could think about was getting some of my property back."

She placed her hands back into her lap. "Sometimes I leave stuff in his glove compartment—like sunglasses and makeup. While he was outside the car, I dug in there. Sure enough, I found my sunglasses, but they were on top of something else. So, here's why I think I may have broken the law. I took this item and stuffed it into my pocket. When he got back, he didn't suspect anything."

Michelle reached into her purse, which she had placed on the floor. She pulled out a clear bag. Inside the bag was an item Lasek couldn't discern.

"Does this look familiar?" she asked.

Lasek extended his arm and took what she gave him.

In black marker, "Cefalo Trial" was printed on what looked like a freezer bag. Inside was a diamond pendant with the letters 'PJC' inscribed.

Penny Jane Cefalo. He remembered that item from the trial. It was found on the floor next to her boyfriend's head. It had been ripped off Cefalo's neck during their struggle. The item had never been returned to Cefalo because the DA was deciding whether to retry the case.

Lasek looked up. "Why did you decide to present this?"

Michelle sat up straighter in her chair, clearing her throat and brushing her hair from her forehead.

"At first, I wasn't sure what I was going to do," she said. "I called Tom two days later. I told him I took something from his glove compartment. I wanted to hear his side. But I'll be damned if he didn't play dumb, telling me he didn't know what I was talking about. I even played along and asked him if he wanted it back. So, get this. He said if whatever I took meant so much, I could just as well keep it. And that pissed me off. He acted like I stole cash or something."

"So why bring this to me now?" asked Lasek.

"Since we're not an item anymore, I thought you should know. I can't imagine Tom committing an awful crime, but with those attacks, I wanted to come clean."

From the view of his office window, Lasek could see the snow falling a little harder, although there was no significant accumulation.

"Did Tom ever speak to you about the so-called vigilante attacks?" he asked. "Or did he offer his opinion about the perpetrator?"

Michelle frowned in concentration. "We discussed what was happening," she said. "But he never gave an opinion."

"Mitsoff not having an opinion. That certainly doesn't sound like him. What about co-workers? Did he say much about them?"

"No," she said. "Only a funny story here or there. The only thing I can remember bothering him was when that female cop was taken hostage in that back room."

"Sydney Livingstone," said Lasek.

"Yes, Syd. He felt she'd made an error by entering that room with her gun. He said that no *male* cop would have ever done that."

"How did you feel when he made statements like that?" asked Lasek.

"He used to say things half-jokingly, so it was difficult to know when he was being serious," she shrugged. "But as a woman, I resented those remarks."

Walking to the small refrigerator in the corner of his office, Lasek removed two bottles of water. He placed one in front of Michelle. He unscrewed the cap of his own and chugged until the container was empty. "I'm going to have to keep this pendant as evidence," he said. "Do you have any other information for me today?"

After thinking for a brief moment, Michelle shook her head.

"I hope I didn't waste your time, sir. Deep down, I still care for Tom."

Lasek stood, which prompted Michelle to also rise. "I cannot express how grateful I am," he said. "Every piece of evidence moves us one step closer."

After Michelle left, Lasek sat in his office, examining the evidence bag. Tonight, he'd give Pratt a call. And they would decide whether to confront Mitsoff on Monday morning.

CHAPTER 22

Syd wasn't feeling lighthearted in the five days before Christmas, as her first stint as a detective allowed for little time off between holidays.

The holidays held no significance for criminals, who often took advantage of the trusting nature of those caught up in the festive spirit. In fact, this time of year was when they were most active.

It had been days since she observed activity from The Enforcer on the dark web. It was highly probable that The Enforcer had loved ones too. Being a crazed assassin with a twisted sense of justice didn't exempt someone from holiday obligations. Maybe everyone could take a break and then restart the game of chase after the New Year. Enzo would return to Ohio soon, and they needed time together to plan their future.

She'd spent an hour shopping at the Belden Village Mall in Canton. Despite being off work for the weekend, she found herself a little stressed.

Syd had set her phone alarm for 1:45, although she knew

she was unlikely to forget her 2 o'clock appointment. She expected the meeting with Lieutenant Gil Trent, from the Franklin County Homicide Division, to be bitter-sweet.

Several years earlier, Trent had played a major role in stopping a deranged killer who stalked Syd while she competed in one of the final tournaments of her career. She and Trent had developed a close relationship by the end of that case. In fact, he had been the one to suggest she consider law enforcement when her tennis career ended.

Trent had phoned unexpectedly a few days earlier. He'd expressed concern after hearing details of the vigilante case. He even mentioned her hostage predicament with Cutter. "We should meet," he said. "You've been through a lot for a first-year cop."

Now, she spotted Trent sitting in the food court, surrounded by the enticing smells of stir fry and cinnamon rolls. She was almost at his table before he finally looked up from his laptop. He rose from the table and extended his arms to embrace her.

"Lieutenant Trent, you must be psychic. I think about you all the time. I wanted so badly to call you. I'm glad you decided to come up to Canton."

"Happy to do it," said Trent. "But you've got to cut the 'Lieutenant' crap. I'm Gil, okay?"

He smiled and waved at a server, who brought several plates to their table. "I hope you don't mind, but I ordered the sample platters," said Trent. "I figured this would be a good opportunity to try a variety of food."

Syd looked into Trent's eyes and smiled. "You saved my life. I'll call you whatever name you like. And this is perfect. Thanks."

The waiter also brought a full teapot and a pair of cups to their table.

"How's Enzo?" asked Trent. "I was surprised to hear you two haven't tied the knot yet."

Syd cleared her throat. "Still working out some details. No firm date yet."

Trent gave her a penetrating look. "I've been a detective for over twenty-five years. Are you holding back something?"

"There have been a few bumps in the road. Hopefully, we can smooth them out over the holidays."

Trent nodded. "You know, he was on our radar a few years ago when you were being stalked. I was relieved when we found out he wasn't the perp."

"If you would've just asked me, I could've told you," she said. "He's not the dangerous type, unless he's on the tennis court."

"Sometimes I catch him on TV," said Trent. "Your case converted me into a tennis fan. I still miss watching you play."

"I serve the community now, not tennis balls," said Syd. "What made you contact me after so long?"

Trent slid a bowl of rice toward Syd and poured a cup of tea. "Basically, I'm worried about you. The hostage situation had to be harrowing, especially after what you experienced before becoming an officer. And now, some crazy vigilante is running rampant in your backyard."

Syd smiled. "It makes the stress of competing on the tour seem like child's play. But I knew what I was getting into."

"I'm not so sure," said Trent. She heard his phone buzz and watched him dismiss the call before setting it on the table. "I also read about your suspension. And that's one of the main reasons I contacted you."

"Which is?" asked Syd.

"Maybe a new start is what you need," he said. "You've been to our precinct in the Columbus area. I've seen your tenacity and dedication. You'd be ideal for our department. You could put the whole suspension thing behind you. And, as far as I know, there are no vigilantes prowling our streets."

"I'm flattered," said Syd. "But there's more to it, Gil. The vigilante may be a member of our department."

Trent fumbled with his spoon. "What the hell. A cop?"

"Possibly," said Syd. "Or someone associated with the department."

"Syd, aren't you concerned about your safety?"

For a moment, Syd was grateful that Enzo wasn't here. He'd be in full agreement. "I've never been one to run from difficult situations," she said. "As crazy as it sounds, I like my job and, for the most part, the people I work with."

Trent let out a sigh, his brow furrowed. "This isn't a game. Syd."

Syd put her lips to her cup, making sure the tea wasn't too hot. "And that's why I was thrilled when you called. I feel safe speaking to you."

Trent gave a small nod before pushing his half-eaten plate away. "I've done a little research, mostly off-duty. Tell me what you've discovered."

For the next half-hour, Syd unloaded. She discussed the depth of her relationships with Montenegro, Mitsoff, and Griffith, which soon led into the management styles of Lasek and Pratt. She talked about Fosterno's strange behavior during the awards ceremony, his supposed stalker, and the way he reacted to the threatening note. And finally, the strange relationship between Fosterno and Cefalo. She also mentioned the previous attacks that were more than likely perpetrated by the vigilante. Trent never interrupted, occasionally scribbling a few notes.

When she finished, Syd sighed. "I'm sure I've left out a few details," she said. "But I wanted to give you a bird's-eye view."

Trent glanced at his notes. "Damn, that's a lot of shit. I'm always available to help. Just pick up the phone. But I do have a few questions."

Syd leaned forward; her eyes fixed on Trent. Taking a deep breath, she braced herself for what she knew would be a difficult conversation. She was used to facing tough opponents on the court, but this battle was different. It was a tangled web of deception and danger that threatened not just her career but the lives of those she cared about.

"Ask away, Gil."

Trent tapped his pen against the table. "Let's start with Montenegro. You mentioned a close relationship with him. How close are we talking?"

"He's my best friend on the force. We're friends. I'd trust Stuart with my life."

"Is it possible he feels differently about you?"

"No way," said Syd. "His wife, Stacey, is lovely, and they seem happy."

Trent's phone buzzed again. He pushed the button to let the call go through to voicemail. "You mentioned a breach in the department - evidence stolen and later reappearing. Have they questioned Mitsoff since he was in charge?"

"They've questioned everyone, but so far, there's been no evidence linking anyone to the theft," Syd explained. "Mitsoff swears he didn't do it, and no one has been able to prove otherwise."

"Let me see if I can dig up any dirt on this character," said

Trent. "Maybe someone in our precinct knows him. Also, anything to indicate whether this so-called vigilante is a man or woman?"

Syd thought for a moment. "Whoever this person is operates like a professional, leaving few traces behind. We honestly don't know."

Trent placed his elbow on the table and massaged his forehead with his fingers. "Captain Wilma Griffith. You've established a certain type of friendship with her as well?"

"You could say that," said Syd. "When she's not working undercover, she's with us. She's a wonderful soul, but damn tough if anyone gets in her way."

Trent flipped a page. "And that brings us to Pratt having a great deal of money, at least according to Griffith. Who knows? Maybe he's greased the palms of organized crime or invested extremely well in stocks or real estate."

"And don't forget about Lasek's past," said Syd.

"I'd heard of Lasek before you even started with the department," he said. "He got into trouble in Flagstaff. Has he ever shown a penchant toward violence?"

"Nope," said Syd. "Not even a hint."

"Okay. A couple more observations," said Trent. "You say this Fosterno character has been acting irrationally. I don't know if someone is really following him, but you need to keep your distance. And, Penny Cefalo, that woman he is 'protecting', - and I'm using that word lightly - she's already proven to be dangerous. Putting the two of them together is a powder keg."

Trent picked up the dirty plates and placed them on an adjacent bus table. When he returned, he sat beside Syd, speaking in a low tone. "Have you considered that maybe this vigilante is targeting specific individuals within the department for a reason? Could there be a pattern you're missing?"

Syd sat motionlessly, wanting to respond but unable to find the words. Trent stood up and extended his hand.

"I know we've shared a lot, and I've given you some stuff to think about," he said. "If you think of something we haven't discussed, call. On the drive back, if I have any amazing revelations, I'll give you a call."

Trent took a couple of steps in the opposite direction and then stopped. Looking over his shoulder, he said, "Syd, please be extremely careful."

CHAPTER 23

Three days after Christmas, Syd rolled over in her bed, reaching for Enzo. He wasn't there. His flight to the next tournament was leaving Cleveland at 7 am. He'd probably left her place around 4, being careful not to wake her.

She still had some time before she had to shower and leave for work. She thought about the time she and Enzo had spent together. While they had enjoyed some special moments over Christmas - exchanging presents, drinking wine, and being intimate - she still sensed something amiss. She could barely discuss her work. Whenever she brought up a vigilante or The Enforcer, he shut down emotionally.

"My biggest fear is that I'm going to receive a call about something tragic happening," said Enzo. "If this psycho is someone involved with the police or county, they're right on your doorstep."

Were they still engaged? Yes, according to Enzo. But Syd hated the fact that he was under such stress. Although Enzo never suggested it, she wondered if his anxiety over her was hurting his career. She knew first-hand of the fragility of the mind, especially when it came to competing against the world's top athletes.

Syd's mind reverted back to the dark web. She hadn't slept especially well. When she finally succumbed, she dreamed about her virtual travels there. She had encountered The Enforcer several times in the past week, using the "DarkMistress" designation. She'd mostly gone along with whatever The Enforcer was posting, pretending to be an interested admirer. The Enforcer had amassed quite a following.

Something wasn't sitting right about the forum chat the previous night. As always, she'd captured the conversation by performing a 'Print Screen' function.

She rose from bed and moved to the kitchen, where her laptop sat on the table. Her hands trembled as she reviewed the screenshots. There was an eerie sense of familiarity about the conversation. In her sleep, her mind had tormented her, trying to reconcile something. Whatever it was, she wasn't sure.

Flipping through several pages of material, she searched for something incongruous. A piece that didn't fit. After reading several pages, she convinced herself that she was being irrational. Imagination overload. Overthinking. Then, she found what had been gnawing at her. The Enforcer had been chatting with several people about a group of vigilantes from Oregon who had banded together to track down a family of killers. There was a contribution by someone named "BoredChairman" that caught her attention.

The Enforcer: Pooling efforts is the best

```
method to stop people who are doing evil
things.
BoredChairman: It takes a village.
Teamwork.
The Enforcer: Whenever stuff like this
happens, I become overwhelmed with
excitement.
BoredChairman: You're excited because
you're experiencing the "Big O." And the
"O" stands for "Organization."
```

Now she knew exactly what was causing her to lose sleep, other than Enzo's early-morning flight. She'd heard that phrase before. The Big O, standing for "Organization." There was only one person she'd known who'd ever used that phrase: Detective Tom Mitsoff.

While she'd never heard Mitsoff discuss a desire to take down criminals through unconventional means, she remembered how his eyes burned whenever he became upset. Perhaps the pieces of the puzzle were falling into place. The evidence of his participation was right in front of her, staring back from the paper she held in her hand. Enough proof for an arrest and conviction? Of course not. But her first visit this morning would be with Montenegro. Perhaps they could put their heads together and decide how to proceed.

CHAPTER 24

A little more than three weeks after his hospital discharge, Frank McBride was beginning to go stir-crazy. He'd spent most of his time in his man cave, a secluded room in the basement equipped with a wide-screen TV, two laptop computers, a double bed, a pinball machine, and an authentic carnival popcorn maker, which he won in a bidding war on eBay.

Surfing the internet for three straight weeks had become boring, even laborious. Frank found himself staring at his stationary bike and the twenty-year-old stepping machine, which he'd relegated to a remote corner because it bothered his knees. He'd give anything for an hour, or even 30 minutes, on either device. A workout fanatic, Frank had always spent a great deal of time in his basement, riding his specialty bike (accompanied by an automated trainer), pumping iron with free weights, and stretching and meditating. His mind and body were used to the endorphin rush spawned by intense exercise. But now, it had been months since he'd experienced those feelings. The hospital doctors had revealed that he was quite lucky to be alive; at one point in the ER, he had flat-lined for more than a minute.

The closest thing to a workout high he'd had was the pain management medication administered - both orally and intravenously - in the hospital. With the doctors cautioning him against exercise for at least another couple of weeks, he found himself longing for the medications again. But before his hospital stay, Frank had eschewed drugs most of his life. While he enjoyed imbibing on special occasions, anything drug-related was a no-no in his book.

Andrea had returned to work on a full-time basis, now that Frank's health allowed him to take care of himself. She worked in retail, which meant her working hours were while he was off. And vice-versa.

Sundays, like today, were often spent alone, watching football during the fall or basketball in the winter. Today was an off week for his favorite team, the Pittsburgh Steelers. His favorite sport to watch was mixed martial arts. If he were 10 to 15 years younger, Frank would have loved to have competed. He felt he could have been world-class.

Climbing the stairs to exit his basement, it became more apparent that his conditioning had deteriorated. By the time he reached the first floor, he was sucking air, eager to park his butt on the living room couch. Frank had only been out of the house three times since he returned from the hospital, with Andrea driving him to a restaurant for a quick bite on each occasion.

He started thinking about his garage, where his '85

Mustang GT seemed to beckon him. If he couldn't get the endorphin effect via exercise, then perhaps speed and power would suffice…anything to break out of his current mindset.

Andrea would be pissed if she found out that he took the car for a spin, especially since doctors had warned him against driving for at least another week. But she wouldn't have to know. And even if she found out, he'd overcome bigger obstacles in the past…including the death penalty, thanks to twelve gullible jurors.

Frank hadn't touched his car keys in over a month. He found them hanging where he expected, on a hook in the laundry room. As he grasped the keys, Frank flashed back to another time when he frantically clutched them, fumbling to the trunk of his car to place the body of his dead wife inside. He'd strangled her quite efficiently that day. No blood or other body fluids had stained the fabric lining.

While on the way to dispose of the body, Frank had thought about praying - asking God to allow him to remain undetected. But then he thought about the hypocrisy. He knew he'd crossed the line when he choked her into lifelessness. And God - if such an entity existed - was aware.

In the end, it was easier to believe God wasn't real. And if not, there was no advantage in praying. It was a waste of time. With no God in the picture, there was a good chance he wouldn't have to pay for Sheila's death after his demise.

The thought of a real God was too depressing to consider.

I wasn't unhappy before I was born, and I won't be sad after I die.

The Mustang was a sight to behold. He'd purchased the

car at an auction in 2015. The exterior was cherry red, guaranteed to attract the attention of law enforcement when it rocketed past at 105 mph. Under the hood was a five-liter (302 cid), 210hp engine that could propel this beast beyond 160. The thick black hood stripe transformed the car from a sporty-looking sedan to a bad-ass machine.

When Frank bought it, he severely compromised the budget that he and Sheila created. But that seemed to be the way it always flowed for Frank - living paycheck-to-paycheck, paying one creditor at the expense of another. That is, until his mother passed and left him an inheritance in the mid-five figures. And later, when he was acquitted of murder and received access to Sheila's insurance money, over the vehement protests of her family.

Today, a cloudy Sunday afternoon, he could enjoy his beloved vehicle - free from the constraints of a tight budget and a murder charge. He envisioned a lone country road, pushing its capabilities to the limit, just him and the car. What could possibly go wrong?

As Frank's Mustang pulled out of the driveway and made its way down his residential street, the unexpected activity alerted someone waiting nearby. There would be no home invasion this afternoon. Instead, The Enforcer followed McBride in a vehicle.

Frank wondered where he should go on this impromptu joyride. Maybe drop by Rex Cutter's apartment? He quickly dismissed the idea. He hadn't told Andrea about the call he received from the man he'd fought with at the theme park. In fact, McBride had little memory of the incident, just hearing a harsh word or two from someone he considered a pipsqueak. The next thing he knew, he was waking up in a hospital bed. It was the police reports he read after emerging from his coma that let him know someone had injected him with a potentially lethal dose of insulin before the confrontation.

Rex had seemed contrite on the phone, inviting Frank to his home for what he called a "kumbaya coffee." It had been an unexpected, bizarre conversation.

"I thought you'd died, and they were going to frame me for murder," said Cutter. "But we both know I barely tapped you. The next thing I knew, you were doing a nose-first face plant on the floor. And now I'm facing ten years for attempted murder on some rookie girl cop. What kinda shit is that?"

McBride's natural aggression kicked in to cover his surprise.

"You actually have the stones to call me at my home? The last thing you want is me at your door."

Five seconds of silence. Then Cutter spoke again. "I'm not calling to piss you off," he said. "I want to apologize. And I'd like to do it in person."

The few people McBride had ever trusted had betrayed him. He was not about to trust Cutter now.

"There's something you're not telling me. I don't believe you want to kiss and make up."

McBride heard Cutter's attempt to suppress a chuckle.

"Okay," the man admitted. "There is another reason. I want you to testify. You know, tell them our scuffle was nothing. Then, my lawyer can show how the police set me up to take a bigger fall. You and I have more in common than you think."

"You should feel fortunate that someone slipped me a mickey," Frank growled. "Consider yourself blessed and move on. I'm not here to cushion your fall."

With that, he had clicked off the phone, fully expecting Cutter to call back. Perhaps if he had, McBride might have been amenable to a compromise. But then again, he wasn't sure. But the point was moot. Cutter never called back.

After today's cathartic drive, maybe McBride would show up at Cutter's place, unannounced. Not for exacting revenge, although he was up for anything if Cutter pushed it. Perhaps they had more in common than he initially thought. McBride knew all about facing charges from an unreasonable prosecutor, whether they were justified or not. Wouldn't it be ironic if he struck up a friendship with Cutter after all? Frank had few friends. Most of the people in his martial arts class wanted nothing to do with him. And in the eyes of the public, he was a pariah for murdering his wife and beating the rap.

McBride turned off Westerly Lane and onto Cavanaugh Street. He was five minutes or so from some of the country roads, where he planned to see what the car could do. As McBride approached a four-way stop, the cell phone he'd placed on his seat lurched forward and hit the floor. As he hit the brake, the phone slid under the passenger seat.

After uttering an expletive, he looked for other cars. With none around, he put his car in park and leaned to grope under the seat. The tip of his middle finger struck the edge of his cell, but he couldn't quite grasp it. Damn!

Frank pressed the lever in front of the passenger seat to initiate its backward movement. He extended his arm, feeling arthritic shoulder pain that had worsened considerably over the years. Grunting while reaching, his middle and index finger finally clutched the end of the phone. He pulled his hand back slowly, not wanting to loosen his grip and restart the entire process. Inch-by-inch, the phone moved forward. Finally, McBride had it with his hand.

Crisis averted.

He hoped no one had pulled up behind him. But then again, screw it. They'd just have to be inconvenienced.

He sat back up in his seat and grabbed the shift, ready to put the vehicle back into drive. His thoughts were interrupted by a knock at the window.

Someone was standing next to the driver's side. A dark helmet, like those worn by motorcyclists, concealed his face.

Shit! A cop? Are they going to write me up for parking too long at a stop sign?

Is that even illegal?

If this was a cop, he or she was about to get a piece of his mind. A real beat down - worse than what the prosecutor had done to him on the stand. The person at the window was reaching downward.

Sit back. The fireworks are about to begin.

Frank had already begun cursing before pressing the button to lower the window. Suddenly, his expression changed. He wasn't angry anymore. He was trying to comprehend what was happening. Why was this person pointing a gun at him?

Am I going to be removed from my car at gunpoint? For dropping my damn phone?

Frank would never find out. The flash of light was sudden, and he never even heard the half-lowered window glass shattering. His final vision was Sheila's face, her body still in the trench where he'd left her.

Was she really smiling at him?

CHAPTER 25

A songbird - bright yellow, but a black wing running down the length of its body - darted in the sky above Syd as she sat in a field of flowing white daffodils. It hovered above her for a few seconds before landing gently on the back of her hand.

The bird didn't seem nervous or skittish, but Syd remained motionless. It stared at her with eyes like black beads, reminding her of the obsidian necklace she once purchased from a Cancun Street vendor.

The bird chirped as though trying to talk to her. She stretched out her free hand, hoping to befriend it before it flew away. Her hand seemed to pass through its body as the chirping grew louder and more pronounced.

Despite Syd's attempt to stroke it, the bird remained motionless. The chirping grew louder, angry. Then, without warning, the bird darted at her face.

Syd sat up in bed, feeling the rataplan of her heart. She grabbed her cell phone off the nightstand and stared at the screen, which read 5:07. Her Monday morning alarm had been chirping for seven minutes.

Shutting off the alarm, she noticed two texts. The first was from Montenegro at 3:17 am.

McBride dead. Murder. See ya in the AM

Syd read the message again to make sure she didn't misinterpret it. *WTF?*

The next message was from Pratt. It arrived at 4:29.

McBride's dead. Let's talk tomorrow.

Syd checked the news on her cell in search of the McBride story. The media hadn't caught wind of it yet. Rex Cutter came to mind. He remained on house arrest.

Did Cutter search out McBride and terminate him? Could he have been the vigilante killer all along?

Not plausible, with that band strapped to his ankle. There was no evidence he harbored a vendetta against murderers who had beaten the rap.

Syd removed her beige night dress and dropped it on the bathroom floor. She'd always found a hot shower to be great therapy, allowing her the opportunity to reflect on the upcoming day.

She recalled how she and Enzo would make a special effort to rise at least 30 minutes early so they could enjoy it together. She missed the feeling of Enzo's hands rubbing her shoulders, gliding smoothly with the assistance of lavender body wash.

She couldn't help but think about Montenegro's dubious plan to catch the vigilante, involving a fabricated story about

McBride's returning memories. Did Montenegro's actions cause The Enforcer to take out McBride? How would Stuart feel about that?

As she massaged shampoo onto her scalp, her mind wandered to the thought of murder - the chase, the capture, and ultimately, the killing. Montenegro never mentioned a suspect. It had to be The Enforcer or someone working for them, fulfilling the prophecies posted on the dark web. She wondered about any witnesses. So far, the descriptions of anyone who might have been the vigilante were sketchy at best.

If the killer was someone working for Walsh County, they were busy last night and probably didn't get much sleep. She made a note to search for anyone who called in sick or seemed excessively tired. It was worth a try.

She couldn't help but think about Fosterno. Was he in danger, being chased by someone who wanted him dead? Or was he attempting to shift the focus off himself? She liked Kevin, and even Griffith trusted him, but neither were experts in psychology. And even if they were..

If someone was pursuing him, who were they? Loan sharks? Gamblers? Blackmailers? Gang members hellbent on revenge? For the moment, he wasn't talking.

Syd shook her head to release the water from her hair. She resolved to put her theories on hold for the time being. At the meeting, she'd let Lasek and Pratt lead the way.

Her instincts told her something was about to break. But with only limited police experience behind her, were her instincts valid?

CHAPTER 26

As the holiday season drew to a close and the year ended, things began to settle back into place. But in Walsh County, the situation was far from normal. When Lasek approached the podium for the year's first meeting, it became obvious that change was on the horizon. He kicked off the gathering with a whopper of an announcement.

"As you may have heard, there's been a development in the vigilante case." Lasek paused for a moment, letting the news sink in. He cleared his throat before continuing. "Everyone remembers Frank McBride. He was the first attack, the victim who started all of this vigilante nonsense. He was murdered last night in his car."

As Syd canvassed the room, it seemed most officers were startled by the news. Griffith appeared completely taken aback. Syd wondered why they would keep the news from Griffith. As a captain, you'd think she would be the first to be informed. Apparently, the good-ol'-boy network in Walsh County was still alive and well.

Fosterno, who had kept a low profile since the incident at The Majestic, exited the room. She wanted to follow, but Lasek continued speaking.

"We've interviewed a witness," he said. "Hopefully, the information they provide will be helpful."

"I thought McBride was in a coma," said a voice from the left corner.

"He left the hospital several weeks ago," said Lasek. "He beat the odds by surviving his first attack. Last night, apparently, the odds evened themselves out. We'll post details about the crime on our website and ask anyone else who may have seen anything to come forward. Once the media gets hold of this, I expect a huge reaction."

Syd could see Fosterno pacing in the hallway. He showed no signs of returning.

"Can we go back to the witness?" asked Griffith. "What kind of information did he provide?"

Lasek took a sip of coffee from a foam cup. "Actually, it's not a man. Her name is Jessica R-I-D-G-E-W-A-Y. She pulled behind McBride's car at a stop sign. The car wasn't moving, so she gave her horn a courtesy tap. She looked closer and couldn't see anyone in the driver's seat. She got out of the car and saw McBride slumped in a pool of blood. She panicked obviously, but thought she remembered someone driving away on a motorcycle in the opposite direction. The only thing she recalled was that they wore a dark helmet and fled at a high rate of speed."

Did she provide other details about the assailant?" asked Griffith. Male, female, tall or short?"

"She claimed there was no way to tell," said Lasek. "Because of her trauma, she couldn't provide us with anything else."

She scratched "Motorcycle" and "Mitsoff" on her pad, followed by a large question mark. She showed it to Montenegro. He nodded and shrugged.

"I want everyone to prepare for a media blitz," said Lasek. "Chief Pratt and I are hosting a press conference this afternoon. Please do not talk with the media. I expect your cooperation on this matter."

Silence.

"There is another matter that you should know about," said Lasek. "I'm going to turn it over to Chief Pratt."

Pratt thanked Lasek and took his place in front of the podium.

Then, someone blurted out, "Is Mitsoff a suspect in the murder of McBride and the other attacks?"

Pratt raised a hand. "Accusing our fellow officers of a crime is unwarranted at this time. But there is a killer out there who's trying to influence the scales of justice. It's our job to stop them before they kill again.

"Unfortunately, there's a segment of the population who identify with this wacko. They feel this person is justified in ridding our community of criminals. As officers, we can't support this narrative. Our job is to enforce the law."

As the meeting drew to a close, Syd spotted Fosterno in the hallway. He stood near a window, staring out into the street below with a furrowed brow.

"Everything all right?" she asked.

Fosterno watched Lasek and Pratt head to their offices. Syd wondered if they'd even noticed when he left the meeting.

"Sure," he replied, "besides that a killer may be one of us. And while I'm in this meeting, someone is probably in the process of stalking my girl-" Fosterno broke off.

"I'm sorry," he continued. "I meant to say 'Penny.' This vigilante killed McBride. We all know Penny is next. And I'm here in this building, miles away."

Syd put her hand on Fosterno's shoulder. "Penny's a tough cookie. She's more than capable of handling herself."

Fosterno moved Syd's hand away. "Are you saying that because she killed her boyfriend in self-defense? Or are you calling her a murderer?"

Syd stepped back. "Kevin, I'm simply saying she can handle herself. Don't read any more into it."

"The department doesn't think so," said Fosterno. "They have me protecting her to prevent this vigilante thing from exploding. Well guess what? With McBride's execution, it already has."

"But Penny's still safe," said Syd.

"For now," said Fosterno. "They already shot out her window when I wasn't around. It's only a matter of time."

As Fosterno grabbed his briefcase and rushed out the door, Syd considered talking to Lasek about getting him some internal counseling.

Pratt had announced during the first meeting of the year that Mitsoff had taken a "self-imposed leave of absence." No time frame was given, but rumor was that Mitsoff would remain off at least until February.

News of the discovery of Cefalo's pendant had spread through the precinct, eliciting a mixed reaction among the officers. Few were convinced of Mitsoff's innocence. Syd couldn't tell if they truly believed in his guilt or if their dislike for him influenced their thinking. To Syd's surprise, one of

Mitsoff's biggest defenders was Griffith. "I smell a setup," she confided to Syd and Montenegro. "I don't like him, but I don't buy that he's some kind of vigilante."

"Where do you stand?" Montenegro asked Syd. "Do you think he's been stealing stuff from the evidence room to harass Cefalo?"

"I wish I knew," Syd shook her head. "Even if he was the one pilfering the Cefalo evidence, that doesn't make him a killer."

"It would get him fired," said Montenegro. "That's a big gamble for such a small payoff. Do you think he might be working with somebody?"

Syd shrugged. "Damned if I know. I don't see him as the killing type, but he could be someone's sidekick. Then again, why? What would he have to gain? He seems too self-centered to worry about punishing strangers who beat the rap."

Syd hesitated, unsure of how to ask Montenegro a question she knew would make things awkward between them. "How are you feeling about what happened to McBride?"

Montenegro paused, placing his head into his hands. "Why are you asking?"

Meeting Montenegro's gaze, Syd attempted to suppress a nervous smile. "I think you know why," she said.

Montenegro nodded. "Do you believe it's my fault that McBride's dead? You think my little trap backfired?"

Syd didn't respond.

"My plan to lie about McBride's memory was meant to elicit a reaction. Whether it caused McBride to be murdered, I guess we'll never know."

Syd shook her head. "You're my friend, Stuart. I want to make sure you're okay."

Montenegro's expression turned serious. "We all know McBride killed his wife. He got exactly what he deserved. If I set the wheels in motion, I can live with that."

Syd took a deep breath. "Did you ever interview McBride a second time? Everyone was expecting that."

"No. I was in a quandary because he didn't remember anything. But now I don't have to keep up the facade. Remember, I told you that off the record."

Syd felt her stomach tighten. She had always admired his dedication and investigative skills, but this conversation unsettled her.

"Don't worry," she said. " "It'll remain our little secret."

Monday morning's 7 o'clock meeting began promptly, with Pratt beginning the briefing.

There was a new video of an individual who had broken into the foundry on Wisconsin Ave. They'd be posting it online later today.

A carjacking on Highsmith St. had left a woman and her adolescent son shaken, but uninjured. She was in the process of working with a sketch artist to develop a composite.

A house fire on Crittendale Drive was being investigated as arson.

As Pratt paused, Detective Cataldi raised his hand at the back of the room. Cataldi had kept a low profile since the incident with Fosterno. As far as she could tell, everyone seemed content with letting the incident go. "Quick comment," he said. "Channel 8 is reporting that Mitsoff was suspended because he may have taken items from the evidence room. They mentioned a patch of clothing and a pendant. Is that factual?"

Pratt looked toward Lasek, who remained in his chair, expressionless.

"Mitsoff has taken voluntary leave of absence," said Pratt. "There's no proof he took anything. We're still investigating."

Syd knew about the patch of clothing, but the pendant was new information. She remembered in the Cefalo case files that Penny's pendant was part of the evidence presented. Had someone removed that, too?

"Okay," said Cataldi. "I'm not trying to create controversy. I wanted to let you know what's being reported."

Lasek stepped up to the podium. "I'm glad you brought that to our attention, Cataldi. Lots of information seems to be leaking from our office, and a good portion is not accurate. Let's not take what the media says as gospel. Most of it is hearsay."

Everyone remained silent.

A 90-minute lunch, consisting of delivered pepperoni pizza and chicken wings, followed the meeting. After that, the detectives and patrol officers were sent back to their normal duties, except for Syd and Montenegro, who were called into Lasek's office.

During times of high anxiety, she often suffered from what her counselor termed "What If" thinking. What if they had found out that she was aware of Montenegro's bluff concerning another McBride interview? Syd could not afford another suspension.

She focused on her breathing as she waited for Lasek and Pratt to enter the room.

Everything's going to be okay. Stop imagining things that aren't going to happen.

Lasek entered and sat behind his desk, plopping a steaming mug of coffee in front of him. Pratt followed, occupying the sofa on the right side of the room that Lasek normally reserved for dignitaries.

"I'll get straight to the point," said Lasek. "I'm putting both of you on the McBride murder."

Montenegro, always cool under pressure, nodded calmly. Syd admired his composure. "Why us?" she asked.

"Normally, I would have placed Mitsoff with Montenegro," said Lasek. "But with him out, I decided to give you this opportunity, Livingstone."

Montenegro caught her gaze and smiled. Syd felt a flicker of doubt. Could she trust her friend completely?

"We need fresh perspectives on this case," said Lasek. "There have been some new developments, and I've seen the way the two of you interact. I'd like you to focus on the McBride case and the vigilante situation as your top priorities."

Montenegro leaned forward in his chair. "We'll do you right, Commissioner." he paused before continuing. "Can you tell us about this pendant thing? I know nothing and I'm sure Syd doesn't either."

"I'll brief you," said Lasek. "You also might want to interview Michelle Watson, Mitsoff's former girlfriend. She's the one who turned over the pendant. I would also recommend a conversation with Rex Cutter."

"Will you share what you've uncovered so far?" asked Montenegro.

"Certainly," said Lasek. "Fosterno and Griffith were working the case until Fosterno was assigned to Cefalo. Now he's too close to the situation to continue. I'll give you their notes. Now before I kick you out of my office, any questions?"

Syd looked over at Montenegro, who shook his head. "I have a question," said Syd, "although I'm hesitant to ask."

"This is an open forum," said Lasek. "Ask away."

Could she be overstepping? Syd took a deep breath and closed her eyes.

"Okay, Commissioner Lasek. As you know, there have been leaks in the department, leading people - including you - to speculate that someone on the inside may be involved. Have you ever thought about calling in an outside agency?"

Lasek reached into a drawer, pulled out a file, and handed it to Syd. "Please read through this. It will explain the visit from Mitsoff's former girlfriend. Regarding your other question, no. Chief Pratt and I don't feel this investigation requires outside intervention.

"So Detective Livingstone, are you up to the challenge? Do you feel comfortable working with Sergeant Montenegro on the McBride case?"

"Yes sir," said Syd. "And I appreciate your faith in us."

Montenegro stood up from the sofa, flashing a confident grin at Syd before extending his hand toward Lasek. "Thank you for this opportunity, Commissioner."

As they exited Lasek's office and made their way back to their desks, Syd felt a surge of excitement. This was the kind of opportunity she had been waiting for, a chance to redeem herself and showcase her investigative skills.

Syd spent the next few hours reviewing the Watson file and wondering why Mitsoff would be careless enough to leave stolen evidence in his glove compartment for his girlfriend to find. She requested the password for Mitsoff's computer, and Lasek provided it.

Her tired mind drifted to last night's bird dream. Then she remembered the early texts. She rechecked her phone, examining both and the times they arrived. She found Montenegro at his desk, absorbed in his computer screen.

"Stuart, can I have a word?" she asked. She looked around at the other officers shuffling by. "Let's talk in the hall."

Montenegro tapped at a few more keys. His screen went dark, and he stood to follow her.

"We'll hit the ground hard on the McBride case tomorrow," he said. "What's on your mind?"

"Thanks for alerting me about McBride this morning," she said. "But I'm a little curious about something."

Montenegro said nothing.

"I received your text about McBride's murder at 3:17 this morning. I was asleep, so I didn't open it until later."

Montenegro nodded. "You were the first person I wanted to share the news with," he said.

"I appreciate that," said Syd, now beginning to regret the question she was about to ask. "But I also received a text from Pratt about an hour later, mentioning that there were new developments in the vigilante case. I assume that he was talking about McBride's murder."

Montenegro nodded.

"Stuart, how did you know about what happened to McBride so early, more than an hour before Pratt's text?"

Syd's question seemed to surprise him.

"That's an easy one," he said. "Because I was the guy on the motorcycle. I shot McBride."

Five seconds later, Montenegro burst out laughing. He put his left hand on Syd's right shoulder and gave it a strong squeeze. "I had you for a second. Sorry, but I couldn't resist."

Syd stared at him for a long time before responding. "That was funny, I have to admit," she said. "But you didn't answer my question."

Stepping backward, Montenegro's eyes narrowed.

"You're seriously asking me that question? You really think that I might have-"

"I'm not thinking anything," said Syd. "When something doesn't add up, I ask. Blame the academy."

"Did the academy also teach you to question the veracity of your friends?"

Syd wasn't sure if he was still kidding. She decided to take him at face value.

"You're the closest friend I have here, Stuart. But I would like an answer."

Montenegro removed his hand from Syd's shoulder and folded his arms defensively. "All right," he said. "Although I'm not thrilled about what your question implies. Patrolman John Malas is a friend. He's not as close as you and I are, but we watch some football games and drink a few beers. Anyway, he was one of the officers on the scene. He sent me a text, once it was determined the victim was McBride. Evidently, McBride kept his wallet under the floor mat of his car. It took hours for an officer to locate it. And the car was listed in his girlfriend's name, so we had trouble cross-referencing that."

Montenegro's voice grew louder. "Do you want me to

show you the text?" he asked. "It's time-stamped before I sent a message to you."

For a moment, Syd struggled to breathe. She wished she'd been more tactful.

"No, Stuart," she answered quietly. "I don't need to see it. And you don't need to verify anything. I trust you. And I'm sorry."

Montenegro shook his head and began walking away. "I'll get over this," eventually," he said. "I'm going to have to."

CHAPTER 27

The car ride to Frank McBride and Andrea Pierce's home was tepid at best. Syd and Montenegro had hardly talked since the conversation about the texts. But Lasek felt it would be prudent to speak to Pierce before interviewing Cutter.

After Syd pulled into Pierce's driveway and cut the engine, Montenegro turned to her from the passenger seat. "I'm going to break the ice," he said. "The question you asked about the timing of my text was a good one," he said. "It shows that you were trained well and have natural instincts. I guess it shocked me."

Letting out a sigh, Syd turned her sights from the windshield and looked at Montenegro.

"I didn't mean to offend you, Stuart," she said. "And I trust you as much as anyone. But the question gnawed at me, so I thought it was best to ask. I face things head-on."

Montenegro nodded, a smile appearing. "That's the best way," he said. "Next time, I'll try not to be so sensitive. Stacey says I act like a little boy sometimes."

"I don't think so," said Syd. "I would've taken offense if the roles had been reversed."

Before Montenegro could respond, Pierce appeared at the front entrance and waved at them to come inside.

"Sergeant Montenegro, I presume," she said as both detectives entered the house. "When you called, I didn't know you were going to bring someone else."

"Yes, Ms. Pierce," said Montenegro. "This is Detective Sydney Livingstone."

The two women reached to shake hands. Pierce's black hair was freshly cut in a bob, brushing the shoulders of a green-and-white striped turtleneck sweater. Her beige corduroy pants fit snugly from the waist down to her calves. On her feet were a pair of cognac suede chain loafers with no socks.

"Nice to meet you both," said Pierce as she escorted them to chairs at the kitchen table. After everyone was seated, Pierce spoke again. "Now what can I offer you? There's still a half pot of coffee left over from this morning. I also have soda and bottled water."

Both detectives shook their heads. "Thanks, but we're good," said Montenegro. "My sympathies about Frank. That must have been painful."

Pierce opened the cupboard and took out a beige mug, filled it to the brim, and placed it on the table with a hard thump.

"Let me ask you both a question," she said. "Do you think my Frank murdered his ex-wife?"

It was a startling question, and Syd replied with caution. "As far as the law is concerned, Frank is innocent."

Sitting back in her chair, Pierce sipped at her coffee. "Thanks for the happy horseshit, Detective Livingstone." She gestured at Montenegro with her mug. "That was a non-answer, so I'll ask him. Do you think my Frank killed his ex-wife?"

"All right, I'll tell you the truth," said Montenegro. "Yes, I think Frank killed his ex-wife. And I think he got away with it."

Pierce smiled. "Finally, I've found an honest man! Too bad I see a ring on your finger, detective, or we might be entering into a different type of conversation."

"And since you're being completely honest, detective, what do you think of my new haircut?" she asked. "I had it styled, so I'll look good at Frank's funeral; that is if the coroner ever releases his body."

"I think you found an excellent hair stylist," said Montenegro. "I'll ask you the same question. Do you think Frank murdered his wife?"

Leaning forward, Pierce nodded. "Fair question. Let me say there's a difference between thinking and knowing. If I go on record saying I *know* he did, perhaps I could be charged with something like - I don't know - accessory after the fact? But if I say I only *think* he did it, then I believe I've covered my butt. So yes, I *think* he killed her, although he always shut me down when I tried to discuss it."

"Ms. Pierce," replied Syd. "We appreciate you sharing this information with us. But we're not here to discuss whether Frank was a murderer. We're attempting to find out who may have murdered *him*."

"Of course," said Pierce. "And don't think I didn't know that. I was simply pulling your strings - trying to find out how honest the two of you are. And so far, I'd say I'm moderately impressed."

Syd gazed toward the living room, spotting several

pictures of Frank on the wall behind a couch and coffee table. A 42" TV on a stand took up the opposite wall. This was the same home Frank had owned with his first wife, Sheila, the place where the investigating officer believed she had died. She wondered how Andrea could live there, knowing that Sheila had probably fought for her life and begged for mercy in one of those rooms. Maybe Andrea wasn't affected by that type of stuff.

She nodded toward the living room. "May we go in?" They all stood and walked through.

Syd pointed at a picture of Frank holding a rifle, with a dead buffalo at his feet.

"I see Frank was a real outdoorsman," she said, not letting on that, as an animal lover, she was repulsed by the photo. "Did he have a group of friends he liked to hunt with?"

"Not really," said Pierce. "He was always a loner-type. Hunting, fishing, and hiking… He mostly preferred to be alone."

Next, Syd pointed to a photo of Frank wearing a martial arts uniform. "It looks like he was into some sort of self-defense. He must have made some friends during that activity."

Pierce shook her head. "He sparred with a few fighters and entered some competitions. It's the sport that's on TV all the time."

"Ultimate fighting?" asked Montenegro.

"That's it," said Pierce. "But he never hung around with anyone outside of class. He did his stuff and came home."

Montenegro continued. "Besides Rex Cutter - who we think Frank met by happenstance - do you know anyone else that may have wanted to hurt him?"

Pierce closed her eyes and sighed. "There's something

else," she said. "That's why I was willing to speak with you here. I need to show you something in the basement." She motioned for them to follow her.

As they headed down a set of wooden stairs, gripping an unsteady handrail covered in peeling black paint, Syd found it difficult to breathe. She recalled and felt Cutter pressing the gun to her head. She struggled to dismiss the disturbing thought that Pierce was leading them into an ambush.

If there were armed assailants waiting for her and Montenegro at the bottom of the stairs, they were disguised as an elliptical machine, a treadmill, and a weight bench. The cement walls desperately needed a fresh coat of paint, while the unfinished ceiling displayed interior plumbing lines, wires, and a stand-alone light bulb. Pierce directed them to a far corner where a room had been converted into an office.

"When Frank wasn't working out or watching television, he spent most of his time here, especially after he was acquitted. I think he liked reading the news stories that were popping up about him. He even joined some of the discussion groups based on Sheila's murder - under a fictitious name, of course."

A desktop computer sat atop a wooden desk. The letters and numbers on the keyboard appeared dirty, while the mouse pad was missing sections of its soft outer layer.

Montenegro wiped a dust bunny off his shoulder. "Is there a reason you asked us to come down here, Ms. Pierce?"

"Call me Andrea," she replied. "We're past the formalities now. But yes, I found something after his murder that I thought might interest you. Frank didn't like me to enter this room. That is, unless he wanted spontaneous sex. But besides that, he made it clear I was to stay out. I found this while I was clearing out his desk."

Pierce pulled a yellow folder out of a drawer and tossed it on the desktop.

Montenegro sat down in McBride's chair and flipped open the folder. Syd stepped to look over his shoulder. She saw several printed email messages with the sender's name listed as "Unknown Subscriber."

"Evidently, Frank printed these emails as he received them," said Pierce. But he never said anything about them. I don't think he wanted to worry me."

There was a total of four, each with the same subject line:

Do not delete. You're about to die.

Bending down to read the emails, Syd noticed the name of the sender at the bottom. The Enforcer.

Syd inhaled quickly when she read the moniker but played it off by breaking into a cough. "I apologize," she said. "It's a little dusty down here."

If Montenegro was disturbed by Syd's reaction, he didn't reveal it. He examined the pages. "So, you knew nothing about this while Frank was alive? He never said a word?"

"Nothing," said Pierce. "But Frank was accustomed to crack pots, before and after his trial. People would come into the store and gawk at him. Some were extremely rude - pointing at him and even taking photos. Once, Frank's co-workers had to restrain him from attacking a guy who made a joke about 'killer prices. ' Frank didn't see the humor.

"I understand why," said Syd. "But I'm surprised he never sent any of this to the police department."

Pierce paced to the other side of the room, then turned to face them again.

"Frank knew the police were angry that he beat the rap.

He didn't trust them. The police and the prosecutors were the ones who tried to put him away for life."

"In hindsight, did you notice Frank acting strangely - maybe slightly paranoid?" asked Montenegro.

Andrea stared at the floor for a moment, fingering her chin. "I would say the only time I noticed anything different was at the amusement park. It was the day someone shot his ass full of insulin. Before that fight, he seemed distracted. He mentioned that someone was following him. He never got a good look, though."

Montenegro asked Pierce if he could keep the contents of the folder. She nodded.

"We'll also be sending a technician to examine this computer," he said. "But I have another question. After Frank emerged from his coma, did he express any idea about who may have tried to inject him?"

"Again, he didn't trust the police," said Pierce. "He thought maybe a cop was trying to impose the death penalty outside the courts. But he also didn't trust that guy he fought, Rex Cutter."

Syd glanced at Montenegro. "He thought maybe Cutter shot him up with insulin. And then instigated the confrontation?"

"It was just one of his theories," said Andrea.

She led the detectives back up the stairs. As they opened the door to leave, Syd thought of another question.

"Was there ever any correspondence between Frank and Cutter, either while Frank was in the hospital or after?"

"Frank never mentioned anything," said Andrea. "But there was one phone call I overheard. Frank didn't know I was listening."

"What do you remember?" asked Syd.

"He sounded surprised. Then he said, 'You're lucky to be alive.' I moved away so he wouldn't catch me eavesdropping, and when he returned to the room, he said the call had been from work. I doubted it, but Frank wasn't a guy you wanted to make angry. I wondered if it had been Cutter. Unfortunately, I never asked."

"We'll check Frank's phone records," said Montenegro. "If Cutter called from his personal phone, we'll find out."

"What about me?" asked Pierce. "Do you think I'm safe?"

The two detectives glanced at each other. Syd responded first.

"As far as we know, the only people being targeted have been those who have evaded punishment of the law. You don't fit into that category. However, I wouldn't take anything for granted."

Montenegro nodded. "If I were you, Ms. Pierce, I'd make sure your doors and windows are locked. And if you have the means, I'd consider arming yourself."

Andrea nodded and smiled. "Frank didn't leave me much," she said. "But one thing he did leave was an impressive gun collection. Someone may eventually take me out, but they'll have to survive one hell of a firefight first."

CHAPTER 28

It was already dark at 6:45 pm as Syd pulled into her neighborhood. After interviewing Pierce, she spent three hours reviewing notes and compiling a list of questions for tomorrow's interview with Cutter.

She massaged her forehead while driving her F-150, unsure if the headache was from eye strain, allergies, or stress. As she pulled into the driveway, her phone flashed, alerting her to a text message.

> Sweet Sydney. Flying back from Italy tomorrow. Home for a week. Can't wait to see you.

She'd watched the progress of his tournament in Rome. She had been waiting for news since his loss in the third round.

The sting of her confrontation with Montenegro had mostly subsided. They were getting along better, at least on a superficial level. Perhaps she should suggest making dinner plans with the Montenegros.

After parking in the driveway, Syd walked into the garage. She scolded herself for not clearing an area to park inside and fumbled with her house keys. As the garage door closed behind her, the light grew dimmer, making it difficult for her to locate the slot. She gripped the doorknob to steady her hand, it turned, and the door swung open.

When she'd left her house this morning, she had a lot on her mind…Enzo's impending return, and her disagreement with Montenegro, and whatever was going on with Fosterno. Maybe she'd forgotten to lock it. She felt for her revolver, which she knew was loaded and ready. No need to remove it from the holster.

The kitchen seemed to be as she left it. Ditto for the living room. As she walked down the hall toward the bedrooms, she thought she could hear dripping. It wasn't from the half bathroom on the right side of the hallway. The sound was coming from the direction of her bedroom.

She remembered taking a shower in the morning. Perhaps, in a rush, she hadn't tightened the spigots. Or maybe, her shower had developed a leak. But academy training had kicked into full gear now, and she approached the room with her revolver drawn.

Syd silently cursed the creaky wood floor in the hall, which might have cost her the element of surprise. Now she heard someone else's footsteps, and the door to the bathroom opened. A figure stepped into her line of fire.

A thin, muscular black man with hanging dreadlocks walked toward her, scrubbing at his back with a towel. It took a second to realize he was staring into a gun.

"Mother of ass!" he screamed, dropping the towel. "Don't shoot! I was hoping to surprise you."

Syd lowered the gun and placed it back into the holster, her thumping heart intensifying her existing headache.

"Enzo! What the hell? You said you'd be home tomorrow."

He took a step toward her. "If I told you I was coming home today, then it wouldn't have been a surprise."

Taking a deep breath, Syd eyed Enzo head to toe. She noticed his robe on the bed, picked it up, and tossed it against his chest.

"Time to get dressed, Tarzan," she said. "I know you enjoy jump out surprises, but doing them when I'm carrying a pistol might not be the best idea."

Enzo slipped the robe over his arms and tied it around his waist with the belt. "Syd, the plan wasn't to jump out at you. It was to greet you at the door. I didn't expect you to surprise *me*."

Syd placed her gun and holster on a table. "This one nearly cost you your life."

Enzo walked over to Syd, grabbed her right arm, and placed a kiss on her cheek. "I'm not accustomed to thinking of you as a cop," he said. "I'm still trying to wrap my mind around that."

"Glad you brought it up," said Syd. "Let's talk over pizza. How does Johnny's on Richter Street sound? I'll let you pick up the tab."

Syd wondered how Enzo would feel about her heading up one of the biggest investigations in Walsh County history. Their future together might depend on it. As they headed out for dinner, Syd made extra sure that she locked the door leading into the house.

The next morning, 'Bad Boyz' was in rare form on the RealVigilante website. He ranted about a case in California in which a mother of five drove her car over a cliff - and into the ocean - with all her children in the vehicle. Two of her five kids perished.

The California case seemed to be the topic du jour on RealVigilante.

Bad Boyz: Bitch is blaming postpartum depression. Some lib jury will give her a cushy sentence, like probation.

Creatine Fueled: Wish we could offer probation to those two dead kids. Another is paralyzed, I hear.

Bad Boyz: Who's going to keep track of this lady once she's out? I'm already following four others. Anyone want to pitch in?

Justice4all: Got her dead to rights. She ain't getting out.

Nothing from The Enforcer yet.

Bad Boyz: You don't understand the system. Or you're some lawyer disguising your identity. Either way, take your dissociative disorder and shit opinions elsewhere.

Justice4all: Bet you wouldn't say that to my face.

Bad Boyz: I eat pansies like you for lunch.

Justice4all: Everyone's a tough guy in their basement, typing on grandma's keyboard.

Suddenly, The Enforcer appeared in the feed.

The Enforcer: Knock it off. We have the same goal - punishing the unpunished. You two need to take a step back.

A minute passed before someone commented.

Justice4all: I'm out.

Half a minute later…

Bad Boyz: Sweet dreams.

Syd saw an opportunity to join the conversation and typed in:

DarkMistress: Anyone want to talk about Ohio? They're biting the dust there.

Five, ten, and twenty minutes passed. In the kitchen, she could hear Enzo fumbling with dishes.
C'mon. Respond.
Almost on cue, a post appeared.

The Enforcer: Ohio is where the

unpunished are brought to justice... either by the courts or one of us.

Curtains For Crimes:

DarkMistress: Justice has been served in Ohio. The guilty have paid the price.

The Enforcer: Ohio is on the right track, but the job is not finished, especially in the Northeast. More2Come.

DarkMistress: Aren't the guilty parties already dead?

Seven minutes passed.

My question was too forward. He knows I'm not one of them.

She could let it go, but decided to try again.

DarkMistress: Haven't the Northeast Ohio's villains already bit the dust? Do we need to focus elsewhere?

Three dots immediately appeared. The Enforcer was typing.

The Enforcer: There's More2Come in this neck of the woods. Supreme justice will prevail. It's the way our universe works. Cause and effect.

DarkMistress: Who else needs to be punished in Ohio?

The Enforcer: Do your research.

BoredChairman: So, you're going to right all these wrongs?

The Enforcer: Me, the universe, the cosmos, whoever. Justice matters. It will be done.

BoredChairman: Suppose someone you're punishing is innocent?

The Enforcer: Do you believe McBride was innocent? How about that wife-drowner Babson? And don't even get me started on Cefalo, who's still alive and breathing.

BoredChairman: Who's next on your list?

The Enforcer: Gotta go. Sit back and get comfortable.

Coroner Melissa Pennington was in the middle of a postmortem examination - a 71-year-old man who had died from a fall at a foundry - when Syd and Montenegro were ushered into the lab. Seeing the two detectives, Pennington waved them forward.

"I was a little surprised to hear that you were coming to see McBride," said Pennington. "Isn't this Fosterno's and Griffith's case?"

Montenegro removed his coat and placed it on a chair nearby. "Initially, but now Syd and I are taking over."

Pennington's mood seemed too cheerful for her line of work. "Probably speaking out of school but based on how unstable Fosterno acted at the awards, I understand. How's he doing?"

Syd forced herself to ignore the cadaver and meet Pennington's gaze. "He's treading water," she said. "The Cefalo assignment has knocked him off-balance."

"He needs to focus on his mental health," said Pennington as she playfully patted the foot of the deceased. "Not everyone's blessed to have an upbeat job like me."

Syd and Montenegro exchanged a smile.

The body was covered with a sheet from the torso down, but bruising and disfigurement on the upper body were evident. "This poor guy was on a tower doing repairs," said Pennington. "An explosion sent him hundreds of feet to his death."

Pennington finished making a few notes on a body diagram and then whispered a verbal message into a recording device. After covering the body, she nodded for her assistant to take it away.

"With McBride, I didn't find anything earth-shattering," said Pennington. "He was shot at close range, through the driver's side window."

The assistant moved McBride to the forefront and whisked the sheet all the way down. His eyes remained open, and his mouth was agape, as if something in the ceiling puzzled him. A large circular opening - presumably a bullet hole - was located just above his left eyebrow.

"Was that the only shot?" asked Montenegro.

"One shot," said Pennington. "The shooter knew what they were doing."

Pennington moved to the left side of the table and manually examined a spot on McBride's neck.

"I've heard the assailant wore a black helmet," said

Pennington. "If that's true, McBride probably never knew who pulled the trigger."

"The suspect pool couldn't get any larger," said Montenegro.

"Everyone knows McBride waxed his wife. Anyone carrying a vendetta had a motive."

"What about his late wife's family," said Pennington as she set down a chart. "Could they have taken matters into their own hands?"

Syd cleared her throat. "Do you have any reason to believe that's the case from a forensic point?"

Pennington smiled. "Nope," she said. "Maybe I've watched too many episodes of Timeline. The bullet is going to forensics. We checked the body for fluids and stuff but didn't find anything. I wish I had more."

Pennington pulled the sheet back over McBride. "We took an inventory of his pockets. Loose change, a money clip with fifty-five bucks, and brass knuckles. He was ready for anything."

"The element of surprise is the weak's weapon against the strong," said Montenegro. "As officers, we have rules, giving the criminals an advantage."

Pennington escorted the two detectives to the exit. "Don't get overly obsessed with the rules," she said. "The last thing in the world you want to be is 'dead right'."

CHAPTER 29

The next day, Syd spent more than an hour interviewing Cutter inside his house with Montenegro, who referred to the interview as "a big nothing burger."

"I noticed you kept your hand near your gun," she observed.

"I remembered what almost happened to you in that interview room," said Montenegro. "For a brief period of time, I thought we might lose you."

Syd removed her right hand from the steering wheel and gave Montenegro a pat on the knee.

"Thanks for being the overprotective big brother I never had," she said. "I appreciate your concern."

Montenegro snickered. "I wasn't being totally selfless," he said. "If that psycho grabbed your gun, he could have wasted us *both*."

Syd laughed. "Cover your ass first and watch over me second."

"A slight exaggeration," he said, smiling. "But I know what he's capable of."

Slowing down behind a car turning left. Syd said, "It seems like there's psychos all around us.".

"Yeah, maybe both inside and outside of our precinct," said Montenegro.

They both laughed, but Syd wondered if Montenegro was referencing anyone in particular.

"Do you think someone in our department is involved in these vigilante killings?" she asked.

After taking a moment, Montenegro nodded. "It's possible since shit's been disappearing from our evidence room. But my instinct tells me whoever is stealing isn't acting alone."

They both sat silent for a moment before Montenegro spoke up. "At least we extracted one important piece of information from Cutter. He admitted trying to meet up with McBride."

"But the meeting never took place," said Syd. "Did you ever get the data from Cutter's ankle bracelet?"

"I got a text during our meeting with him. He's never left his house."

Syd shook her head. "Another dead end."

Montenegro removed the gum from his mouth and placed it in the ashtray. "When are the four of us going to dinner? Stacey's dying to meet Enzo. She watches him on television."

"Soon, I promise," said Syd.

"And how's your friend, The Enforcer? Have you run into him lately on the dark side?"

"Interesting you should ask," said Syd, taking a paper from her visor and handing it over. "I didn't want to bring anything up until after our chat with Cutter. I tried to goad him this morning."

Turning on the inside light above him, Montenegro pursued the paper's contents.

DarkMistress: Vague information is all you supply. Not sure you're involved.

The Enforcer: The guilty will pay. Bank on it.

DarkMistress: We know someone's out there. Offer some proof it's you.

The Enforcer: The next victim in Walsh County will be a copper.

"What the hell?" he said. "Did you show this to Lasek?"

"Texted him this morning, but I've heard nothing else."

"'DarkMistress'. That's you, right?"

"Yep. Not original, but the best I could do in a pinch."

Sighing and turning back to face the road, Montenegro said, "I have a theory. Probably doesn't hold water, but that pendant thing has been bothering me. We don't really know Michelle. What if she's trying to throw us off?"

"How so?" asked Syd.

"Maybe she's working with someone else - possibly in the department. They're setting up Mitsoff to take the fall."

"That's a possibility," said Syd. "Our evidence room was in disarray until we were tasked to spiff it up. Despite having to fight off that little perv, I think I got the place pretty well organized. But prior to that, I'd say that anyone in our precinct could have gained access."

Montenegro nodded. "Or any county employee who regularly visits. Mitsoff was pretty careless with those keys."

"Okay," said Syd. "Let's build on that. Michelle receives

the pendant from someone. Then, she brings it to the police, claiming she found it. Now the light shines on Mitsoff - a guy nobody likes anyway. Then, her accomplice hunts down McBride."

"Or, maybe Michelle does it herself," added Montenegro, "using a motorcycle because that implicates Mitsoff."

They met eyes for a second and began to laugh.

"Maybe we should take a creative writing class," said Syd.

"Or write the next great crime novel," said Montenegro.

The sun set and the streetlights flickered as Syd and Montenegro made their way back to the station and reported to Lasek's office.

"Interesting find regarding The Enforcer," said Lasek. "We probably should alert the rest of the force about the threat."

Syd thought about the irony of the situation. At first, the prevailing theory was that the suspect could be a cop. Now it seemed an officer was in the crosshairs.

"I'll have Pratt notify all officers," said Lasek. "I don't necessarily believe whoever is putting this shit online, but we need to take it seriously."

"Is someone going to notify Mitsoff?" she asked. "He's not working right now, but he's still a cop."

Lasek took a deep breath. "I suppose I'll text him.

"And since we're discussing Mitsoff, I have an assignment for you, Livingstone. The leave of absence happened quickly and there's some unfinished business he was working on. Use his computer to wrap up any loose ends. I have his login information."

"On it," she agreed.

"I'm freeing up Griffith to assist you and Montenegro," said Lasek. "Her undercover assignment has concluded."

Syd felt a sense of relief as she left Lasek's office and headed for Mitsoff's desk. A few minutes later, Griffith pulled up a chair next to Syd, with Montenegro looking over her shoulder at the screen.

"I'm going to conduct a little research," he said. "I'll let you two comb through Mitsoff's files. If you need help, you know where to find me."

Syd flashed a thumbs-up as he walked away, then handed the passwords to Griffith and stood.

"I have some tidying up to do in the evidence room," she said. "Since I'm the only one working there now, I've got to make sure we aren't falling behind."

"Give me a couple of hours," said Griffith. "By the time I'm done, we'll know more than we ever wanted to know about our friend."

Syd requested the evidence room key from Arledge, then spent a good part of an hour separating an area for evidence procured in an industrial arson case. She used a ladder to bring several marked boxes up to a second-floor landing. The last one was the heaviest, and she struggled to lift it. As much of a pain as Mitsoff was, she almost missed him.

After catching her breath on the second level, she began her backward descent down the ladder. Nearly halfway, she felt a wobble. As she was steadying herself, she felt a large hand on her lower back. Holding on tightly with her left hand, she swung her right elbow out and caught someone squarely on the jaw.

The figure fell away from her, crashing into a stack of

evidence boxes. Syd gasped, seeing Montenegro groaning as he lay on the floor, both hands cupping his nose.

"Damn, Stuart, I'm sorry," she yelped. "Why are you sneaking up behind me?"

Montenegro rose to his feet as he attempted to stem a trickle of blood leaking from his right nostril.

"Nothing wrong with your reflexes," he said. "Now I see why you were one of the world's top 50 players."

Syd pulled a tissue out of her pocket and handed it over.

He blew his nose, and a good portion of the tissue was covered in red. "I wasn't sneaking," he said. "I came in here to see you, and I saw the ladder shaking. I was offering a hand."

"Next time, make a little noise," said Syd. "The Enforcer is residing rent-free in my mind."

Montenegro nodded. "I'll keep that in mind. Thanks for the Kleenex, by the way." He looked around for a trash can and tossed it.

"So why are you here?" asked Syd, her voice still trembling.

"Thinking about your last interaction with The Enforcer," said Montenegro. "Something's not adding up. They've gone from attacking unpunished criminals to threatening officers. What gives?"

Syd pulled a chair up to a table and motioned for Montenegro to sit. "It could be different. But then again, maybe not."

"How so?" asked Montenegro.

"Maybe someone in law enforcement has gotten away with an offense. We obviously wouldn't know who or what crime they committed."

Montenegro leaned back in his chair. "It's not looking

good for Mitsoff. If he's behind this nonsense, he's got more time on his hands now to develop a plan."

Massaging her forehead, Syd responded. "I'll take you one step further. What if The Enforcer knows that Mitsoff has been set up, and is going after the person who's responsible?"

"That's reasonable," said Montenegro.

Syd nodded and placed her hand over Montenegro's. "Stuart, if it's Mitsoff, we need proof. No one likes him around here. The perfect ending would be that Mitsoff confesses before anyone else dies, and we're all happy to be rid of him. But that almost seems too convenient. Too tidy."

Montenegro laughed. "True, things usually don't tie themselves into a perfect little bow. At least, not in my world."

Syd's phone buzzed. It was Griffith.

"Whatever you and Montenegro are doing in that evidence room is none of my business," she laughed. "But I need you both to get your asses up front right away. "

"How'd you know we were both back here?" asked Syd.

"It's my job to notice things," said Griffith. "Anyway, I found something important on Mitsoff's computer, and it might help us solve this damn case."

"What did you find?" asked Syd.

"I can't explain over the phone," said Griffith. "Meet me at Mitsoff's workspace. And, Syd, I'd rather you come alone."

As she tucked her phone away, Montenegro asked, "What's that about?"

Syd hesitated before replying, "I need to meet with Griffith for a second. Did you need to speak with me about anything else?"

"Nope, I just wanted to compare notes. We should always know what each other is thinking."

"Agreed," said Syd as she escorted Montenegro from the evidence room. "No secrets."

"I gotta hit the restroom," he said. "I'll see you in five."

Well, that was one problem solved. Syd headed straight for Mitsoff's desk.

CHAPTER 30

"Pull up a chair," said Griffith.

"Shouldn't Stuart be in on this?" she asked. "It sounds big, whatever it is."

Griffith tapped her forefinger against her lips.

"There'll be time for that," she said. "For now, just you and me."

Syd felt awkward not including Montenegro, but she understood where Griffith was coming from. Paranoia was running rampant in the department.

"Turns out you ain't the only one who's been exploring the dark web," whispered Griffith.

She tapped a few buttons as Mitsoff's screen illuminated. She opened one file and then another one within it. A listing of nearly 20 websites appeared on the screen. But the one that caught Syd's eye was "RealVigilante."

"Looks familiar, doesn't it?" said Griffith. "Glad we got the passwords for this creep's computer."

Feeling her heart pound, Syd tried to maintain her composure.

"That's the site we've been monitoring!" she said. "The one used by The Enforcer."

"I know," said Griffith. "That's why I called you."

Listed next to "RealVigilante" was a username, "Tough Guy", and a password.

"Have you done anything with those?" asked Syd.

"Nope," said Griffith. "Wanted you here with me. I figured we could plug them in together. Kind of share the experience."

Tapping a few more keys, the RealVigilante website filled the screen, with bright colors and eye-catching graphics jumping out everywhere. It was a sight all too familiar to Syd. Griffith logged in with the ToughGuy credentials.

From what they could determine, only two people were on the site at the moment. And then a third.

Syd scooted her chair closer. "It's not exactly primetime at 3:40 in the afternoon," she said. "Not many people on. It'll look a lot different after 11 at night."

"That's when the weirdos appear," laughed Griffith.

Now Mitsoff's handle appeared on the screen: Bored Chairman. Her skin prickled with goosebumps. She reached for Griffith's paper coffee cup and downed the contents before saying, "Sonofabitch! Mitsoff's username and screen name are two different things." She pointed at the screen. "See, you typed in ToughGuy, but the display name is Bored Chairman."

Griffith nodded. "Okay, the names are different. What's the big deal?"

Syd closed her eyes and exhaled. "The big deal is that I've seen the name 'BoredChairman' plenty of times before. He's a friend of The Enforcer. I'd go so far as calling him a confidante."

Griffith's eyebrows shot up to her hairline. "Wait, you mean…"

"Yes," said Syd. "Mitsoff has been working with The Enforcer."

Griffith's jaw clenched before a smirk appeared. "I never would've pegged Mitsoff for someone who chased ultimate justice," she said. "He seems like a selfish prick to me."

Syd remembered BoredChairman's reference to the "Big O" on the website. "Do you see any other passwords or screen names on that website that Mitsoff may have used?"

"Nothing else," said Griffith. "Why do you ask?"

It had seemed odd that someone else besides Mitsoff had used that phrase. But it wasn't what mattered most at the moment.

"It's nothing," she said. "We need to show what you've discovered to Lasek and Pratt. There's a good chance Mitsoff's planning his next move."

Griffith wasted no time in uploading copies of the files she'd found to a memory stick, and then they headed for Lasek's office.

Syd felt the weight of the situation as they prepared to present their findings. What if Pratt or Lasek had tasked Mitsoff to investigate The Enforcer's activities on the dark web?

Pratt gave the answer within the first minute. "Neither Commissioner Lasek nor I instructed Mitsoff to search for information about the vigilante on any dark web sites. If he did, it was on his own."

Syd felt confident that if they hadn't asked Mitsoff to investigate, he wouldn't have taken it upon himself. She glanced at Griffith, who nodded with a steely determination in her eyes.

"Commissioner, we've uncovered proof linking Mitsoff to The Enforcer's activities on the dark web," Syd began. As she detailed their findings, Griffith handed over the USB stick, and Lasek plugged it into his own computer.

Lasek's expression darkened as he examined the files. Pratt leaned forward, his face a mask of incredulity.

"Has anyone discussed this with Montenegro?" asked Pratt.

Syd felt a twinge of regret. Maybe she should have insisted that Griffith include him.

"Not yet," said Griffith. "But we'll get him up to speed."

"What do you think this all means?" asked Lasek.

Without hesitation, Griffith responded. "It means that Mitsoff has a personal relationship with whoever The Enforcer is. He's complicit and the key to solving this case."

"Do you want Montenegro and me to pick him up?" asked Syd.

Lasek motioned for Pratt to step into the hallway with him. When they returned, Pratt said, "Let's see how the situation develops. Syd, continue with your investigation. Montenegro and Griffith can take turns keeping an eye on Mitsoff, who's been told not to leave town."

Griffith looked from Syd to Pratt and Lasek. "You're all serious? Don't we have enough to pick him up and charge him? Or, at the very least, make him tell us what he knows?"

Lasek shook his head. "Captain Griffith, I know there's a lot of evidence pointing toward Mitsoff; however, it's not airtight enough to procure an indictment. We need to gather more information. And once we brief Montenegro, no one else should know anything about this."

CHAPTER 31

Three days before her fiancé was scheduled to leave for Argentina to compete in the Cordova Tennis Open, Syd organized a night out with the Montenegros at Breakers, one of Canton's finest seafood eateries. Syd liked that it was elegant but not stuffy.

Syd and Enzo arrived ten minutes early and were shown to the table. They were sharing a cocktail when Stuart and Stacey walked in. She turned to him and quipped, "We might need to step up our fashion game." She gestured to her own sundress and his button-down shirt and khaki pants, then pointed to Stacey, who glided across the floor in a knee-length, emerald-green dress and gold jewelry.

Enzo smiled and whispered back, "I think we're fine. Anything goes at Breakers."

"So glad we could finally make this happen," said Stacey as she exchanged hugs with Syd and Enzo.

"I'm going to warn you, Enzo," said Stuart, as he pulled his chair to the table, "Stacey is a huge fan. Ever since I told her that I knew you through Syd, she always seeks you out on television. We've even subscribed to the Tennis Channel."

Stacey nodded. "Besides Syd, we're your biggest fans in Ohio."

Enzo laughed aloud. "I accept fans wherever I can find them."

Syd chuckled at the exchange, grateful for the lighthearted atmosphere that had settled over their table. She took a sip of her cocktail and leaned back, feeling content in the company of her fiancé and the Montenegros.

They were chatting as they perused their menus when their server, a brown-haired girl named Corrine, approached with a platter. She put down plates of appetizers, a bowl of steamed mussels, and a bottle of champagne. Everyone made appreciative sounds as she began to pour the wine into glasses.

"What a pleasant surprise," Syd smiled, taking the glass she was handed. "Stuart, Stacey, thank you."

The Montenegros looked astonished. Stacey turned to her husband. "It wasn't me. Was it you?"

He shook his head. "When I saw the spread, I assumed that Syd and Enzo had ordered it."

They turned their attention to Corrine, and Stuart said, "I think this might be some kind of mistake. As far as I can tell, nobody here ordered any of this."

The young woman smiled. "My manager told me to bring it over." Seeing their expressions, her smile faded. "Is there a problem?"

Syd noticed stress on the server's face. "No problem. It's very nice of your manager."

"I don't think this is a gift from management, at least as far as I know," Corrine replied. "I was instructed to bring out this free stuff and then present you with an envelope after the meal."

Montenegro held up a hand. "Wait a moment. Syd, did you tell anyone else that we were coming here tonight?"

"Not that I can think of," she said. "Did you?"

"No," said Montenegro. "Stacey? Enzo?"

They both shook their heads.

"Would you mind bringing out that envelope now?" asked Syd.

Corrine shrugged. "I guess that wouldn't be a problem."

Corrine disappeared into the kitchen, leaving the foursome in a state of perplexity. Syd could see Stuart scanning the room as Stacey leaned close to Enzo and whispered, "This is all quite mysterious, isn't it?"

Enzo nodded. "Definitely unexpected. I can't wait to read the card."

They both seemed more amused than troubled, but Syd knew that she and Stuart were thinking along the same lines.

Before long, Corrine returned with a small envelope in hand. She passed it to Stuart. "Thanks," he said. "Could you give us a few minutes?"

After the young woman had walked away, Stuart tore open the envelope and removed a white card. Syd could see what looked to be a series of letters cut from magazines and pasted unevenly across the paper.

·   ·   ·

He put the card in the center of the table where all could read it.

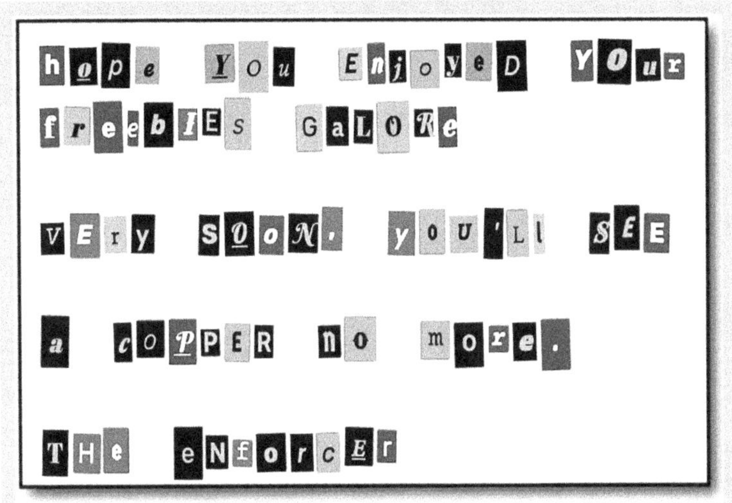
hope You EnjoyeD YOur
freebIEs GaLORe

VEry SOoN, you'll SEE

a coPPER no more.

THE eNforcEr

CHAPTER 32

The words sent a chill down Syd's spine, and she exchanged alarmed glances with the rest of the group.

"What does this mean?" Stacey whispered, her voice barely audible above the ambient restaurant conversation.

Enzo leaned in closer, his expression grave. "It sounds like a threat... directed at Stuart and Syd."

"We need to leave," said Syd.

"Not quite yet," said Montenegro as he rose and walked to a table where Corrine stood. Syd followed.

"Ma'am, we would like to see your manager immediately," he said, flashing his badge. "Police business."

Corrine started to talk but stopped. She gestured for the detectives to follow her into the kitchen. She led the way to a slender middle-aged man in a shirt and tie, sorting through job applications. He seemed surprised as he looked up and spotted Montenegro's badge.

Standing up, he said, "I'm sorry. Is there something wrong?"

Syd quickly scanned the kitchen. The cooks were busy at the grill, while servers were bustling around, grabbing plates off the counter and bringing them to customers in the dining area.

"You're the manager, right?" asked Montenegro. The man nodded. "Your name, please?"

The man cleared his throat and then spoke. "Steve Rowland. I've been the manager here for almost four years."

"Steve, who instructed you to bring the envelope to our table?" asked Montenegro.

The manager glanced at Corrine before answering. "To be honest, I don't know."

"I need a better explanation," said Montenegro.

The manager motioned the server away with his hand. "Corrine," he said. "I can handle this." After the young woman walked away, looking back over her shoulder, he spoke.

"I opened up at around 2 this afternoon," he said. "The restaurant opens to the public at 4, but we keep the doors unlocked for vendors and employees. It's like that on weekdays."

"Who brought the envelope?" asked Stuart.

"I don't know. I know that sounds weird," he said. "After working in the kitchen, I returned to the front, where our staff greets customers. On the server's stand, there was a list of instructions with my name on it. The envelope was sitting on top."

"Where are those instructions now?" asked Syd.

"I tossed them hours ago."

"What did they say?" said Syd.

"The note said there was a reservation for Livingstone," said Frank. "It instructed me to bring this free stuff to your table once the party was situated. There was $500 in cash, thanking me for my help."

Syd could tell Montenegro was having trouble digesting the explanation. He crossed his arms and said, "So you have absolutely no idea who brought this envelope?"

"No," said the manager. "They were gone by the time I found the note."

"Do you have camera footage?" asked Syd.

"Unfortunately, not," he said. "Our cameras are timed to be operational during regular restaurant hours. Can I ask what it said?"

Ignoring the question, Syd asked, "Mr. Rowland, is there anyone else who may have seen the person who brought that envelope in here?"

Rowland shook his head. "None of the cleaning staff remembered anybody. At the time, it was only them and me."

They instructed Rowland to contact them if he remembered anything else and asked him to stay in town for the time being.

As they headed for the door with their significant others, Montenegro addressed Syd. "Once we get these guys home safe and sound, I need you to meet me at the office. We have a lot to discuss."

"All right," said Montenegro while sitting next to Syd in her cubicle. "So, you made the reservation?"

"Yes."

"We know Enzo and Stacey didn't tell anybody about our

plans," said Montenegro. "So how would The Enforcer know we were going to be there?"

Syd furrowed her brow. "Maybe they've been following us," she suggested. Then she interrupted herself. "But that makes no sense because the envelope was dropped off before we arrived."

Stuart tapped the desktop with his fingers. "When did you reserve the table, Syd?"

"Yesterday."

"Do you know anyone who works at Breakers?" asked Stuart. "A friend or anything?"

Syd shook her head.

"It makes no sense," said Montenegro.

Syd took a deep breath. "I know, right? How would someone know where we were going to be?" After hearing herself ask the question, the answer came to her. She placed her left hand over her mouth.

"Syd, what's going on?"

"Oh shit," said Syd. "It couldn't be, could it?" She dropped her head into her hands, placing her elbows on the desk. "I think I figured it out."

Montenegro stared at her, waiting.

"It's that damn CRM."

Appearing confused, Montenegro asked, "Our Customer Relations Management software?"

"That's exactly what I'm talking about," said Syd. "All of the county offices use that shit. It gives all employees access to everyone else's schedules and contacts."

"Wait a minute. You put our dinner appointment on CRM?"

"Yep. Several months ago, I began entering my

appointments into my office calendar - even personal ones," said Syd. "It's easier to keep everything in one place."

Montenegro nodded. "That's how they knew we'd be there. They had access to your schedule."

"It's the only explanation," said Syd."

"That lets the manager off the hook," said Montenegro.

"I wish I could tell you I feel better now."

CHAPTER 33

It was Enzo's last night in town before he would travel to Argentina for his next tournament. Syd had prepared a special meal for the both of them. Candles flickered on the table, casting a warm glow across the dining room. A bouquet of colorful flowers served as the table's centerpiece. She'd even cleaned up her fine china plates and arranged them with sparkling silverware and elegant crystal glasses.

She'd made Enzo's favorite tonight, a plate piled high with steaming hot spaghetti and meatballs, topped with grated Parmesan cheese and fresh parsley. A side of garlic bread and a tall glass of red wine completed the meal.

Even though she had put in extra effort to make the meal a memorable one, their conversation was awkward. They hadn't discussed what happened at Breakers in any kind of detail. She knew the subject needed to be addressed.

As she brought out dessert - a towering slice of double chocolate cake with vanilla ice cream on top - she reached for Enzo's hand.

"I know what happened at the restaurant has been on your mind," she said. "We should talk about it."

After sampling the cake, Enzo nodded. "Dinner was delicious. Thank you for making tonight special."

Syd leaned and kissed him.

"But Syd, you need to know this Enforcer thing is difficult for me, near impossible. I find it paralyzing. There's a real chance I could lose you." Enzo leaned back in his chair. "You seem calm about all of this. Almost too calm."

His statement took Syd by surprise. "Enzo, just because I'm not outwardly panicking doesn't mean I'm not taking this seriously. I understand the danger."

Leaning back in his chair, Enzo said, "Sometimes I wonder if you do."

Syd stared at Enzo, waiting for him to continue.

"You and Montenegro are in the crosshairs of some psycho," he said. "And that's assuming that Montenegro himself isn't The Enforcer. How do you know he's not?"

"He's a friend. I trust him," she said.

"Boy, do you ever have a short memory," he said. "When you were stalked as a tennis player, you trusted that nutcase as well. Am I right?"

Syd hung her head and nodded quietly.

"Look, I'm not saying it's Montenegro," said Enzo. "But it's someone close to you. Someone you probably could reach out and touch."

"I have to do my job," said Syd.

Enzo rose. "What if it wasn't your job?" he asked.

Syd shrugged, waiting for an explanation.

"We don't need the money," said Enzo. "I've made enough for us to live comfortably, probably for the rest of our lives. Come with me. We'll get married and travel the world together. We'll welcome kids and enjoy everything that goes with that."

Syd's heart ached. She wanted to assure him that she'd remain safe but couldn't.

"Syd, if something really bad happened to you, then they might as well go ahead and bury me too," he said.

Syd could feel the pain in his eyes. She removed a wallet from her pocket, opened it, and showed Enzo her badge. "I took an oath," she said. "I made a vow to serve and protect the citizens of this community. Those weren't meaningless words to me, Enzo."

"You've honored those words, Syd," he said. "But now it's time to put all of that behind you and come with me. It's about us, our life together."

She longed to place her arms around Enzo's neck but refrained. "I can't walk away, Enzo, especially not now," she said. "I know your concern for me is genuine, from the heart. But I can't give in to evil. I need to stay here and fight. I'm needed."

Enzo winced. "So, I'm supposed to travel to South America and concentrate on tennis while my future wife is threatened by someone named The Enforcer? I go on as usual, worrying about my forehand, backhand, serve, and volley. Do you really believe I'm capable of compartmentalizing that well?"

"You don't have to go to Argentina," said Syd. "You can take a month off and stay with me."

Enzo sat down and exhaled. "I need those ratings points. You know how that works. If I don't play, I'll drop in the rankings. Then, I won't qualify for other tournaments."

Syd placed her elbow on the table, her chin in her hand. "Enzo, you just said we have all the money we'll ever need."

"That's assuming that I keep competing for a few more years. I'm trying to secure a future for us."

As the silence settled between them, a sense of resignation crept over Syd. She lifted her gaze to meet Enzo's, searching for the right words to express the turmoil within her. "We're obviously on different paths. I hope you win down there and accumulate as many points as possible."

After several uncomfortable seconds, Enzo said. "Are you sure you won't come with me?" When Syd didn't answer, Enzo said, "I guess neither one of us is ready to abandon our goals and dreams."

Syd felt the war within her - her love for Enzo versus the dedication to her calling. Catching the next plane for Argentina would be the easy solution. But was it the right one?

He stood from the table, his movements slow and deliberate. As he gathered his belongings, he said, "I think I'll stay at a hotel tonight. When I get back from Argentina, we can talk more. Until then, please be careful."

Syd sat in silence as Enzo gave her a peck on the cheek, grabbed his bags, and exited. She knew the road ahead would be challenging and filled with uncertainty, but she also knew she couldn't compromise who she was for anyone, not even for love.

CHAPTER 34

S yd and Montenegro met the next morning at Dillard's Pancake House to discuss their investigation. Montenegro appeared disheveled; his hair was ruffled, and he needed a shave. Syd figured he had a rough night trying to convince Staccy that everything was under control. She could certainly commiserate.

"Stacey would be destroyed if anything happened to me," he said. "That's all she talks about. She wants me to go back to school and become a teacher. Could you imagine me working with seventh graders?"

"Actually, I could," said Syd. "You'd be stern but likable and respected."

Montenegro laughed. "Ain't going to happen." Then he added, "How's it going with Enzo?"

She paused, her gaze drifting out the window before she continued, "Enzo asked me to accompany him on the tour. And now he's off to South America, with both of us confused about where the relationship is headed."

Montenegro reached across the table to give Syd's hand a

squeeze. "I know it's tough. But put your emotions about Enzo aside until this Enforcer thing is over. If you're not focused, it could mean the end for you, me, or another officer."

She took another bite of pancake before pushing the dish aside. "You're right. We can't be distracted."

"We have to be extra aware, extra diligent," he said. "Whoever wrote that note is seeking a reaction. We need to sit back and observe. They'll slip up, ask one too many questions."

"I know your mind never stops, Stuart. I want to know who The Enforcer is, or who among us is aiding and abetting?"

Montenegro poured another cup of coffee, then added two creams and a packet of sugar before responding. "I think Mitsoff's involved, but I may be biased because I don't like the guy. The other person I'm not sure about is Fosterno. He's been a paranoid basket case for months. I want you to keep an eye on him. Maybe he'll reveal something."

CHAPTER 35

With Lasek and Pratt out of town for a few days at a conference, Syd enjoyed a mild reprieve from the daily pressure of digging up dirt on The Enforcer.

She shadowed Fosterno discreetly while he was in the office. Once jovial and fun-loving, Fosterno now seemed pensive and distant. He spent a good part of the day on his cell phone, presumably texting Penny. Inside the precinct's walls, Fosterno appeared less paranoid than he did on the outside.

She felt sorry for him and wanted to offer her assistance as a friend but had to maintain a degree of impartiality amid the investigation.

She monitored the RealVigilante website periodically, but there were no updates from The Enforcer. She wasn't surprised since The Enforcer typically logged in after business hours, preferring to operate under the cover of darkness.

After a day passed without a word from Montenegro, she dialed his number.

"Syd," answered Montenegro. "I hope you're calling to tell me that someone has blown their cover. I need some good news."

"I wish," said Syd. "Unfortunately, it's been almost too quiet, especially since Griffith's been bugging out early since the brass aren't here."

"She's probably rehearsing for a performance," said Montenegro. "What's up?"

"Haven't heard from you today," said Syd. "Anything I can help you with?"

Montenegro snickered. "You can bring me a cup of coffee. I've been sitting in a car for hours waiting for Mitsoff to leave his house."

"Stuart, what if Mitsoff discovers he's being watched?"

There was a pause before Montenegro responded, "Syd, I've been at this job a long time. I know what I'm doing."

"Okay, then," said Syd. "Did anything happen yesterday?"

"Since you asked nicely, I'll tell you," said Montenegro. "At around 6 pm, he leaves his house on his motorcycle. I follow him to Canton, hoping he'll lead me somewhere important. Instead, he pulls into the parking lot of the Lucky Charm Casino."

"Never pegged Mitsoff for a gambler," said Syd.

"Trust me, he's no gambler," said Montenegro. "He spent two hours playing the roulette wheel, which has terrible odds unless you compare them to the slots. The dumbass must've dropped five- or six hundred."

Envisioning Montenegro hovering close enough to observe Mitsoff's losses, Syd said, "He must have spotted you. He's a trained detective."

Montenegro's laugh did nothing to calm her.

"You underestimate me," he said. "Griffith isn't the only

one who's a master of disguise. You should have seen me. I looked like a hippy from the Sixties, long hair, beard, everything."

"Yeah, I'm sure you blended in with everyone else," she said.

Montenegro chuckled. "You have to think outside the box to catch a criminal," he said. "The only thing criminal about yesterday, though, was how much money he threw away."

"So, if you found nothing, why are you tailing him tonight?"

"If I catch him in the act, we can end this whole thing without anyone else getting killed."

Syd asked if Stacey knew about Stuart's plan to tail Mitsoff and if she was bothered by his late hours.

"I haven't told her what I'm doing," he replied. "She's a lot calmer than she was at Breakers, but she's adamant about me being careful."

As Syd was in the process of asking another question, Montenegro interrupted. "Wait - his garage door is opening, and he's backing his sedan out."

"Hang on, Stu, he knows your car," said Syd.

"I'm one step ahead of you," he said. "I rented a brown sedan. And I'm not dressed up as a hippy. I'm a chameleon in human form - dark glasses, a fake 'stache, and a Red Sox cap. He knows I hate Boston, so he would never think of me."

Syd shook her head. "He's probably on his way to his mother's or going to dinner. Stuart, you can't let him see you."

"As my father used to say, 'Never underestimate a Montenegro.' If anything worthwhile happens, I'll call you. Otherwise, we'll touch base in the morning."

After the call, Syd felt restless. But after thinking more, she convinced herself Montenegro would probably discover little if anything. They would more than likely share a laugh tomorrow at the office.

After traveling nearly two miles on Clementine Pike, Mitsoff's Honda took a left on the less-traveled Ainsworth Rd. Instead of turning left directly behind Mitsoff, Montenegro's vehicle passed Ainsworth before making a U-turn to get back onto the road. He followed as Mitsoff took a left on Cherokee Court and then a quick right into an apartment complex called The Woods.

Parking in front of weathered, brick townhouse apartments that formed an inverted U-shape, Mitsoff exited his vehicle and walked down a concrete path that led him to a courtyard. Carrying a duffel-shaped green bag, Mitsoff stopped for a moment to look behind him. Then he continued forward, arriving at the doorstep of Unit #145. He pressed the bell several times, but no one answered.

Mitsoff paused before reaching into his pocket to extract something. After a few moments, he thrust his shoulder into the door, and it swung open. He walked inside, closing it behind him.

Montenegro lowered a pair of tiny binoculars and entered the street name and the 145 address into his phone. Michelle Watson's name appeared on his screen.

A moment later, a rumbling, late-model maroon Mustang with a white racing stripe running down its side pulled next to him. The sound of its exhaust rattled the doors of Montenegro's car. A young woman emerged from the passenger side. She hoisted her middle finger and yelled obscenities at the male driver. The man emerged from the car and confronted her on the sidewalk. They were nose-to-nose, screaming.

Leaving his car, Montenegro approached. The driver jumped to attention once the more chiseled Montenegro was upon him. The man mumbled something to the woman and returned quickly to his car. Without saying another word, the man fired up the engine and backed out in a jumble of noise and flying gravel. In a moment, his car was gone. The woman smiled at Montenegro and mouthed a silent thank you before making her way into a nearby apartment.

By the time Montenegro had shifted his gaze back to the original surveillance site, another young woman clad in a black-and-white fleece coat was standing at the front door. In a moment, Montenegro's binoculars were focused on Michelle Watson, who entered her apartment after briefly fumbling with her keys.

Montenegro began to dial dispatch but then hung up. Then, he began composing a text to Syd.

CHAPTER 36

Turning a normal 20-minute ride into 15, Syd's F-150 quickly pulled into a parking spot next to Montenegro's. As she exited her vehicle, Montenegro motioned for Syd to join him in his car. She jogged to the passenger side door and entered.

"Why'd you call *me*?" she asked, wiping away a strand of hair from her eyes. "If this is a kidnapping, someone could already be dead."

Montenegro clutched the steering wheel. The bags under his eyes made it seem as though he hadn't slept in a while.

"I'll take responsibility for whatever happens," he said. "If I call in the cavalry and this turns out to be nothing, then my career's over."

"I'm already on thin ice with the department," said Syd.

Montenegro began explaining his plan. "These townhouses have sliding glass doors as back entrances," he said. "I want you to knock on the front door and move away. I'll be waiting around back. When I see movement, like

Mitsoff heading toward the front door, I'll enter through the back."

Syd squinted her eyes, trying to comprehend. "I don't think they're going to let you in."

Montenegro pulled out a black, V-shaped knife with a pointed edge.

"I keep this handy in case my car ends up underwater," he said. "It's a guaranteed glass-breaker. One firm poke, and I'm inside."

Syd remained silent, staring ahead at the windshield.

"I realize you don't like this," said Montenegro. "But I saw him break in."

"Look, Stuart," she said. "I know Mitsoff is a creep. But it's a stretch to think of him as a kidnapper. Are you sure?"

"That's why I called you and not the department," he said. "We'll keep this low-key. If it's a misunderstanding, we'll get through it. And besides, your part's easy…knock and then back away."

"Promise you won't break in unless there's no other choice," said Syd. "If nothing's going on, we'll explain that we're here to ask Michelle a few questions. That'll be our way out."

Montenegro nodded, but Syd wasn't convinced he was listening.

"I've had a bad feeling about this guy for months and now there's evidence I've been right all along," he said.

Syd closed her eyes for a moment, attempting to gather courage. She left the car and walked slowly toward the front door, providing Montenegro with enough time to move to the back of the complex. Instinctively, she felt for her pistol with her right hand. She'd never used it in action and hoped today wouldn't be different. As she approached the door, she decided to deviate slightly from Montenegro's plan. She'd wait for someone to answer the front door and simply engage. Perhaps peering through the door, she could assess the situation without Montenegro having to enter forcibly.

Looking down at her phone, she reads Montenegro's text:

Proceed.

Syd knocked. And then knocked again. After a minute, she heard footsteps moving toward the front door. Mitsoff answered, a puzzled look on his face.

"Syd, what the hell are you doing here?"

Syd's reply was interrupted by the sound of breaking glass.

CHAPTER 37

"Our department has been completely embarrassed, and you both have some explaining to do," said Pratt, pacing back and forth in one of the precinct's interview rooms. "Commissioner Lasek and I had to leave an important conference.

"The media is hounding Commissioner Lasek for a statement," said Pratt as Lasek sat behind a table with his arms folded. "Maybe one of you can give me a quote that's suitable for printing about what the hell happened."

Syd and Montenegro sat silently in front of Lasek, their backs against the wall, both literally and figuratively. Mitsoff and Michelle had already been interviewed and were sent home, with Pratt and Lasek offering apologies.

"The media is reporting that two officers were locked in a standoff, pointing their weapons at each other. Would either of you like to comment?"

Montenegro rose from his seat, both hands in the air.

"I take responsibility," he said. "Detective Livingstone shouldn't be scrutinized. She simply did what I asked."

"Do you feel you followed proper police procedure?" asked Lasek.

"Not exactly," said Montenegro. "But both of you were suspicious of Mitsoff after evidence appeared in Michelle's car. And we were told to investigate."

Pratt looked to Syd. "Detective Livingstone, do you have anything to add?"

"What would you like me to say?" she asked.

"Well, for starters, what was your role besides creating a diversion?"

"I was there to support my partner," she said. "Right or wrong, I accept responsibility." Her mind reverted to her last conversation with Enzo. Maybe she simply should have left with him.

"What happened after you knocked on the door?" asked Lasek.

"Detective Mitsoff answered," she said. "But when he heard the glass breaking behind him, he turned and confronted Montenegro. They both drew their guns."

"Did you attempt to mediate?" asked Pratt.

"I tried, but Mitsoff was concerned that he was being targeted. He felt that Montenegro might be the vigilante."

Pratt shook his head and made his way to a small water cooler. He inhaled a cup and turned his attention to Montenegro.

"Detective, why didn't you drop your gun and de-escalate?"

Montenegro repositioned himself in his chair. "Mitsoff was acting crazy," he said. "He threatened my life. And I could detect alcohol."

"Did you happen to look around the room after you broke into Ms. Watson's apartment?" asked Lasek. "Did you notice the sign that read 'Happy Birthday'? Or the balloons and streamers?"

"The only thing I was focused on was the barrel of his gun. Detective Livingstone was telling me to drop my gun but, as I said before, I didn't feel safe."

"What about Ms. Watson? Didn't she tell you that this was consensual?"

"I was sure Mitsoff was going to pull the trigger. That's why I kept my gun drawn - until the officers arrived."

Lasek looked to Syd, who was leaning forward in her chair, her hands between her knees. "Detective Livingstone, did you ever attempt to convey to your partner that he simply interrupted a surprise birthday party?"

"I said something to that effect," said Syd. "But it isn't fair that Sergeant Montenegro takes all the heat. I was there, too."

Lasek motioned to Pratt, and the two exited the room. After fifteen long minutes, Lasek returned alone.

He stood with his eyes closed and rubbed his chin before speaking. "We have major problems in this department," he said. "Evidence has been stolen from storage, a detective was held at gunpoint in our interrogation room, and two officers almost killed each other tonight. And that's not to mention that we have another detective possibly dating a murder suspect he was tasked to protect. With a vigilante murderer still on the loose, I'm surprised the *National Enquirer* isn't calling."

As Syd let this sink in, he continued. "What happened tonight is an egregious act of malfeasance and insubordination. With that in mind, I am suspending you from the department, Sergeant Montenegro, for an indefinite period. Chief Pratt and I, along with the input of our county commissioners, will soon decide your future."

Lasek continued. "Your conduct, Detective Livingstone, while certainly unbecoming, can be excused with a firm warning to never bypass our office again. I understand supporting your partner. I really do. But considering your past actions, one more infraction will result in your immediate termination. Sergeant Montenegro, I'd like you to turn in your badge and gun before you leave my office."

Syd felt conflicted as she watched Montenegro stand up, hand over his badge and gun, and exit the room without a word. Left alone with Lasek, Syd took a deep breath and met his gaze. "Thank you for not terminating me," she said. "I understand the severity of the situation and it won't happen again."

Lasek grimaced. "I hate to be the heavy, Syd, but we can't afford any more missteps," he said. "Moving forward, everyone is going to be under stricter supervision. I'm going to have you work more closely with Captain Griffith."

Syd pondered the irony of both Montenegro and Mitsoff being off work at the same time. Griffith always mentioned that the guys in the office stuck together, but she couldn't have meant this. Hopefully Griffith would begin working full days now that Lasek and Pratt were back. No part-time effort was going to take down The Enforcer.

CHAPTER 38

When the new work week began, Griffith entered Syd's cubicle precisely at 8:15 am with two cups of coffee in her hands.

"You like it black, if I remember," she said, placing a Styrofoam cup on her desk.

"Good memory," said Syd. "Noticed you bugged out early on several occasions last week. More undercover work?"

"Definitely not," she said. "I'm done working undercover for the foreseeable future - at least until we get this vigilante thing under control."

"Are you ready for a big week, tracking down the most notorious criminal in Ohio?"

Griffith pulled up a chair next to Syd's desk. She blew at the surface of her own steaming, creamer-laced coffee. "I would say yes, considering that I'm your partner now. At least until Montenegro is reinstated."

Syd sat back in her chair and took a deep breath. "Not sure that'll happen. Lasek and Pratt weren't happy."

Griffith shook her head. "Between us, I wouldn't put too

much weight on what they say in the heat of the moment. They're a pair of lions who roar occasionally to see if anyone's listening."

Syd took a taste of her coffee, swirled the cup around in her hand, and then finished the remainder.

"We embarrassed the department pretty badly this time. I hope they give him another chance."

"I know," said Griffith. "Never had a problem with him. It's Mitsoff I have no tolerance for."

Syd nodded but saw no reason to trash Mitsoff any further. "May I ask you a question?" she asked. "You know, being that we're partners?"

"Anything," said Griffith. "Nothing's off limits."

"Okay," said Syd. "I was wondering, the last time you were undercover, were you gathering information on The Enforcer?"

"Nope," said Griffith. "I was busting a narcotics ring in a nearby town that'll remain nameless. Why do you ask?"

"I want to stay up to date," said Syd. "The Enforcer has indicated that a cop is next."

Griffith paused for a moment, weighing her words. "I think it's reasonable to assume that we are as likely as anybody to be the next target."

Syd sighed deeply. She knew Griffith might be right.

"I'm worried but not scared," said Griffith. "I'm always locked and loaded. And remembering how you laid out that Cutter character, I'm willing to bet you and I remain safe."

CHAPTER 39

Everyone invited filed into Pratt's office for the Tuesday morning meeting, with Lasek closing the door behind them. In person attendees included Fosterno, Griffith, and Syd. Stuart Montenegro, despite his suspension, and Stacey attended via Zoom.

Lasek began the meeting by addressing the Montenegros. "I want to thank you, Sergeant, for joining us despite difficult circumstances. Because you and Stacey were present at Breakers, your perspectives and thoughts are essential."

Stuart Montenegro nodded but didn't respond. Syd wondered how Stacey felt about assisting a department that had suspended her husband.

Lasek got straight to business. "We conducted background checks on the manager and employees who worked that night at Breakers. They checked out and were cleared. A few minutes ago, Captain Griffith asked me if any cameras at neighboring businesses caught any images of the suspect. Chief Pratt recently received the videos. We can't glean any discernible information from them."

"I have them on my computer," said Pratt. "They were sent from the spa next door. The videos are grainy. We can see a shadowy figure ducking in and out of the restaurant. Can't tell who it is or even the gender."

"What about a video at Breakers?" asked Fosterno.

"They didn't have their cameras operating at that time," said Lasek. "I know. It sucks."

Griffith raised her hand to speak. "I wasn't at Breakers that night," she said. "But somebody must have noticed something, whether it was on the way in, during the meal, or on the way out."

No one responded.

Pratt finally spoke up. "Griffith, you're experienced when it comes to tracking people without being noticed. What should they have been looking for?"

A slight grin came to Griffith's face. "That's hard to say," she said. "Maybe someone sitting by themselves at a nearby table. Or a person hanging around, pretending to be an employee."

Montenegro's voice emerged from the computer screen. "I definitely would've noticed something like that. Maybe not at the beginning of the night, but certainly after we realized something was amiss. Besides what happened, everything else seemed normal."

"Ms. Montenegro, is there anything you noticed?" asked Lasek.

"No, nothing at all, sir," she said. "Of course, I've had no police training."

Seeing Stacey's face on the computer screen brought a wave of warmth to Syd. Even through the pixelated video chat, her radiance and charm were evident.

Lasek thanked her and then continued. "How about Enzo? I know he couldn't be with us today, but did he happen to notice anything?"

"Not at all," said Syd. "He would've told me."

Syd's eyes diverted to Fosterno, who had raised his hand. She was surprised to see him participate since he'd kept such a low profile for the past week.

"The situation's changed," said Fosterno. "Threatening a cop anonymously on the dark web is one thing, but Breakers made it real. I don't feel anyone here should feel safe." He looked around the room.

"Did anyone think of inviting Mitsoff to this meeting, either in person or remotely? Considering what was discovered in his girlfriend's car, he's pretty involved."

All eyes focused on Lasek.

"Chief Pratt and I thought it was better that he wasn't here," Lasek replied. "But since we're discussing him, he claims that someone planted that pendant."

"Anybody believe that?" huffed Griffith. "How about a show of hands?"

"He also owns a motorcycle," interjected Fosterno. "Don't forget how that McBride character died."

Pratt rose to his feet, waving his hands to stop the chatter. "If we're going to discuss Mitsoff, we'll do it in a civilized manner," he said. "We've run a check to determine how many employees in the department own motorcycles. So far, we have a list of three. Mitsoff does, as you are aware. Commissioner Lasek also owns one, although it's been out of commission for a while. And Officer Cataldi. But my question for you is whether anyone else has one. Maybe it was given to you, or you bought it from someone without registering it. I frankly don't care if your registration is up to date. I need to know if you have one. And please, don't make us discover that later."

The room grew silent.

"Okay, then, I'll assume nobody else has one," said Pratt. "If you know of anybody in the department who either has or had one, please let us know immediately."

Syd remembered the last time she was on a motorcycle. Enzo had allowed her to ride his bike during her trip to England. Since it was overseas, she didn't feel obligated to say anything.

"I sold one about five years ago," Montenegro said. "All done legally, with the proper registration."

"No problem," said Pratt. "Anyone else?"

Nothing.

"Okay, we are going to hold you to that," said Lasek. "As Commissioner Pratt stated, I own a bike, but it hasn't been on the road in years due to mechanical problems. I should've got rid of the damn thing years ago."

Griffith raised her hand. "I hate to keep beating on a guy who's not here, but I'll ask anyway. Did anyone ask Mitsoff if he's been riding his bike lately?"

Lasek responded. "That subject came up. He said he rode the night McBride was killed, although nowhere near the crime scene."

Syd now understood why Mitsoff hadn't been invited to the meeting. It would have been awkward discussing such matters in his presence.

"I have a question that nobody's asked," said Griffith. "If Mitsoff's girlfriend turned in damning evidence against him, how the hell are those two back together again?"

Syd could tell that Lasek and Pratt were caught off-guard.

She surprised herself by breaking in. "Relationships can be complicated. When love is involved, you shouldn't expect things to make sense."

Nervous laughter filled the room.

Lasek resumed control. "I need to know where everybody was during the early afternoon on Saturday, around the time when the stranger entered the restaurant. Fosterno, would you like to begin?"

Fosterno smirked. Syd couldn't tell if he was irritated or inconvenienced. "I arrived at Penny's in the morning, but I'm not sure about the exact time," he said. "I stayed with her through the evening."

"More precisely," said Lasek, "what were you doing between 1 and 3 in the afternoon?"

"Not exactly sure. More than likely watching sports or Netflix."

"If we contact Penny, will she vouch for you?"

"Guaranteed," said Fosterno.

Very tidy, thought Syd.

"Captain Griffith," continued Lasek. "I'll bet you were doing something much more interesting during that time. Tell us about it."

Griffith grimaced as if trying to recall. "Spent some time lifting weights in my basement," she said. "Made some lunch afterward. I was alone."

Lasek and Pratt also shared their whereabouts: Lasek at a soccer tournament, Pratt shopping for a car.

"Do you know where Mitsoff was?" asked Montenegro. "I'd say that's pretty important."

"We're attempting to tie that down," said Lasek. "But I'd like to finish up here. Tell us about your whereabouts during that time, Sergeant Montenegro."

On-screen, Syd could see Montenegro shifting in his chair.

"Stacey and I got out of bed late that morning, around 10. We had breakfast and completed a few chores. Sometime in the afternoon - not sure what time - I went for an hour jog. We were pretty much together until we went to dinner."

Lasek nodded while Pratt scribbled notes. "Detective Livingstone, it's your turn."

Syd had already jotted a few notes on her pad. "Enzo woke up before me at around 8. Breakfast was ready when I got up an hour later. We didn't do much after that, just hanging around the house. At noon, I hit the gym for a couple of hours. Enzo told me he found an interesting show on TV. That's pretty much it until dinner."

As Syd finished, Lasek scanned the room. "Thank you, everyone, for being forthcoming. I know this isn't easy."

Fosterno once again lifted his hand to get Lasek's attention. Syd's and Fosterno's eyes met before he spoke.

"I understand why it's important to gather this information," he said. "But there are at least 40 to 50 other people who work in the department. If, as Syd believes, they got the information from our software, everybody's a suspect."

Pratt shook his head in agreement. "Commissioner Lasek has tasked me with gathering that data. As you know, it's a tedious task. Verification is going to take some time."

The answer to Fosterno's question overwhelmed Syd. They were no closer to finding out which, if any, cop was involved.

Lasek took over again. "You've all been briefed about the Breakers situation. Would anyone like to ask a question to anyone who was there that night?"

Fosterno spoke up. "I've met the manager. I've dined there

with a couple of different ladies. Seems like a decent guy. Did anyone there previously know him?"

Syd shook her head, as did Stuart and Stacey.

"Okay, one more thing," said Lasek. "The media has gotten wind of what happened at Breakers. If you're asked, please don't comment. We need to get more answers."

CHAPTER 40

Lasek arrived earlier than usual on Friday morning. The Cleveland Browns were hosting the Kansas City Chiefs for a playoff game the next day, and the town was buzzing with excitement. Lasek was looking over a sheet entitled "NFL Fantasy" and typing vigorously. As he was finishing up, Pratt strolled into his office.

"I've been thinking about the suspension all week," said Pratt. "You know, Montenegro's a good guy. Everyone likes him. I think he got a little protective about Livingstone. I've heard Mitsoff mistreated her."

Flipping a paper aside that included the list of his fantasy players, Lasek looked quizzically at Pratt.

"Are you saying he was justified in breaking into Watson's apartment? Did you know she was lying in bed naked when he barged in?"

Pratt smiled. "Never heard that part," he said. "But Montenegro witnessed Mitsoff breaking in."

Lasek nodded. "Yeah, breaking in to decorate for her birthday. Possibly the most heinous crime of the year."

As he took a chair, Pratt said, "You're right. But no one ever dreamed those two would get back together. Do you think they planned this whole thing out?"

"I've thought about that," said Lasek. "But you know how weird relationships can be. Off today, on tomorrow. But we can't have officers pulling guns on each other. The media is loving it."

"I get it," said Pratt. "I'd just like to see the guy get another chance…after he's learned his lesson."

"Give me another week," said Lasek. "I'm pissed right now. Fosterno offered me a pair of tickets for the Browns' playoff game, a rare occurrence in Cleveland. But I can't go. My wife made plans to attend some bullshit art show in Akron. If you can find Fosterno, he might still have them."

"Why can't he go?" asked Pratt.

"He's on Cefalo duty this weekend. With this vigilante situation heating up, he wants to lay low."

Pratt strolled toward the window in Lasek's office and gazed outside.

"The evidence seems to be stacking up against Mitsoff. Are we going to make an arrest?"

Lasek pulled out an orange stress ball from his drawer and squeezed it. "It's possible, but we don't have enough to present to a Grand Jury. A competent defense lawyer would tear the case apart. Virtually any county employee could have ventured into that evidence room."

Lasek stopped squeezing the ball and tossed it to Pratt. "I can get you a great deal on one of these," he said. "They're super-effective if you don't mind a little carpal tunnel."

Pratt squeezed the ball a couple of times and returned it to Lasek's desk. He removed a wallet from his back pocket and thumbed through it. He presented a picture of a man in a firefighting uniform.

"Whenever I am at a loss, I always think about what my dad would say," said Pratt. "He was a firefighter and a perfectionist. God rest his soul; he saved many lives before he succumbed to an arsonist's blaze."

"Sounds like a great man," said Lasek. "What words of wisdom would he offer?"

There was one saying he used to mention occasionally," he said. "I think it applies here. It goes something like this - *Sometimes we're not fighting fire; we're playing with fire.*"

CHAPTER 41

To Syd, the first eight-hour shift she'd completed in the field with Griffith seemed like three. They found out all kinds of new and interesting information about each other, all while ticketing speeders, breaking up a bar fight, and responding to a call about two rottweilers romping near kids in a schoolyard.

Something about Griffith appealed to her. She loved her enthusiasm and spontaneity, especially during tense situations. She was tough when she had to be but fair when dealing with a subject. She could disarm the angriest person by employing good judgment and a quick wit.

"If you even think about picking up that pool cue, you'd better have a good proctologist," she told an aggressive man in the bar. A minute later, he was laughing.

"If those dogs get off that leash again, then we're going to come back and collar *your* sorry ass," said Griffith. "And if you think they bite hard, then you haven't met our jail clerk."

Taking pride in being a good listener, Syd enjoyed hearing stories from Griffith's perspective.

"I always believe in giving someone a second chance," said Griffith. "That is, if they are truly contrite. But as for those who take innocent lives, I'd just as soon ice every one of them."

The next day, as Griffith drove the squad car, Syd checked her phone constantly, wondering if Montenegro would respond to her multiple texts. He didn't. She hoped Montenegro was okay. After all, something bad was supposed to happen to a police officer. And soon.

Syd liked that she and Griffith could multitask together: serve the community while discussing theories about The Enforcer. They traveled silently as they headed back toward the precinct, pensive after a long day. She reached into her briefcase and extracted one of the last posts submitted by The Enforcer. It was one she had shared with Griffith.

The Enforcer: There's scuttlebutt the police are involved. The next victim in Walsh County will be a copper.

As she read the text, something gnawed at her brain. Whatever it was, it was staring her in the face, but she hadn't made the connection yet.

The squad car pulled up to an intersection where a man sat on a curb, wearing tattered and dirty clothes. His hair was greasy and matted, and a blanket was draped over his shoulders. After noticing their car, he rose to his feet and approached the driver's side window.

"Captain Griffith," he said while tapping on the glass. "It's been a few weeks. I was hoping you'd come around."

Griffith glanced over at Syd and winked. She rolled down

her window. "Cecil, you ain't been misbehaving, have you?" she said with a grin.

"No, ma'am," he said. "Haven't touched the stuff for sixty-five days straight now. Clean and sober from now on."

"So that's all you wanted?" said Griffith. "Just comin' to say hello?"

The man smiled, exposing several missing teeth. "Captain, I said I'm sober, not stupid." He put his hands out.

Griffith reached into her console and grabbed a handful of change, mostly quarters with several dimes, nickels, and pennies mixed in. She handed them over.

"No foldin' money this time, Captain Griffith?" the man asked.

"That'll come at the end of the month when I get paid," she said. "Until then, you take care of yourself."

After stuffing the coins into his pockets, the man spoke again. "Guess what, Captain. My daughter's coming in next month. She says she's gonna take me out for dinner and buy me some clothes."

Griffith nodded. "Glad you two are talking again. I'll see you at the end of the month."

She rolled up her window and waved. "Poor fellah," she said. "He made a few wrong choices and that started the ball rolling."

Syd hoped the man would remain safe. She thought about the way he was dressed, his friendly smile, and the way his trembling hands had accepted the money.

But then she froze for a second, her eyes growing wide. It was something one of her criminology teachers in college had termed an "Oh Shit moment." She looked to Griffith who appeared lost in her own thoughts, as she slowed down for a red light.

"Captain," said Syd. "I need to ask you something. Do you follow football? I'm talking about the pros."

Griffith turned to make eye contact. "I'm a lifelong Browns fan. That's probably one of the reasons I'm always cranky."

Although not a football fan herself, Syd was aware of the Browns' struggles over the years. "Do you know they're on national TV tonight?"

Griffith laughed. "Yeah, of course I know. I've got burgers and dogs in the fridge, along with wine."

"Would you be interested in watching the game with me tonight?" asked Syd. "And maybe with…"

She stopped.

"With whom?" asked Griffith. "Montenegro?"

"I was thinking of Fosterno and Penny Cefalo."

Pulling off the road and into a store parking lot, Griffith slammed the vehicle into park. "Have you lost your mind, girl? Why would I want to do that?"

Syd glanced at the text one more time to make sure she was thinking clearly. "We could consider it police work. You know, overtime."

Griffith shook her head. "How are you going to correlate the Browns game with a case we're working on?"

"That's something we can discuss on the way," she said. "The scuttlebutt is that Fosterno won't be attending. He plans to watch the game with Penny."

"Why do you care, and more importantly, why should I?"

Syd grabbed Griffith by the arm. "Because everyone in the damn office knows that he's going to be watching with her tonight. We've got to find out where they're going to be."

"I assume they're going to be watching at home," said Griffith. "He can't take her out in public."

Syd thought about Fosterno's propensity to bend the rules. "Can you call him and find out where they are?" asked Syd.

"Again, why would I want to do that?"

"Because everybody in this damn city is fixated on that playoff game," said Syd. "The Enforcer is threatening to strike. What better time than during the biggest game of the year when everyone's distracted?"

"For your information, Miss Rookie Cop, I don't need to call him to find out where the hell he is." She held up her smartphone. "We shared locations when we were partners. I can track him."

Griffith hit a few keys on her phone. She looked at Syd with a surprised expression. "Oh shit. He ain't nowhere near home."

"Where does it say he is?"

"A restaurant bar in Cleveland called the Silver Salamander," said Griffith. "Been there once before. Huge Browns bar."

"Call him and tell him you know he's there," said Syd. "Tell him we're coming to watch the game. Just for fun."

Griffith looked at Syd with her eyes wide and mouth open but said nothing.

"Roll with me on this one," said Syd. "I'll explain everything on the way."

Griffith shook her head. "Tell you what, I'll meet you halfway on this one. You explain everything to me along the way. But I want to surprise his ass when we arrive."

Syd wasn't entirely sure Griffith was buying into her revelation, but she drove toward Cleveland anyway. Traveling on I-71, Griffith pushed the speedometer past 80, zipping around four cars in the middle lane. If she broke a few traffic laws, they might arrive an hour before kickoff.

"The Silver Salamander's a couple of blocks from the stadium," said Griffith. "He's probably drunk already. I just hope we don't scare him when we arrive. Because theoretically, either one of us could be The Enforcer."

Looking over at Griffith and smiling, Syd said, "He trusts me."

"Aren't we a little bitchy today?" laughed Griffith. "He was my partner long before I was yours, and he trusts me the most. But he never said Cefalo was with him."

"Trust me, she's there," said Syd.

Griffith winced. "If we're risking our lives just to sit with a bunch of partiers, I'm going to be pissed."

Taking several deep breaths before responding, Syd replied, "I'm going with my gut on this one. If I'm wrong, forgive me."

Traffic was exceptionally heavy entering the city for the game. Syd and Griffith arrived at the Silver Salamander an hour before kickoff, using their lights and siren to bypass a significant part of the congestion.

Griffith pressed the button on the key fob to lock the car, and they walked quickly through several large groups of bystanders in the parking lot. "We definitely broke a few laws," she said. "We're tearing through this city basing everything on what? A hunch? A riddle that you may have solved?"

In the door to the bar, Syd bumped into a large man with dyed orange hair and dressed head to toe in Browns paraphernalia. The man grunted and pushed her aside with a shoulder as he hurriedly passed. She turned and whispered to

Griffith. "If I'm wrong, then I've been overthinking," she said. "But for now, let's assume I'm correct."

The surroundings of the Silver Salamander looked familiar. Syd remembered being there one other time before a country concert at the football stadium. On that visit, she remembered a more relaxed ambiance. Tonight, all the tables were filled while servers scurried to keep up with the high volume of orders. The bar area was overflowing with raucous fans, making it difficult to navigate to the dining area.

During their walkthrough, she noticed a couple huddled at a table near the corner of the bar area. She could see Fosterno's unmistakable profile, his dark hair standing out amid the sea of jerseys and team colors. They made their way through the crowd, determined to get closer without causing a scene.

As they approached, Fosterno glanced up, surprise flashing across his face before it settled into a guarded expression. Beside him sat Penny Cefalo, her features a mix of wariness and curiosity as she looked from Fosterno to the two visitors standing before them.

Syd took the lead, offering a tight smile. "Mind if we join you for a drink?"

Fosterno hesitated, exchanging a quick look with Penny before gesturing to the empty chairs at their table. "Have a seat," he said.

Griffith shook hands politely with Cefalo before embracing Fosterno. "Greetings, former partner," she said. "I hear you sold your tickets."

Fosterno took a deep breath as Syd and Griffith pulled their chairs to the table. "Sometimes you gotta do what you gotta do," he said, sweat glistening on his forehead. "What are you two doing here?"

"An unexpected pleasure," said Cefalo.

Syd wasn't sure if Cefalo was kidding, but she could tell they both had been imbibing for a while.

"Browns are underdogs," said Griffith. "Are you gonna be okay if they don't win, Fosterno?"

Fosterno chugged beer from a fresh pitcher before pouring a glass for Penny. "I love the Browns, but I've got bigger things to worry about. I'm only here for the party."

Syd performed a quick scan of the room. Fosterno had chugged a mug of beer from a fresh pitcher and had poured another to share with Penny. "Kevin, have you seen any sign of your stalker recently?"

"Here?" he asked. "No, but I haven't exactly been watching that closely. Why?"

"Just asking," said Syd.

Cefalo spoke up. "I haven't noticed anyone. But it makes me nervous that you're asking."

"No reason to worry," said Griffith. "As long as you haven't noticed anything weird."

Cefalo laughed aloud. "Look around you. People are wearing fright wigs and dog masks and dressing like werewolves. Nothing abnormal."

Fosterno stood from the table, his legs wobbly. "I want to find out why you're here," he said to Syd. "That is, once I return from the facilities." Then he turned to Cefalo. "Penny, make sure these women are comfortable. Their first round is on me."

"Do you need help?" asked Cefalo. "You seem unsteady."

"Got this," said Fosterno as he walked away, bumping into several revelers on his way to the men's room.

Griffith leaned in closer to Cefalo as Fosterno disappeared into the crowd. "Listen, Penny. We didn't come here for the party. We need to talk about something important."

Cefalo raised an eyebrow. "Okay, I'm all ears."

"It's the vigilante," said Syd. "We believe they might be planning something big, and we're concerned about your safety."

A shadow passed over Cefalo's face as she glanced around the crowded bar. "You mean The Enforcer? Here?"

Griffith nodded. "There's been some signs that The Enforcer is getting closer to the endgame."

Frowning nervously, Cefalo turned her head from side to side. "How do you know?"

Syd glanced at Griffith before answering. "We think you might be the next target. Is it possible someone followed you here?"

Cefalo opened her purse and briefly looked inside before answering. "I guess it's possible," she said. "Off the record, we had a few drinks at home before we drove here, but nothing over the limit. Kevin probably wasn't as attentive as normal."

A commotion from the direction of the restroom interrupted their conversation. Syd could detect Fosterno's massive frame heading toward them. He was wiping his face with a paper towel while banging into several patrons.

"Watch where the hell you're going!" said one slightly built man. Another, decidedly more bulky, had gotten into Fosterno's face. "Not a good idea to crash into my wife," he said. "I'll mess you up."

Before Syd and Griffith could reach the stranger, his wife had pulled him back, whispering something into his ear. The man disappeared into the crowd.

Penny got up and put both hands on Fosterno's cheeks. "Kevin, you don't look so good."

Fosterno let out a belch. "I just lost it all in the bathroom. Several times." He removed Penny's hands from his cheeks, took a backward step, collapsed on the floor, then lay motionless.

An off-duty EMT came over from a nearby table, and the bartender hurried over with a defibrillator, which the man applied to Fosterno's exposed chest. "An ambulance is on the way," the EMT said. "He's not breathing."

Cefalo gripped Syd's shoulders. "I don't understand," she said. "A heart attack?"

The rescue squad placed Fosterno on a stretcher and loaded him into their vehicle. Several guards cleared the area of onlookers, and the ambulance eased its way out of the parking lot before speeding off on a side road. The driver had requested Cefalo to stay back.

"I can't leave him," said Cefalo. "You need to take me to the hospital."

Syd nodded. "That's exactly where we're going."

Griffith took Cefalo by the hand, the other holding her cell to her ear, and the trio circumvented the crowd to return to their squad car. Once inside, Cefalo turned toward Syd, her face strained. "Please tell me he'll be okay," she cried. "How is it that you showed right before he collapsed?"

Griffith ended her phone call. "This seemed like Cutter's MO," she said. "But I checked, and they told me he's still confined to his home with his leg bracelet secure."

Cefalo poked a finger in Syd's face. "You knew something,

didn't you?" she screamed. "You knew someone was going to attack Kevin tonight."

"Calm down!" said Griffith, removing Cefalo's hand. "We didn't know anything for sure."

The two detectives met eyes before Syd responded. "I felt something bad might happen. But now, I think I may have been mistaken about the circumstances."

"What are you talking about?" asked Cefalo. "Something bad *did* happen."

Syd shook her head. "I didn't think Kevin would be the target."

"What are you talking about? Who did you think would be?"

Turning around to face Cefalo in the back seat, Syd responded. "I thought it was going to be you, Penny."

"Me?" she said. "Why did you think it would be me - especially today?"

"A person claiming to be the vigilante has been bragging online," said Syd. "They seemed to hint that the next victim would be a 'copper'."

"I've heard that," said Cefalo. "But there are a hundred cops in this city. And what the hell does that have to do with *me*?"

Griffith looked at Syd. "Want me to take this part?" she asked.

"No," said Syd. "I can finish. Everyone assumed that meant a police officer. But as I thought about that phrasing, I wondered if they meant you."

Putting her head into her hands, Cefalo exhaled. "But I'm not a cop. Why me?"

Griffith interrupted. "I always keep coins handy so I can

help out people on the street. Today, as I handed some to a homeless guy, Detective Livingstone had a revelation."

Cefalo's eyes darted back and forth between them. "Okay, maybe it's because I watched my boyf-, er, bodyguard being carried away on a stretcher," she said. "But, detective, what the hell are you talking about?"

Syd cleared her throat. "The coins. Pennies. My boyfriend's English, and over there, at least sometimes, they refer to pennies as 'coppers'."

"What does that have to do with anything?" asked Cefalo.

"Okay," said Syd. "Coppers. Pennies. That's your name. The same word The Enforcer used in the threat. The Enforcer wasn't talking about attacking a police officer. They were talking about you."

Penny's jaw dropped. "That's a great thought," she said. "Wildly creative. But if I was the target, why am I sitting here while Kevin is fighting for his life?"

Using the automatic control to lower the window, Syd took a breath of the cold winter air. "Well," she said, "I thought you may have been the target tonight. But now that I think about it, that threat may have been posted before someone shot out your car window at the gym."

CHAPTER 42

When Syd and Griffith walked into the morgue, Lasek and Pratt stood over the cold, naked body of Kevin Fosterno. Seven hours after his death, rigor mortis had spread into his face and down through the chest, abdomen, and limbs. Pennington was pulling a white sheet over his waist.

Lasek scoffed. "I liked Fosterno. But keeping his drawers upright was never a priority in life, so why should it be any different now?"

Griffith gave a stern shake of the head. "Easy there, commish. That's my partner you're talking about. His zipper problem was one negative trait among many positive ones."

"I meant no disrespect," said Lasek. "Sometimes, I have to employ a little levity to remain sane in this business."

Syd watched Pratt pace back and forth, a clipboard in hand. "I see your report uses the word 'toxicity'," he said.

"How can you know that before the blood results come back?"

"There are definitely signs," said Pennington. "According to a report, this guy shits his pants and vomited on his shirt. And his skin was unusually pale."

"Isn't it possible that he ate something bad?" asked Lasek.

Pennington squeezed the gland area directly underneath Fosterno's chin. "Not in this case," she said. "I'd bet my reputation on something chemical."

Syd put her right hand over her stomach, trying to ignore the urge to vomit. "How painful was it?"

Pulling the sheet over Fosterno's head, Pennington instructed her young female assistant to take the body away. "It certainly wasn't pleasant," she said. "Besides the purging of liquids from various orifices, his female companion said he was complaining of head pain."

Lasek glanced at Pratt. "That would be Cefalo," he said. "Pratt and I assigned Fosterno to watch over her despite his reputation, so the buck stops with me. But he wasn't supposed to become emotionally attached. That decision may have gotten him killed."

Griffith downed a paper cup of water, swallowing noticeably. "By trying to protect an unpunished criminal, we've now lost one of our own."

"Hold on," said Pratt. "Why do we think this is the work of the vigilante?"

Syd chimed in. "I believe Cefalo was the intended target, but Fosterno ended up being collateral damage."

Griffith shook her head and pinched the bridge of her nose with her left thumb and forefinger. "Nothing like hearing your former partner being referred to as 'collateral damage.' That's not the way I want to remember him."

"I'm sorry," said Syd. "Just talking here - not weighing every word."

"We get that," said Pratt. "Finish your thought."

"Griffith and I interviewed Penny in the hospital after the doctor informed us of Kevin's death. Once she stopped crying, we were able to gather some viable information."

"Like what?" asked Lasek.

"Penny mentioned that Fosterno had been drinking pitchers, but they were surprised by the last pitcher that showed up. Fosterno didn't remember ordering it."

Lasek interrupted. "So, is she implying that the last pitcher was tainted? Because if that's so, wouldn't both Fosterno and Cefalo be dead?"

"That's logical," said Syd. "But according to Penny, she only took a small sip. She's not a big fan of draft."

"When did that last pitcher arrive?" asked Lasek.

"Shortly after we did," said Syd. "I remember it showing up on the table."

"Did you notice who delivered it?" asked Lasek.

"I wish I could tell you, but I don't remember. Neither can Griffith. The place was brimming with people."

Pratt laughed. "How convenient," he said. "She just happened to drink little or nothing from that last pitcher."

Lasek reached into his pocket, removed a red stress ball, and squeezed it. "Where is Cefalo?" he asked.

"She's scheduled to come into the office tomorrow," said Pratt. "Apparently, she's taken it upon herself to start planning for his funeral."

"Let's not release the body yet," said Lasek. "Interesting how Cefalo continues to survive this vigilante despite escaping justice in a monumental way."

Syd thought that shifting the attention to Cefalo was

premature. The evidence against her didn't add up. Why would the vigilante be someone who had skirted justice herself?

Pratt flipped over a page in his notebook. "If she took a few sips of the beer, wouldn't she have gotten sick?"

Syd nodded. "On the way to the hospital, she complained about her stomach. They examined her and performed a blood test."

"So, she ingested enough to make her sick but not kill her?" Pratt snorted. "Funny how that takes the spotlight off her."

Griffith smiled and looked over at Lasek and Pratt. "It seems like you'll have plenty to discuss when you interview Cefalo. Push her buttons and get some real answers."

Lasek and Pratt rose from their seats. "Anything else?" asked Lasek.

"Since you asked, I have one more thing," said Syd. She pulled a penny from her pocket and held it up. "I've been working on a theory. Do either of you know what this is made of?"

CHAPTER 43

Syd and Griffith were seated behind the glass, staring into the interrogation room at Penny Cefalo. For the moment, she was sitting quietly, bent over in a chair with her head in her hands. But as Lasek opened the door to join Pratt inside the room, a loud wail resonated from the aperture and down the main hallway.

"Stop accusing me!" she screamed.

Pratt reached into a manila envelope and removed two pictures, placing both in front of Cefalo. One was a picture of her partially decapitated former boyfriend, Derek Stovall. The other was a naked photo of Fosterno lying on the examination table.

It was obvious to Syd that Pratt was in full-court-press mode, using every tactic in his arsenal to break her down.

"We all know you caused the death of the person on the left," said Pratt. "So why is it completely out of the question that you also killed the person on the right?"

"I didn't kill Kevin. I loved him."

Lasek joined in. "I believe you said the same thing about your former boyfriend during your trial."

"That was different. It was self-defense."

Syd was surprised at the directness of Lasek's statement. Usually, they employed the good cop/bad cop routine. That obviously wasn't happening today.

"You were with Fosterno for the entire day," said Lasek. "And now he's no longer with us. That's a mighty big coincidence, isn't it, Ms. Cefalo?"

Taking a tissue from a box sitting on the table, Cefalo wiped tears from her eyes and cleared her throat. Her expression had changed to anger.

"What motive would I have to poison him?" she snapped.

"Why don't you tell us and save yourself the stress of another brutal trial?" said Pratt.

Cefalo suddenly grew silent. She looked to Pratt and then to Lasek. "I didn't kill him!"

"It fits your pattern," said Lasek. "Maybe he pissed you off like your last boyfriend did."

As much as Syd longed for the truth, she found Lasek's demeanor to be distressing, even over-the-top.

Cefalo's fists clenched. She began to rise but caught herself.

"I want an attorney," she said. "No more insults or questions from you two clowns."

Pratt and Lasek didn't say another word, rising and then exiting the room. Syd met them in the hallway. She longed to ask why they were so harsh but knew it wouldn't do any good.

"She's refusing to answer any more questions and has requested counsel," said Pratt. "We beat her down pretty good in there."

"Do you think she's a part of this vigilante thing?" asked Syd.

"Truthfully, I don't know," said Lasek. "It's odd how every boyfriend of hers ends up in a cemetery." He frowned anxiously.

"I think she's more likely to be the intended victim than The Enforcer," said Syd.

Lasek shrugged. "I know you like that 'penny-copper' theory of yours. But I think she may be involved."

"Are you going to arrest her?" asked Syd.

Pratt responded. "No, we're actually going to let her stew in there while she phones a lawyer. Then we'll allow her to go home."

"I want to speak with her," said Syd. "Before she has a chance to phone an attorney."

"Waste of time," said Pratt. "She's made her decision. She's not going to say any more."

"Then it won't hurt for me to try," said Syd. "We'll enjoy a little chat. Let me go in."

Lasek nodded at Pratt. "She's yours," he said. Then he extended his hand.

"Do you want to shake?" asked Syd.

"Hand me your gun. As officers, we must learn from previous mistakes."

Entering the interrogation room, Syd felt stripped of both her weapon and dignity. The mistake she'd made with Cutter was probably going to haunt her for the rest of her career. She pulled her chair across the table from Cefalo and placed a hand on top of hers.

" "I know you're going through an awful lot," she said.

"I've barely processed what happened," said Cefalo. "Now they're suspecting me."

Syd squeezed Cefalo's hand a little more tightly. "They're doing their job. But I need to speak openly with you so we can determine what happened."

"I already told them," said Cefalo.

"I need to clarify a few things," said Syd.

"I want you to catch whoever did this," said Cefalo. "If someone actually poisoned him."

"The coroner is sure he was poisoned."

"If that's the case, I'd say there are about 200 suspects to interrogate," said Cefalo.

Looking into Cefalo's face, Syd noticed dark circles below her eyes. "Did you share the same food and drinks?"

"For the most part," she said. "We both nibbled on the same appetizers - you know how couples do."

"I need to ask you about that last pitcher," said Syd. "Before it arrived, were either of you feeling sick?"

Cefalo looked down, attempting to recall. "Not that I remember. After you arrived, that's when Kevin became sick. You witnessed it. My stomach was messed up, but nothing major."

"They found traces of strychnine in your blood at the hospital," said Syd. "But not enough to harm you. Be thankful that you didn't drink any more than a sip."

"Your superiors think it was all calculated on my part," said Cefalo.

"Why would Kevin drink from that last pitcher? He was careful, at least when he wasn't drinking."

"I can't speak for him, especially now, "said Cefalo. "But I think he figured he'd forgotten that he ordered it."

Syd sat quietly, musing, as Penny continued. "Our relationship wasn't supposed to turn romantic. It was probably my fault. I insisted that he share a drink with me in my living room one night. It was one of those green olive martinis. One turned into three and then…"

Syd nodded. "Was that the only time you two were intimate?"

Cefalo smiled briefly. "Are you kidding? After that, we could hardly keep our hands off each other."

She paused to grab a tissue and wiped her eyes. "Kevin was loud but funny. I'm going to miss that story-telling windbag."

Syd leaned forward. "I know it's hard, but I need you to stay with me. Did you recognize anyone you knew in the Salamander besides Griffith and me?"

"Not that I remember," said Penny. "And certainly not the guy that had followed Kevin before."

"You've seen his stalker before? In person?"

"On one occasion," said Cefalo.

"Okay," said Syd. "Did Kevin know who that guy was?"

"He claimed he didn't."

"Would you recognize him if you saw him again?" asked Syd.

"Probably," said Cefalo.

Before Syd could respond, she heard a tap on the door. She excused herself and left the room.

Lasek met her outside with another folder. "I was up till four in the morning examining videos of people coming and going at the Majestic that evening. I've printed stills of about ten people who were unidentifiable to me. Run these by her. Two of them resemble felons in our database. The pictures are labeled 'A' through 'J'. The ones labeled 'D', and 'I' are the ones that resemble known criminals."

Syd pulled the folder from Lasek's hand and headed back toward the room. "I'll see what she says. Stand by."

For five minutes, Cefalo shuffled through the printed pictures of the unidentified men. She kept returning to one image of a man with brown hair and a beard. The subject had aquiline features, his sharp chin and pronounced jaw plainly visible from a side view.

"That's him," said Cefalo as she picked up the photo and placed it down firmly on the table. "I'm sure. He usually doesn't have a beard. I've seen him before, in a bowling alley. We'd drive miles out of our way to a small town where we thought no one would notice us together. Kevin made us leave in the middle of a game. It was a shame since I'd made three strikes in a row."

Flipping over the photo, Syd looked on the back for the letter. It was an 'I'.

I'll be damned. Are we finally going to solve this case?

Syd held up the back of the photo to the glass so Lasek and anyone else witnessing could clearly identify the letter 'I'.

After a minute or two, Lasek entered the room. "Thank you, Ms. Cefalo," he said. "I appreciate how forthcoming you were with Detective Livingstone. If Chief Pratt or I offended you today, I'd like to apologize."

Lasek motioned for Detective Dave Roberts to enter. Roberts escorted Cefalo from the room.

Once they were alone, Lasek turned toward Syd. "She ID'd Curtis Marksbury. He served four years for racketeering and also has a previous B & E. He's known to be associated with 'The Warlords.' Does that ring any bells?"

"I don't know," said Syd. "Should it?"

"A big drug cartel that originated from the central part of Indiana. A few years ago, two members died in a car chase. And I'll bet you can guess who the officer in pursuit was."

"Kevin Fosterno," said Syd.

"If he was at the Majestic that night, he was probably leaning on Fosterno."

"Can we pick him up?" asked Syd.

"We have his mother's address on file. There's been a warrant out for his arrest, but we don't know if he's still in town. If he happens to be visiting Mama for some good ol' fashioned home cooking, we'll have him in custody in a few hours."

At the next morning's meeting, Lasek announced that Walsh County detectives had served a warrant on Marksbury and found him sleeping on a sofa in a back room of his mother's house. They could hold him on existing charges, but they'd have to gather more evidence before filing new ones. "We may be nearing the end of this ordeal," he proclaimed. "My hunch tells me we've got the right guy."

But Syd wasn't convinced.

CHAPTER 44

Syd was at her desk when Penny Cefalo walked into the precinct and asked for her. After a moment of small talk, she placed a small cartridge tape into Syd's hand.

"I don't know if you'll believe me, but I haven't listened to this," said Cefalo. "God, this feels so surreal. Kevin wanted me to bring it to you in the case of his death. I thought he was being paranoid. For some reason, he wanted you - and only you - to listen to it. He said you were the one he could trust."

Syd studied the tape in her hand. There was no label on it. "How long have you known about it?"

"Less than a month," said Cefalo. "After he told me that criminals were tracking him for shooting those two guys."

Syd could see the pain in Cefalo's eyes. Fosterno had definitely won her over in their short time together.

Cefalo continued. "This is the way Kevin wanted it. If

you'd like to discuss it later, that's up to you." She got up to leave.

"Where are you going?" asked Syd.

"Home," she said. "I need some alone time. The world keeps going sideways."

Before reaching the door, she stopped and turned back to Syd. "I know it doesn't look good for me, with another boyfriend dying. But I truly loved Kevin."

Syd acknowledged her statement with a nod.

"I've done a lot of self-reflecting since my trial," Penny said. "That last night with Derek was so emotional. Sometime, when I look back, I wonder if I could have made another choice. But I really thought he was going to kill me."

She stopped for a moment and smiled. "Anyway, I wanted you to know that I'm sorry that Kevin is gone. He liked and trusted you."

Syd nodded again as Cefalo turned and exited the building. Her first thought was to bring in the usual suspects to hear the tape, but she decided to honor Fosterno's final wishes. She located a small recorder and headed into a vacant interrogation room. She pressed the "Play" button.

After a brief shuffling sound, Fosterno's voice filled the room.

I guess I should start by saying goodbye, Detective Livingstone because if you're listening to this, I have more than likely been offed. I'm asking Penny to give this tape to you, and only to you, because this vigilante situation has left most of us unsettled, and it looks like someone in the department may be involved. You may already know who. I certainly don't. But there's one thing I am 100% certain of. You are not The Enforcer.

I leave it up to you, Syd, whether you wish to disseminate this information. I trust your instincts as a cop, and I admire your integrity. I was once like you as far as integrity goes. (Here, Syd heard Fosterno's voice break.)

I have let everyone down: my community, my fellow officers, and even myself. Having said that, my story needs to go on the permanent record. I am not doing this to name names or to rat people out. In fact, the only person I'm calling out on this tape is myself. There's a major player in all of this, but whatever happens from here on out is between them and God.

Syd switched off the recorder and dabbed at a tear running down her cheek. It was hard to reconcile this serious and somber man with the playful and humorous one she used to know. If someone like Fosterno could be compromised, who else might be? She resumed listening.

You already know a portion of the story, Syd, from the ceremony at the Majestic. But I'm offering my testimony now for the record, from start to finish. I'd do anything to change what happened that night. If I could, you wouldn't be listening to this right now, and I'd probably be working down the hall from you.

As you know, someone has been following me. It isn't my imagination. But it has nothing to do with this vigilante situation. It all goes back to that night when, like an idiot, I decided to pursue those speeding vehicles when I was off-duty.

I was on my way home after spending a good part of the evening drinking with friends. I probably consumed a little too much. I was driving my personal vehicle. I was carrying my revolver, which I know is a big-time no-no. I noticed a black cargo van speeding - maybe 100 - in the left lane, with a white car following. For some reason, I decided to pursue, despite my condition.

When I realized my cell was dead and I couldn't call for backup, I should have aborted the mission. At first, I thought it was some crazy kids. But then I remembered an APB about a black van with a sunshine bumper sticker on the back window. That description matched the lead vehicle. The white sedan drew even, and I saw someone in the van point a gun at the car.

In retrospect, I should've let those scumbags kill each other. You know, thin the herd. But I've never been one to back away from a challenge. I wanted to finish. After I saw a flash from that gun, the white car veered out of control. It spun out, ending up on the other end of the highway, facing traffic. I almost rear-ended the van before it switched to the left lane and sped away. I chased the sonofabitch for 15 miles. You'd think the pursuit might catch the attention of law enforcement, but nothing. It was just the two of us.

We passed Crescentville. Now, Fosterno gave a brief laugh. I know the little old man that's the sheriff there. He would've had a heart attack if he witnessed it.

Picture this, Syd. The van takes a road called Hyden. It's supposed to be two-lane, but you're lucky to fit one car on it. He's doing close to 100, and it's muddy as shit. There's craters and potholes. My windshield is full of gunk, I can barely see, and my car's making grinding noises. We're both having to slow down like crazy, practically crawling. The side panel door on the driver's side suddenly slides open. I see some fat white dude leaning out of there. He's pointing a pistol with a long-ass barrel at me.

So, I, Syd, being the dumb-ass you've always known, start wondering how someone can open the side door while driving. Of course, it finally dawns on me that there are two of those bastards in there. My car is rattling, and I can see smoke billowing from their car. We're both coming to a stop.

Syd could hear Fosterno's breath becoming labored. She longed to reach out her hand and offer comfort.

I'm in the middle of nowhere, without backup or phone. And outnumbered. My hands are glued to the wheel. My gun is at my side, but I'm paralyzed. Then, glass shatters in front of me. Next thing, I'm tasting my own blood. I think it's a bullet, but I feel my face and realize the windshield glass cut me. And I'm not sitting anymore. I'm lying on the front seat, blood everywhere. I can hear the van grinding to a halt. I seize my gun, but don't move, basically playing dead. I see the fat-ass in yellow walking toward my car. He peers in and then looks away. He shouts to his buddy that he took me out with one shot. Jackass.

Another voice shouts, "Make sure he's dead." I can see a little better now, especially in one eye. I hear someone jiggling the door handle, so I pull my gun and fire twice out the driver's side. Fat-ass drops.

I sit up in time to see the van driver's door swing open. Some thin black guy exits with a 9mm. He's firing at me. I get out of my car and there's Mr. Yellow on the ground, gasping. I slip on his blood as bullets are whizzing by. Weirdly enough, that blood may have saved me.

So now, I'm trying to get off the ground. I can hear the guy reloading. Yellow is probably dead. I decide to stay down and give the guy less of a target. He starts shooting again and something strikes my left shoulder. I know I'm hit; I don't feel pain. First time in my career I ever took a bullet.

Black guy stops firing and jumps back into the van. The engine chokes, and he's trying so hard to get it started, it's like he forgot about me. A few seconds later, I'm standing at his window, my gun pointed at his face.

I yell, "Drop your weapon," but the bastard raises his gun. And that was the end.

Clicking off the recorder, Syd marveled that the voice she was hearing belonged to a dead man. If she'd arrived at the Silver Salamander even a half-hour earlier, she might have been able to save him.

For a few seconds, she was bothered by another intrusive thought. Chances were good that this was the only version of the tape. What if it malfunctioned and she never heard the rest of Fosterno's story? Maybe she should have insisted that someone in the department create a duplicate at the time she received it. But that would entail trusting an insider. She clicked to start it up again.

Syd, I had never shot - let alone killed - anyone before. As a cop, I always felt I would handle it better. Maybe I should have felt a sense of accomplishment for neutralizing both suspects, but I felt terrible. Sure, I was glad to be alive, and I realized it had to be done, but damn, two people were dead.

He cleared his throat.

This is the part of the story that I've been dreading. But it needs to be told. Syd, I know you will do what's necessary for justice to be done. So let me take the opportunity to thank you now, before I forget.

One of the best days of my life was when I became an officer. With my hand on the Bible, I promised to hold myself and others accountable for our actions. I vowed to maintain the highest ethical standards while upholding the values of my community and the agency I serve.

I failed to live up to those standards. And for everyone who is either hearing this, or reading these words in a transcript, you need to know that I'm truly sorry for my actions.

Anyway, now I found myself in the middle of nowhere, no way to summon help, while in the presence of two dead criminals. My shoulder was starting to hurt, but it wasn't bleeding bad, so I probably wouldn't die.

I swung open the van's side cargo door. Luckily, the inside light was still operational. I didn't expect to find anyone else, and I was right, but I did find a couple of bags of weed. There were some more disturbing items, too. Rope, zip ties, ligatures, and a couple of ski masks. I didn't know who these guys were, but I knew whatever they were up to wasn't good.

Then I spotted something pushed back toward the corner of the van. I got in and shuffled back there. It was a pair of black suitcases. For a second, I freaked out, thinking they could contain explosive devices. But that seemed unlikely. I thought about walking out to get help, but I second-guessed myself. What if another party stumbled upon the van while I was gone? They could steal whatever was inside. Vital evidence would disappear. I tried to start the van again, but no luck.

I wanted to know what was inside those suitcases. I didn't realize that my life was about to change forever.

Before I say anything more about what happened, please understand that I have served as a police officer for more than 15 years. As you listen to these words, I implore you not to judge my entire body of work based on one event. I am so much more than that.

Both suitcases had three-digit combination locks that I couldn't open. So, I made the decision to leave them in the van, against my better judgment. They were heavy and I needed to find help.

I found a farmhouse, and an old lady answered the door. She was smart, keeping the screen door shut until I showed her my badge. Then she let me make a call. I won't say who I called. But I gave that person my location and - this is the part I'm not proud of - I asked them to bring a hacksaw. Then I walked back to the van to wait.

Syd's concentration was interrupted by a knock on the interrogation room door. She slipped the small recorder into her pocket before the door swung open, and Lasek walked in. "Didn't expect to see you here," he said. "What brings you to the interrogation room? Isn't your cubicle stimulating enough?"

Lasek was smiling, but it looked like he hadn't had much sleep. Maybe the vigilante situation was wearing on him.

"Sometimes I need a change of scenery," she lied. "It's an old technique I used in my tennis days. It gets the creative juices flowing."

Lasek nodded. "I get that. To be a professional in any sport, you must be willing to think outside the box. Speaking of that, anything new in the investigation?"

Syd's heart raced. "We're still reviewing some blurry tape from inside the Silver Salamander," she said. "It was so crowded though, it's hard to recognize anyone."

"I'm around if you need me," said Lasek. She noticed he was squeezing his stress ball. "I'll let you get back to your brainstorming."

After Lasek left, Syd wondered what he might have seen from the other side of the glass. Putting her trepidations aside, she brought the recorder out again and resumed listening. Fosterno's voice once again filled the room.

The hacksaw got us into the suitcases, no problem.

It was cash - spilling out in denominations of 50's and 100's. More cash than I'd ever seen in one location in my life. The second one contained as much or more than the first. I was surprised that the paramedics hadn't arrived yet, or the squad cars, or the coroner. I had told the person who was with me what happened, and said I needed support.

I'd been expecting sirens wailing and cars racing to get here. But instead, there was silence. There was a reason they hadn't been called.

So, here's where I get into trouble. I have always prided myself on being open-minded, making me a sucker for anyone who presents a good argument. And boy was I presented one.

The perps were dead. They were obviously into drugs, and probably human trafficking. And the money in those suitcases was theirs, obviously generated from nefarious activities. The person argued that nobody worthwhile was going to get hurt. Not a cent was taken from the Sisters of Charity, the Girl Scouts, Boy Scouts, or the Foundation to Save the Freezing Animals. The only people getting screwed in this transaction - if we kept the money - were the bad guys. The dregs of society.

I was persuaded that we would be the best stewards of the money. Helping support charities… along with some of the people we loved. It was a simple choice of Good vs. Evil. Right vs. Wrong. The Angels vs. The Antichrist. In the end, I took one suitcase, and the other went to…well, I won't say who.

I take full responsibility for the one suitcase I took. I could have left it at the scene and informed the department that it was the only one. Who would have ever known?

I'm not going to discuss the other suitcase. This recording is only about me - Kevin Fosterno - and not the decisions made by anyone else.

Anyway, we agreed I'd take 15 minutes to separate and find hiding places, then call for backup. I probably walked three-quarters of a mile, northeast. I hadn't decided whether I'd keep the money. A hiding place would provide extra time to decide what I really wanted to do. If I eventually returned the cash, technically, I wouldn't be breaking any laws. Right?

I found a pile of abandoned wooden planks near a pair of trees, and I stashed the suitcase there. I could hear the ambulances and squad cars finally starting to arrive, and I walked back. The bodies were taken to the morgue. After the paramedics checked me out, I was given a ride to the police station, where I was interviewed thoroughly. The next day, news outlets were calling my actions "selfless" and "heroic."

I didn't return to retrieve the money the next day. Or even the next week. I was still telling myself that I'd turn it in eventually. What harm would there be in hiding it while I decided how to proceed? I talked myself into believing that I had suffered a minor concussion and wasn't thinking clearly.

After a couple of months, I couldn't wait any longer. I drove out to the scene of the shootout, then walked to the site with the planks. I prayed that someone had stumbled upon the money by accident.

If someone else now had the money, it was between them and their conscience. I would be out of the equation. Finders keepers.

My heart was beating so hard as I removed the planks. The briefcase seemed like it wasn't where I'd left it. But soon, I could see the corner of it. After removing another plank, I could see some of the currency sticking out from where it had been sliced open.

I sat down behind the stack of boards, sorted the money into piles, and started to count.

Ten, then twenty piles, and I wasn't even close to being finished. Fifty, seventy-five, then one hundred. A total of 150 piles.

The total stunned me, $750,000.

And I had the smaller of the two suitcases. What the hell?

And that was the day I took my first hundred-thousand home.

So far, I have removed at least one-third of the money. The remainder still sits underneath those rotting planks.

Syd, I swear I haven't spent a dime. I'm still trying to figure out how I can return it. Thing is, the people who died in that shootout were not the only members of that syndicate. When the news media made me a hero, they realized that no mention had ever been made about the money. They put two-and-two together and came to the conclusion that I stole it. They were half right.

And now my life is in danger. Those gangbangers want it all back. I'm not sure how much my accomplice has spent, but they are not cooperating. And I'm not sure I should give what I've got to the bad guys. I'm still a cop. I've been followed on more occasions that I can count. I'm scared.

So, there you have it. I've confessed to grand theft and betraying my code of honor as an officer. Now that I've said it, it seems so incredibly real. If you're hearing this because I'm dead, then I have managed to avoid the worst consequences that come with these actions, the legal ones. But please believe me when I say that no judge or jury could ever punish me more harshly than I have already punished myself.

Syd could see that the tape was about to run out. After a pause, Fosterno's voice came on again.

Thanks, Livingstone, for taking the time to listen. I've told you everything I know, except the identity of the other person. I can't bring myself to betray a friend - even from beyond the grave. That would be truly despicable.
And there's one more thing before I close. Please check in on Penny once in a while. She's not the cold-blooded killer the prosecutors portrayed. I've been married three times, but I believe she's the only one who truly loved me.

The tape stopped.

CHAPTER 45

As Syd drove the ten minutes to Montenegro's house on Tuesday night at 10 pm, she couldn't help but question her own judgment and sanity. Going out in the dark of the night to see a suspended cop was not the most sensible decision for achieving her career goals. However, she knew she needed the advice and support of her best friend and former partner.

After she tapped quietly on his door, Stuart Montenegro peered out of the drapes of his front window. Clad in a torn Cleveland Guardians T-shirt and a blue pair of jogging shorts, he seemed surprised. He swung the front door open with a smile.

"Syd, I didn't expect to see you on my doorstep on a snowy night. Please come in."

Stacey Montenegro had emerged from the den, phone in hand, seemingly putting the finishing touches on a text message. "Syd! What a pleasant surprise." She glanced at her husband, "You never mentioned she was coming over."

"In all fairness, he didn't know," said Syd. "If this is an imposition, I can come back another time."

"Gosh, no," said Stacey. "It's always a pleasure, my friend. Can I offer you some coffee or a soda?"

Syd's hoodie was covering her blonde hair, as the third week of January had brought a light snow to Northeast Ohio. After brushing a light layer of snow from her sleeve, she proceeded to give Stacey a hug.

Smiling, Stuart said, "It looks like you two are going to be busy for a while. Maybe I should be the one who fetches the drinks."

"I'm sorry I didn't call," said Syd. "This visit is as impromptu as they come."

"You're always welcome," interrupted Stuart. "Does anyone know you're here?"

"No," she said. "But I'm not thinking clearly. I have some information, and I'm not sure who I can trust."

Stacey again offered coffee. Stuart interrupted. "I'll make it for her," he said. "Stacey, would you let us talk privately?"

"Of course," she nodded. "I'll be in the bedroom if you need me."

Syd hadn't shared the Fosterno tape with anyone yet. She wanted to discuss it with Montenegro before proceeding.

"I normally would have called or texted first," said Syd. "I didn't think I'd have the courage to stop here. But here I am."

"It's probably not a good idea to be interacting with me," said Montenegro. "But I've heard rumors I might be returning to work soon." He placed a pod into the coffee machine and produced a steaming cup a few seconds later.

Syd wanted to give Stuart a hug, but she didn't feel it was appropriate, especially with her showing up unannounced.

"I know you were close to Fosterno," she said. "I think we all were."

"Hard to believe he's gone," said Montenegro. "Is that why you stopped?"

"Not totally. It's just that you and I are partners, and we always share ideas. I respect Griffith, but it's not the same."

Nodding, Stuart took in a deep breath.

"I phoned Police Chief Trent, a friend from the Columbus area," said Syd. "He says I should trust my instincts about you."

"Let's go into the den," said Montenegro. "There's even more privacy."

Montenegro switched off the TV, which displayed a paused World War II documentary. For the next hour, she and Montenegro listened to Fosterno's tape. He listened attentively, occasionally scribbling notes.

"I haven't shared this with anyone," she said. "I will soon, but I need perspective from you."

Montenegro smiled as he stared into his coffee mug. "I appreciate the confidence, Syd, but damn, this could get you into big trouble."

"I understand," said Syd, nodding. "But this case is so different. There's evidence that an insider is involved. It could be anyone."

"Including me?" asked Montenegro.

Before Syd could respond, Montenegro chuckled. "Syd, you know I'm kidding. But you have to promise that no one will ever know about this meeting."

"Scouts honor," said Syd. "I'm on the shortest leash in the department. But I know you aren't The Enforcer or an accomplice."

"You're right," he said. "Now that we've established that, let's discuss that tape. Someone absconded with the lion's share of the money. Maybe someone in the office, maybe not."

Syd reclined in her easy chair. "My first thought was Mitsoff, but that could be wishful thinking," she said. "He showed up with an expensive new bike. And we know the significance a motorcycle has to this case."

"I wasn't following him because I like the way he dresses," said Montenegro. "He'd be dumb enough to flaunt that money too."

Montenegro continued. "Mitsoff had complete access to the evidence room. And we all know about what his girlfriend discovered. Maybe I was suspended because they felt I was compromising the case against him."

Syd smiled, "I think breaking into Michelle's house and pointing a gun at Mitsoff had more to do with it."

For a moment, when they laughed together, things seemed almost back to normal. "Assuming it's Mitsoff," said Syd, "what about his motive?"

Montenegro hesitated for a moment. "He's a prick to almost everybody. Maybe he's an even bigger one to unpunished criminals."

Despite the late hour, Montenegro appeared to be gaining steam. "Something else is bugging me," he said. "If Fosterno knew the tape would only be heard if he passed away, why wouldn't he reveal his accomplice?"

Syd took a moment before responding. "Like he mentioned on the tape, he didn't want to betray a friend."

Montenegro nodded. "Yeah, a friend that talked him into becoming a felon. Hard for me to fathom. Do you think he was the intended target?"

"Can't be sure. It may have been her."

Montenegro sighed and shook his head. "Someone he trusted coerced him into stealing that money."

"Someone we probably know quite well," said Syd.

Tapping his hand on the table, Montenegro raised another question. "Why were you the only one he sent the tape to? He was close with me and several others."

Montenegro's question made Syd a little uncomfortable. "Maybe because I was so new, he realized I didn't come with baggage."

"Weird," said Montenegro. "Maybe he didn't trust his conspirator anymore."

"Considering what happened, I can understand why," said Syd.

"How do we know that Cefalo didn't listen to the tape? And maybe even alter it?"

"We don't," said Syd. "I'm taking her at her word."

"Did she seem despondent when Fosterno died?" asked Montenegro.

Syd nodded her head. "In my opinion, she was devastated."

"Perhaps your instincts are right, Syd. It's possible that she felt grief, but that doesn't mean she didn't have a motive to harm him."

Montenegro rose to his feet to dim the ceiling lights. "Let's continue down the money path. Anyone else displaying abnormal wealth?"

"The obvious answer is Pratt," said Syd. "According to someone I trust, he owns a huge house and an expensive beach property."

"Peculiar," said Montenegro. "Walsh County pays him well, but not like that. Could he have inherited it?"

"Seems unlikely, but possible," said Syd. "After him, I don't know of anybody else."

"Place yourself in Fosterno's shoes. You've come off a high-speed chase and you're still somewhat drunk. Two suspects are dead. Who would be the first person you'd call?"

Syd scratched her chin. "You, my partner," she said.

"So, in Fosterno's case, that would've been Griffith. She moonlights by acting in plays. Is she doing that for love or money?"

"I have a friend who did that in Savannah. She definitely didn't do it for the money."

"Weren't you with her when Fosterno was poisoned?" asked Montenegro. "Would she have had the opportunity?"

"Technically, yes," said Syd. "But I can't imagine she would do that."

"We're not talking about emotion right now," said Montenegro. "Try to put that aside."

Syd knew Montenegro was right. She needed to think like a detective. "It doesn't seem like she has a lot of money. She has to wait until payday just to help out a homeless guy."

Montenegro looked at Syd but didn't react.

The conversation was interrupted by the sound of footsteps. Stacey walked past the entrance of the den in the direction of the kitchen. "Forgot my glass of water," she said. "Syd, is there anything you need before I say goodnight?"

"No, I'm fine, Stacey," she said. "I'll be heading out before too long."

"Take your time," said Stacey. "I know you're talking shop." She turned and walked down the hallway toward the bedroom.

Syd downed the final swig of her now tepid coffee. "I

should go and let you be with your wife. We can finish another time."

"We have more to discuss," said Stuart. "I'll get you another cup." He left the kitchen and returned a minute later with a new steaming mug .

If the forced hiatus had any detrimental effects on Stuart, Syd couldn't tell. In fact, he looked fitter than usual. She assumed he'd been pumping iron at home.

For the next thirty minutes, they went over the specifics of her interview with Cefalo and the resulting apprehension of Marksbury.

Stuart stared at the table for a minute before he spoke.

"Maybe this Marksbury figure is the vigilante? Does that even make sense?"

"Could be," said Syd. "But he'd have to be working with an insider. He would've never had access to our evidence room."

Montenegro said, "True. We should probably be focusing on our insider. Agreed?"

"I think so," said Syd.

"That leaves us with someone else to discuss: Lasek. It's no secret he ran into some trouble in Flagstaff."

"He got physical with an officer there," said Syd. "Although nothing major came of it. Then, his wife was the victim of an attack, but the suspect ended up dead. It was reported as a suicide."

Montenegro smirked for a moment. "And then there's every other employee of Walsh County who could've gained access to your scheduling software. That's a big list."

Syd nodded, letting the gravity of Montenegro's words sink in.

Finally, Montenegro took a deep breath. "Syd, I need to

know something. Around the office, has my name come up? I mean, as a suspect?"

Staring down at her coffee mug, Syd momentarily wished it was filled with whiskey.

"We're required to perform due diligence," she said. "But you're not considered a suspect. Basically, they look at you as someone who made an egregious mistake with Mitsoff."

"That's understandable," said Montenegro. "Wonder if I'll ever get reinstated."

"I think you will," she said. "As long as no one ever finds out about our discussion tonight."

As Syd exited the front door and walked down the driveway, she felt better about her own thoughts concerning the investigation. Her conversation with Stuart had opened her mind to several possibilities. But for now, she needed sleep. It had been a long day, and tomorrow would be just as busy, starting with sharing the Fosterno tape with Lasek and Pratt.

She quickly walked down the driveway and slipped inside her car. For a moment, she questioned her judgment for leaving it in the driveway. She rationalized that the street was dimly lit, so no one probably noticed.

As she drove home, she couldn't help but miss Enzo. She longed for the comfort of him waiting at home, where they could exchange stories about their day and unwind with a warm bath and intimate moments together. As she pulled into her driveway, she pressed the button to open the garage door, allowing her to park inside.

The Enforcer watched Syd exit the car and close the garage door behind her, then turned the motorcycle for home. Tucked safely behind closed doors, The Enforcer logged on to the RealVigilante website for what they determined would be the final time. Even with the precautions used to avoid tracking via the latest software, eventually the hard drive would have to be destroyed, and the computer dismantled. The remnants would either be buried or dropped into the center of a large body of water, firmly anchored down.

Perusing a breaking article online, The Enforcer read a quote from Coroner Melissa Pennington, who confirmed that Kevin Fosterno's death was caused by the consumption of strychnine.

The poison wasn't difficult to acquire. A few brands of yard treatments designed to kill gophers still contain strychnine and were easy to buy - at a hardware superstore in a city ninety miles away.

The playoff matchup had brought all types of characters to the Silver Salamander, including The Enforcer. With three empty pitchers sitting on Fosterno's table, it was obvious he was well into his buzz. Ordering another one and tainting it with strychnine wasn't difficult. Slipping the pitcher on Fosterno's table was a little more awkward but doable.

The Enforcer was present when Fosterno collapsed, but in a car leaving the Silver Salamander shortly thereafter.

The Enforcer smiled. The cryptic threat involving "a copper" was a smart bit of misdirection.

RealVigilante lit up with the familiar sight of the mugshots of famous killers interspersed. After entering a password, The Enforcer began to type:

At the beginning of this quest, the only real goal was to achieve justice for victims who aren't with us anymore. And for the most part, we achieved our goal.

Who among us - beside perhaps the insane - would ever grieve for vermin like Frank McBride and Gabriel Babson? Everyone knows McBride murdered his wife and dumped her body without the dignity of a burial. We did the community a favor by eliminating him. And Gabriel Babson, who beat the rap after drowning his wife on a rafting trip? Do any of you believe he felt any remorse when he held her head under the water until her struggling ceased? Certainly not. But in fishing, and in life, there's always one that got away. And in our case, that person is Penny Cefalo. She used a Chinese cooking knife to decapitate her boyfriend and had the audacity to claim self-defense. A sleazebag defense attorney convinced 3 of 12 jurors to vote for acquittal, resulting in a hung jury. Now the prosecutors are reluctant to retry her. She now flaunts her looks and jewelry in public.

I take 100% responsibility for the death of officer Fosterno, making me every bit as guilty as anyone targeted here. I stated that my goal was to kill "a copper." That threat was only meant to confuse the police. I wanted them worried about protecting their own, while my real target was Penny (Made of Copper) Cefalo. When all was said and done, the wrong copper ended up dying. So sad.

While continuing to track down Ms. Cefalo would be a worthwhile endeavor, I am no longer worthy of the quest. Tonight, tomorrow, or soon, I will quietly and quickly end my life. I am guilty and deserve to be punished. Anything else would be extremely hypocritical.

No MORE2COME.

The Enforcer

As the PC powered down, the hope was that whoever was following the post would buy what The Enforcer was selling.

CHAPTER 46

Syd tapped at Lasek's office door at 8 am with the Fosterno tape in her pocket. She'd texted him a few hours earlier to schedule the meeting. As Lasek opened the door, she was surprised to see Mitsoff on his way out. Mitsoff smiled and nodded as he walked past.

"There's someone I didn't expect to see," said Syd as she sat down.

Placing a file back into a drawer, Lasek nodded. "We're easing him back in," he said. "He'll be working mornings this week and then back to full time."

Syd did her best not to shiver visibly. "Commissioner, how can Mitsoff be back to work, especially after we proved he was corresponding with The Enforcer?"

Lasek sat back in his chair and paused before answering. "I understand your concern. Pratt and I interviewed him last week. He came clean about what he was doing on the dark web. He said he was attempting to befriend the vigilante so that he could solve the case."

"And you both believe him?"

"He seemed very contrite. We both think he was trying to play hero like he usually does. The only thing we can prove is that he has a big ego."

Syd wondered how the rest of the office would react to Mitsoff being back on active duty.

"Your text said that you had something urgent to discuss," said Lasek.

"Can you summon Pratt and Griffith to the conference room?" asked Syd while showing the tape to Lasek. "There's a recorder in there. Everyone needs to hear this."

"What's on the tape?" asked Lasek.

"It was made by Fosterno. He gave explicit instructions for Cefalo to present it to me in the event of his death. It's big."

"When did she bring this tape to you?" asked Lasek.

For a moment, Syd found it difficult to breathe. A great deal was riding on her answer.

"Late yesterday afternoon," she responded.

"So why are you sharing this with us today?"

"I wanted to make sure it was relevant before presenting it," she said. "I had no idea what was on there."

Staring at her without expression, Lasek asked, "Has anyone else heard this tape besides you?"

She couldn't help but gulp and hoped Lasek didn't notice. "Cefalo claimed that she didn't play the tape. I can't be certain, though."

"Anyone else?" asked Lasek.

"Not that I'm aware," she lied.

"Who else knows about the tape's existence?"

"Cefalo and me," said Syd. "Unless she mentioned it to someone else."

"So, we're supposed to believe Fosterno sensed he was

going to die and recorded this secret tape," said Lasek. "Then, after Cefalo got hold of the tape, she gave it directly to you without playing it herself? Am I understanding correctly?"

Syd nodded.

"And then you listened to it on your own and brought it in for the rest of us to hear?"

"Yes, that's right," said Syd, clearing her throat.

Lasek glanced at a board on the wall to determine which employees were currently in the building. "I'm expecting Pratt in about 30 minutes. He and I need to go over this first before anyone else."

Syd shifted in her chair. "I figured since Griffith and I were actively investigating the case-"

Lasek interrupted. "I don't want anyone else to know about this tape until I clear it. That means no one. Do you understand?"

"Yes, Commissioner," replied Syd.

"Once Pratt and I digest what's on the tape, we'll meet again," said Lasek.

"May I ask when that might be?" asked Syd.

Lasek appeared uncomfortable. "Depends what's on that tape," he said. "It'll happen soon enough."

Syd left Lasek's office feeling unsettled. If word got out that she shared the tape with Montenegro, she'd be terminated. Plain and simple. And for the time being, she couldn't even acknowledge the existence of the tape. Whether it had anything to do with The Enforcer case was anyone's guess, but how was she going to hide such vital information from Griffith?

As she sat down at her desk, she noticed Griffith looking over with a curious expression. She attempted to avert her eyes, but it was too late. "Good morning," said Griffith. "Are you all right? You seem a bit unsettled."

Syd attempted to put on her game face. "Fosterno's death and this Enforcer thing have me on edge," she said.

"Saw you coming out of Lasek's office," said Griffith. "Anything specific you can share?"

"Nothing new, just some procedural stuff," said Syd. "Maybe we can compare notes after lunch."

"Okay," said Griffith. "Keep me informed if anything else happens." She moved back in the direction of her desk but turned to glance over her shoulder before leaving the room.

Syd felt bad about not telling Griffith about the tape. If they were going to investigate properly, Griffith needed to know. But with Lasek and Pratt reviewing it, all she could do was wait. She began to wonder if she had done the right thing by sharing the tape with Montenegro. If she turned out to be wrong and he couldn't be trusted, her world was about to turn upside down.

As the day wore on, Syd found herself peering over at Griffith, wanting to tell her everything but bound by Lasek's strict orders. The guilt gnawed at her insides, eating away at her resolve. She was tired of the lies and obfuscations, no longer wanting to keep secrets from anyone.

When Griffith approached her desk later in the afternoon, Syd could sense curiosity in her eyes. "Lasek and Pratt just called a meeting for all officers, starting in 30 minutes. Any idea what that's about?"

"I don't think it has anything to do with the vending

machine prices going up," joked Syd. "Let's say I might have an inkling."

Griffith appeared surprised. "Are you willing to share?"

"I'm not entirely sure, so I'd rather wait. No offense," said Syd.

She wondered how Pratt and Lasek would handle the meeting. Would they tie the recording to the vigilante case? Would they make an example of her for not immediately presenting the tape?

The meeting room was nearly full when Syd and Griffith arrived. Lasek stood at the front, his face grave and unreadable. Pratt was seated nearby, flipping through a file with a furrowed brow. As the officers settled in, Lasek began to speak.

"Thank you for coming on short notice. I have information which is relevant to the murder of Detective Fosterno. It may or may not be relevant to the ongoing Enforcer case. Either way, it is essential that everyone knows about this."

Lasek pulled a tape from his pocket and inserted it into a recorder on his desk. "Yesterday, it seems, Penny Cefalo presented this tape to Detective Livingstone. According to Ms. Cefalo, Detective Fosterno made a request for the tape to be given to Detective Livingstone if something were to happen to him."

Syd couldn't help but notice the surprised looks from officers throughout the room. "As far as we know, the only people who have heard this recording are Detective Livingstone, Chief Pratt, and me."

"What about Cefalo?" asked Griffith.

"She claims she never listened to it," said Lasek.

From the expressions around the room, Syd felt like nobody was buying it.

"Why would Fosterno want Syd to have it?" asked Cataldi.

When Lasek didn't immediately answer, all the officers looked toward Syd.

"Detective Livingstone?" said Lasek. "Why don't you answer that?"

Feeling the hairs stand on her neck, Syd felt a little betrayed. No matter how she answered, she would appear foolish. Or possibly conceited.

"Ms. Cefalo said that I was the only one Fosterno trusted," said Syd. "Why that is, I don't know."

The room fell silent.

As the world seemed to pause, Syd wished she could be anywhere but in that moment. Sitting in a tennis stadium with a drink in hand while watching Enzo compete would have been ideal. She wished she had taken him up on his offer to travel with him.

Lasek broke the silence. "I'm going to allow everyone to hear what's on this tape," he said. "I'd encourage everyone to take notes. Please save your questions for later." He pressed the "play" button.

After the tape finished playing, there were no questions. Only an eerie silence. Syd felt that everyone in the room was focusing on her. Lasek and Pratt ordered everyone in earshot to maintain their silence about the tape. They didn't want anything leaked to the press.

After the meeting, Syd approached Griffith who was sitting motionlessly at her desk and staring at her screen. She knew she needed to address the tape and its consequences with her partner before the situation became even more awkward.

"I'm sorry I didn't disclose the contents of the tape to you," she said, applying a gentle hand to Griffith's shoulder. "I was in a weird predicament. Fosterno requested me, and me only."

Griffith turned her head away from the monitor and looked at Syd. "As far as I knew, you and I were partners investigating one of the biggest crimes in this part of the country. You didn't even disclose there *was* a tape, let alone what was on it."

As Mitsoff strolled past Griffith's workstation, he caught Syd's eye and then cast a quick glance at Griffith.

"So, is that it?" continued Griffith. "You don't trust me now?"

After taking a deep breath to calm herself, Syd replied. "I would never do anything intentionally to hurt you or our partnership."

"Then why didn't you tell me?" asked Griffith.

For a moment, Syd saw a shadow of movement nearby. She was convinced Mitsoff was still in the area. "Lasek was insistent that I keep it quiet. As you know, I'm on a short leash around here. But I'm sorry. I should have been more forthcoming."

CHAPTER 47

er 10 am phone call with Lieutenant Gil Trent from Columbus lasted nearly an hour. Trent said he couldn't find anything nefarious in Mitsoff's past. "But the guy's a real creep who very well could be behind all of this," he qualified. "The problem is there's nothing to show us he's done anything bad. A juvenile arrest for fighting at seventeen certainly doesn't qualify."

They discussed what little was uncovered about Montenegro and Griffith and touched once again on Lasek's troubles in Arizona. But at the end, Trent seemed more interested in discussing Pratt. "The two large properties and his large donation to a charity definitely caught my attention," said Trent. "But now I've got even more to throw on top of the pile. Two weeks ago, he closed on another vacation home - a property worth over $1 million on Hilton Head Island. He certainly has good taste - and a shitload of money."

After Trent stopped speaking, there was an awkward long pause. Finally, Syd responded. "Okay, well, maybe he sold one of his other properties to buy the one on Hilton Head," she said. "Property owners are known to trade up when they find a deal."

"I had the same thought," said Trent. "But all of the properties are currently in Pratt's name, and not a single one is even listed for sale."

Syd felt a rush of adrenaline, and for a moment, it seemed like her head would explode.

"Gil, maybe I'm a little too close to all of this. Please tell me what you think it means."

"Since you told me all about what happened to this Fosterno character and the recording he left behind, I'd say there's a reasonable chance that Pratt could be the accomplice," he said. "If he got his hands on all that drug money, it would all make sense. And get this. All of those major purchases occurred after that shooting incident with Fosterno."

"Pratt somehow got his hands on that drug money," she said. "He was probably the person who was working with Fosterno. There can be no other possible explanation."

"Are you sure he doesn't have rich relatives who bequeathed money to him?" asked Trent.

"I can't find any evidence of that," said Syd.

"Well, if the money didn't magically arrive from some outside source, I would say he's your culprit. At least, that's what my years of law enforcement are telling me. So, what are you going to do?"

"I'm going to expose that bastard," she said. "I'm going to tell Lasek everything. Pratt's never mentioned anything to anyone about any beach homes, at least as far as I know.'

"A fish rots from the head down," said Trent. "You may

have your thief. Not sure whether that has any relevance to your vigilante."

"I have no idea at this point," said Syd. "But the quicker we get to the bottom of Pratt's finances, the better."

"Maybe you should hold back for a little while," said Trent. "You've already had your butt caught in a wringer. Let it all play out a little longer."

Syd smiled. She thanked Trent for his research and help. Her heart was pounding, and she knew she would have to tell Lasek about what she'd uncovered about Pratt. The evidence was simply too damning. Tomorrow morning, she'd schedule a meeting with Lasek.

Near quitting time, Syd heard everyone's phone sounding at once. It was a group text from Lasek:

> Noon meeting tomorrow in the big room.
> Lunch will be catered. Absolutely
> mandatory for all officers to attend. New
> evidence pertaining to the vigilante case.
> Be on time! Lasek.

Syd read the message, her mind still spinning over her conversation with Trent. She sent her reply:

> I will be there. Is it possible we could meet
> first thing in the morning? I may have some
> information that's valuable to the case.

She didn't want to mention Pratt in the text. He might be sitting next to Lasek. She needed to tread lightly.

No mistakes. She was only starting to emerge from the cauldron of hot water she'd been in within the department.

Her phone chimed with a response:

I won't be in until 11:30. Meet me in my office then, right before our main meeting.

She texted back.

Okay, done.

She wondered how Lasek would react when he found out about Pratt's newfound wealth. Hopefully, he would do the right thing.

CHAPTER 48

At 11:37, Lasek motioned Syd to come inside his office. "If this can wait until after our big meeting today, that would be great," he said. "I'd like to have Pratt and Griffith join in as well."

Syd found a seat on a beige fabric couch. "I have something I need to discuss with you alone," she said. "And I'd prefer to do it now."

Lasek rose from his desk, walked over to the door and shut it. "Okay, you officially have my attention. But we'll need to adjourn by 11:55. I have big news to share."

"I'll be brief," said Syd. "I have some information on Chief Pratt. It's relevant to this investigation."

"Pratt? Is that why you wanted to see me?"

Syd felt a buzz in her pocket. A text was coming in on her cell. She removed it from her pocket, felt for a button, and depressed it. It was a text from Trent:

> I've discovered new information. Check
> your voicemail immediately.

She made a mental note to deal with it later.

"Yes, he's who I'm talking about," said Syd. "He's a public servant like we all are," said Syd. "So, it's public record what kind of salary he makes."

"I don't see what this has-"

Syd held up her hand, requesting to interrupt.

"Please Commissioner Lasek. I need you to hear me out. While Chief Pratt does very well compared to the average citizen in Walsh County, there is no way in the world he is filthy rich. Yet, he currently owns three properties valued at around $3 million dollars. And I've also discovered information that he has donated hundreds of thousands of dollars to charities - all worthwhile, I might add. But that's not the point. He's donated hundreds of thousands. Has he ever mentioned anything about those properties or donations to you?"

Lasek placed his left elbow on his desk, resting his chin in his hand. She could see his mind working. "He's never mentioned them. I am aware he likes to travel, but I assumed he rented the places where he stayed. But what are you implying?"

"Commissioner, the information about Fosterno's activities is out there. We all know he took the money. And we also know he split it with someone. Knowing Pratt's financial situation, is it really that difficult to figure out who that accomplice is?"

"You're making some mighty big accusations, Detective Livingstone," said Lasek. "How do you know he didn't inherit it? His parents are deceased."

"I explored that possibility. His parents were not people of means. They lived a simple lifestyle and raised their family in a modest neighborhood."

"How about a rich brother or sister?" asked Lasek.

"Pratt was an only child. Nothing there."

"So, for the record, you're stating that Pratt may have taken some of the illegal drug money?"

"The money's missing, and Pratt owns several luxurious properties. Don't you find it odd that he's never shared any of that with you?"

"I would say it's interesting," said Lasek. "But maybe he's a private person. Someone who doesn't like to brag."

Lasek rose out of his chair and paced across the carpet, then stopped to peer out the window at the street below. "Let's get to the bottom of this right now," he said. "I'm going to delay the lunchtime meeting until 12:30. I'll let everyone eat before we begin. In the meantime, I'm going to ask Pratt to come in here."

As Lasek left his office, Syd could feel her tongue sticking to the roof of her mouth. She breathed deeply to prevent from shaking. Her career in law enforcement was on the line. But she still felt confident. People like Pratt don't get filthy rich out of thin air. Her cell buzzed again, but she once again ignored it, waiting for Lasek and Pratt.

Pratt followed Lasek in the door, appearing confused and slightly annoyed. "I assumed we'd be going into our meeting about now," he argued. "Is this going to take long?"

"I've arranged for us to have a little more time," said Lasek. "Delvin, please bear with us for a few minutes."

Then Lasek turned to Syd. "Detective Livingstone, would you mind sharing the information you discovered with Chief Pratt? I think he may be able to fill in the missing blanks."

Syd took a deep breath. For a moment, she had a flashback to sixth grade, when her social studies teacher lambasted her for not completing her homework. On that day, she vomited on the floor in front of the entire classroom.

Finally, she began to speak. "Chief Pratt, during our investigation into the Fosterno case, I discovered some information regarding your financial situation." She watched as Pratt's face turned from confusion to concern. "We discovered that you own three properties valued at around $3 million dollars and have donated hundreds of thousands of dollars to various charities."

Pratt's eyes narrowed. "I don't see how that has any relevance to the investigation."

Syd pressed on. "Chief, we also know that Fosterno had an accomplice who took more than half of the illegal drug money. And considering you're employed as a public servant in Walsh County, I find it hard to believe that you were not involved."

Syd watched Lasek wipe away a bead trickling down the side of his face, his eyes darting between her and Pratt.

"Whose idea was it to search my financial history?" asked Pratt.

Lasek started to answer, but Syd put her hand up to stop him. "It was me, acting alone," she said. "When it became a real possibility that the vigilante killer may have been one of us, I took it on myself to investigate a number of personnel."

"Well, I certainly applaud you," said Pratt. "And I will tell you that everything you said today is precisely on the mark."

Lasek's eyebrows rose as his chin dropped. To Syd, he seemed shocked by Pratt's admission.

"Well, let me rephrase," said Pratt. "Everything was on the mark except for what you said at the very end when you insinuated that I was on the receiving end of dirty money."

Syd maintained eye contact with Pratt. She sat up, trying her best not to appear intimidated.

"I need to go into my office for a minute. I'll be right back." Pratt excused himself from the room.

For a few long minutes, Syd and Lasek sat silently. When Lasek's eyes met Syd's, he slowly shook his head. She wasn't sure if he was doubting her or was shocked by the news about Pratt.

Her mind raced. Had Pratt already made a run for it? Or was he preparing his firearm for a confrontation right there in the office?

When Pratt returned, he wasn't carrying a gun. A Manilla envelope was in his hand. "I hope this explains everything," he said. "Commissioner, would you open the envelope and share what's inside with Detective Livingstone?"

Lasek removed a double-sided plastic page covering. As he scanned both sides, the color drained from his face. On one side was a small ticket with a stamp of authenticity from the State of South Carolina. On the other side was a newspaper article with the following headline:

SOUTH CAROLINA MULTI-MILLION DOLLAR
LOTTERY WINNER TO REMAIN ANONYMOUS.

Syd's eyes followed Lasek's movements as he passed the page to her. She examined it carefully, attempting not to smudge it with her sweaty hands. As she looked at the ticket, her jaw dropped.

Pratt smiled. "I won it a couple of years ago, several months after Fosterno's confrontation. As a private person, I chose not to reveal it."

Lasek wasn't looking over at Syd anymore. His eyes were fixed on Pratt. For a moment, she felt like an outsider.

"Not that it is any of our business, Chief Pratt, but this is a $3.2 million ticket. Were you part of a group that won this?" asked Lasek.

"That's the ironic part," said Pratt. "I usually entered with co-workers. But I purchased this one myself. I felt a little guilty after I found out I'd won. I kept it a secret from my office mates."

"Congratulations on your good fortune, Chief Pratt," said Lasek with a tight smile. "And I'm so sorry you were forced to reveal this. But the information regarding your winnings will not leave this room."

Pratt shook his head and then turned to Syd. "First of all, I didn't receive $3.2 million. Uncle Sam took a huge chunk right from the get-go. But now, I actually feel relieved that someone else knows. It's been difficult keeping it inside for all these months. But since you already know, I'll reveal a little more. After good luck shined on me, I invested a portion in secure stocks and real estate. I've nearly doubled my wealth, yet I still maintain my anonymity. It hasn't changed me."

Noticing that Lasek's eyes were still fixed on Pratt, Syd raised her left hand, palm out. "Chief, I owe you a sincere apology. Your net worth should have been none of my concern. I am truly sorry."

Pratt nodded but said nothing more. Lasek got out of his chair and escorted him to the door. "I'll handle this matter from here. See you in the next meeting."

Pratt murmured something she couldn't hear.

Lasek pulled his chair back behind his desk and focused his eyes on Syd. "Do you have any other unsubstantiated theories you'd like to run by me? I mean, there's certainly others in this office you could accuse. Maybe I'm the vigilante."

During the time Lasek had walked Pratt to the door, Syd had glanced at the digital version of her voicemail from Trent:

> **I've discovered how our subject acquired his wealth. Don't say another word about it until you speak with me.**

But it was too late now. The toothpaste wasn't going back into the tube. And her days as a detective were about to come to an end.

"It all didn't add up, Commissioner," she said when Lasek returned. "How was I to know he would beat more than one in a million odds? That doesn't happen to people."

Lasek reached into his desk and pulled out a form. He slammed it on the surface of the desktop.

A termination notice, possibly?

"You've falsely accused one of our highest-ranking officers of stealing dirty money," he said. "It doesn't get much more egregious than that. And for some reason, I let you proceed. But here's the ironic thing. He actually left the room smiling, urging me to go easy on you."

Syd remained silent. She was already thinking ahead to other options. She could teach tennis or travel the world with Enzo. But she preferred law enforcement, investigating crimes and punishing lawbreakers.

"We're going to cover some important findings during our next meeting," said Lasek. "I don't want you there, but I have no choice since you and Griffith have been investigating the vigilante case. But I'm not going to lie, Syd. Your future here doesn't look good."

Gathering her folder and other belongings together, Syd prepared to leave. "I understand. Is there anything else, sir?"

"As a matter of fact, there is," said Lasek. "I want to share a few facts we're going to discuss in the meeting. There's some important information about your close friend, Detective Montenegro."

After no response from Syd, Lasek continued. "Are you aware that a motorcycle was seen racing away from the scene of McBride's murder?"

"Yes, of course, I remember that."

"Well, since there was some indication that someone in Walsh County may have been involved due to misplaced evidence, Chief Pratt and I conducted a title search of all Walsh County employees who currently own motorcycles. On the list were a county recorder, Coroner Melissa Pennington, and Mitsoff - which we already knew. Nothing damning or conclusive."

Syd looked at Lasek, unsure where he was going with all of this.

"About a week ago, we received an anonymous tip that Detective Montenegro had rented a storage unit just east of Minerva. I didn't ask, but the way it looked, they'd probably let you rent a unit by the hour. The tip suggested that we might be interested in what was hidden inside."

Syd wondered in what format the tip had arrived.

"So, I go out there with Fosterno - God rest his soul - and we find Stuart's name on one of the units. I ordered the manager to open the door, and guess what we found inside?"

Syd could barely get the words out. "A motorcycle?"

"Bingo! It wasn't new or in particularly good condition, but it's a bike, nonetheless. And the VIN number had been mutilated. Totally unreadable. And no license plate. So let me ask you. Did you know he owned a bike?"

"No," said Syd, feeling her heart pound.

"Okay," said Lasek. "I won't ask you any more questions about Montenegro for now. But I will fill you in on some other developments."

"Like what?"

"Of course, you remember Fosterno's murder," he said. "You were present. Do you remember the chemical agent that caused his death?"

"Yes, strychnine."

"Well, we checked with the local hardware stores after Fosterno died. It was a long shot, but we decided to try. A couple of days before Fosterno died, guess who we saw on tape buying a container of mole killer that contained strychnine?"

No, it couldn't be.

"Stuart Montenegro," said Lasek.

"May I see the video?" asked Syd.

"Hold on. I had it ready just in case you asked."

The video appeared grainy, but she could tell by the walk that it was Montenegro, carrying a product and heading to the checkout. As he placed one container on the counter, she could read the label, displayed among a number of skulls and crossbones:

"Herzog's Fast Acting Mole Killer."

Lasek stared at her across the desk.

"I don't know what to say," she said. "Is it possible he has moles in his yard?'

"And he also has an unregistered motorcycle in a crumbling storage unit facility? My experience is that wild coincidences like that don't simply happen. He was the only employee in Walsh County among five local stores in the area who purchased the same type of strychnine that killed Fosterno. And maybe that's why he tailed Mitsoff and had a gun pointing at his head. Because Mitsoff was onto him."

Suddenly, her own situation didn't seem as dire. Montenegro's was worse.

"Why don't you pick him up if you have such convincing evidence?"

Lasek let out a laugh. "You see, that's just it. Everything favors the criminal. We all know this is damning evidence, but a Grand Jury might disagree. We're being careful. We have a warrant to search his property. We're sending a team there right now. So, I wouldn't suggest calling and warning him. You need to stay on this side of the law."

Syd's shame and embarrassment quickly turned to something else. "You're not suggesting that I'm compromised? Granted, I probably shouldn't have accused Pratt today, but I'm a detective. I took an oath, and those words still mean something to me."

Lasek didn't answer. Instead, he pulled another folder from his desk and opened it. He removed a photo and placed it in front of her. "Once you simmer down, I want to discuss this man with you. It's Curtis Marksbury. Do you remember him?"

"The guy who was tailing Fosterno. Isn't he someone who should be charged?"

"He's in jail already. We really don't have too much on him. He pretty much told us his entire story. He was involved in the same Indiana syndicate that transported the drugs in the Fosterno chase. After Fosterno shot those two thugs, his group expected to hear something about the confiscated money.

Except, there was never any word about it. When Fosterno was lauded as a hero, they figured that he was the one who had absconded with the dough. And it appears they were right."

Lasek left his seat, walked over to a whiteboard, and scribbled the name "Fosterno" in big red letters. He tapped the board with his marker. This is the guy he was following. He was ordered to squeeze Fosterno for the money. He's provided us with the names of his superiors. Eventually, Marksbury is going to need witness protection."

"So why didn't he kill Fosterno?" asked Syd.

"Because dead people never pay. Fosterno promised to make payments but never did.

"Marksbury was a known gang member, and he'll go down for a couple of years before he's set free. But we have no proof that he ever attempted to harm Fosterno, Cefalo, or anyone else. Marksbury was evidently every bit as frightened of his superiors as Fosterno was of him."

"So, what about Montenegro?" asked Syd. "Do you think he's the vigilante?"

Lasek scribbled Montenegro's name on the board below Fosterno's. He drew two lines connecting to Montenegro. One read "Vigilante?" and the other read "Accomplice - money?"

"I think he's one or both," said Lasek. "Maybe Montenegro didn't care about Fosterno and was simply hellbent on punishing criminals. He probably tried to poison Cefalo with the strychnine but got Fosterno in the crossfire. I haven't seen a lifestyle change with Montenegro. Unless he's been funneling all of that dough to his wife."

"Are we done now, sir?"

"Yes," said Lasek. "You're officially up to speed. And Syd,

I'm not sure what the future's going to hold for you in the next few days."

The future. Her entire world was going sideways.

"And now, if you'll excuse me, I need to prepare for our next meeting. I'm not sure how everyone's going to react when they hear about your friend."

Driving home after the all-department meeting, Syd's anger and fear had subsided into emptiness. Her hands and arms felt numb as they maneuvered the steering wheel through various curves and turns. The only thing that made her realize she was still alive was a throbbing headache.

Her cell phone sounded with the name "Lieutenant Trent" displayed on the screen. She thought about letting it pass through but instead answered, putting his voice on the speaker.

"I hope you heard my voicemail before you spoke with anyone about Pratt," said Trent. "Please tell me you did."

"By the time I saw it, it was too late. Safe to say, the shit hit the fan when I confronted Pratt."

"Syd, I am so terribly sorry," he said. "I found an article about the South Carolina lottery winner. And then, I used my influence to drum up some conversations with a few of the people involved in distributing the prize. They didn't mention Pratt by name, but through the process of elimination, I realized it was him."

"At least someone got lucky," said Syd. "He hit his numbers, and now my days are numbered in Walsh County."

There was a brief pause on the other end of the line. "Syd, I got to know you pretty well when that psycho stalked you," said Trent. "I guarantee 90 percent of the other players would have crumbled in the same situation. But you persevered. And you know why, don't you?"

"My guess is you're going to tell me," she said.

"Because you're tough as nails," said Trent. "You didn't quit then, and I know you won't quit now."

Syd teared up as the impact of Trent's words hit her. "But they are probably going to quit on me. I've done some stupid stuff since I accepted this position."

Trent took a moment to respond. "If they let you go, then it's their loss. They'd have no idea what they were losing. I promise you'll land on your feet, whether in law enforcement or anything else."

The conversation with Trent made her smile, although the reality of the situation still weighed heavily. But her life could go on outside of law enforcement. Montenegro, on the other hand, was firmly in the crosshairs of the Walsh County investigators. But was it for good reason? She trusted in her feelings, but unfortunately, her feelings had already betrayed her with Pratt.

She thanked Trent for his time and support and promised to keep him up to date. She knew that Enzo would be in her corner, no matter what. But since she wasn't actually suspended yet, there was someone else she could call tonight. If that person would assist her, she still had a fighting chance as a law enforcement officer.

There was something else gnawing at her. Something that Lasek had shared during their conversation. It was nothing earth-shattering, but it struck a firm chord with her at the time. But right now, as she tried to recall it, she drew a blank. Perhaps it was nothing, but she'd rack her brain tonight. It was certainly worth remembering.

CHAPTER 49

During their call that night, Syd was once again reminded of why she fell in love with him. While he was far from perfect - he could be outspoken, brazen, and even somewhat eccentric - Enzo listened to her for 90 minutes. He listened calmly and without judgment while she informed him about what had transpired with Pratt and Montenegro. She even shared her theories and ideas about the vigilante case, at times against her better judgment. But she knew if they were going to have a future together, he needed to be aware of what was going on in her life.

"I've made some big mistakes, and I'm terrified about what's going to happen," she said. "Not just for me, but for Stuart. And I've got a sinking feeling that this vigilante is going to slip through our fingers."

Then she added, "How could I have been so careless? Accusing a higher-up like Pratt of taking dirty money. But it didn't add up. Winning the lottery? That never happens - well, except the one time I decide to take a stand."

She heard Enzo take a deep breath. "Syd, after listening to

everything you said tonight, I get the feeling that these events might have happened for a reason. I believe in fate. Do you?"

"Um-, yeah, I guess so," she said.

"Maybe someone is telling you that this is the perfect time to get out of police work," he said. "Maybe you should go in tomorrow morning and tell Lasek and Pratt to stick it. Come travel the world with me. We'll figure out what you want to do in a few years. My body's not going to hold out for much longer than that."

Syd longed to place both arms around his neck. "You know, I've fought you on that for a long time, but it's starting to make sense now. Maybe I was never suited to be in law enforcement. It would be so nice to have all of this pressure off, starting tomorrow."

"Let's sleep on it. I'll fly back in a couple of days, or even earlier if I lose in the first round. And promise me you'll stay away from anyone emitting vigilante vibes."

Moments after Enzo hung up, Syd's cell phone buzzed. Her phone didn't recognize the caller. Normally, she would have let it ring through, but she doubted a solicitation would come in at 8:15 in the evening. She answered.

"Syd, it's Stuart," said the voice. "I'm calling you from a burner."

"Stuart? Shit! Are you okay?"

"I'm alive, if that's what you mean. We need to talk."

"I don't know if that's a good idea," she said. "Especially after what's transpiring. You shouldn't be calling me."

"I know," he said. "But I need your help. Stacey is frantic. They enforced a warrant to search our house today."

Syd suddenly found it difficult to breathe. Why would he be worried if he had nothing to hide?

For a few seconds, there was an awkward pause. "They

found some things," he said. "But I'm being set up. You have to believe me."

"Did one of those things happen to be mole killer?"

"Yes," said Montenegro. "They're saying that's the poison that was used to kill Fosterno."

Syd fumbled for the right words; "Stuart, I saw a video of you buying it. Nobody planted that on you."

Montenegro sighed. "I see Lasek's been busy. What he showed you was legit. I did purchase mole killer. But again, someone's setting me up. I mentioned at a meeting once that I needed to purchase a mole killer. Anyone could have used that idea to kill Fosterno. It would be a perfect plan."

"Did they find anything else?"

"Yeah, they did," he said. "But I need to know that you trust me and that you believe what I'm about to tell you."

Syd remained silent.

"Syd, I have a shed in my backyard. I use it for storage - you know, lawnmowers, wheel barrels, that type of shit. There's a little space underneath the shed. Sometimes, I see squirrels and chipmunks slipping in and outta there. Anyway, they checked under the little space and found something."

Break it to me easy, Stuart.

"A son-of-a-bitchin black suitcase," he said. "They say it came from the van of drug dealers that Fosterno stopped. But I didn't put it there."

"Was it empty?" asked Syd.

"The side was sliced open, but there were a few stacks of bills in there. No one's going to believe me. Who actually brings cash to set someone up?"

"Okay," said Syd. "I believe you."

"And there's more," he said.

"What?"

"They found a savings account in my name at a bank that I've never even dealt with. There's $101,000 dollars in there."

"How could anyone accomplish that, Stuart?"

"It's a lot more difficult when you're taking money out. Somehow it was set up online, in my name. Evidently, the statements were funneled to a PO Box."

"People don't just give others a hundred thousand dollars," said Syd.

"I know," said Montenegro. "I can hardly believe it myself."

"This is going to sound crazy, but could Stacey have done that?"

"She'd never do that," he said. "We have a different type of financial arrangement - our accounts are separate."

"So, I assume that's everything?" she said.

"Everything as of now," said Montenegro.

"So let me get this straight. You're in possession of the type of strychnine that killed Fosterno, along with one of the missing briefcases. And over $100,000 in a phantom bank account?"

"Yeah."

"So besides that, how was your evening at the theater, Mrs. Lincoln?"

"Syd, please don't. The police are building a strong case. They're going to arrest me."

"I'm sorry," she said. "If I don't find humor in this, I'll break down. But you need to listen. I believe you. I'll help you get to the bottom of all this."

She decided not to mention what had transpired between her and Pratt. He had enough going on.

"Let me think about how I'm going to proceed. I suggest you get a lawyer and stop talking to everybody else."

"Everyone except you," he said.

Syd hung up and remained motionless for a few minutes, trying to process what was happening. She knew she had to act fast if she wanted to help Montenegro. But how? There was only one other person in the department who she felt she could depend on.

CHAPTER 50

S yd made her way into the office for her scheduled 10 am meeting with Lasek and Pratt. She knew she was on thin ice. If there were any post-Christmas miracles still floating around, she would gladly accept one.

The brass at Walsh County had probably already changed her login password to their computer system. Hopefully, her ally would have burned the midnight oil to uncover the vital information she needed. That was, of course, assuming all of her assumptions were correct.

Syd waited outside Lasek's office for ten minutes before he arrived. "I will be leading this meeting," said Lasek as he slipped behind his desk and opened a file drawer. "I've asked Chief Pratt to sit in as a witness and assist if necessary. Any questions?"

Syd glanced at Pratt and back at Lasek, then nodded. "I'd like to ask you about the search of Montenegro's home," she said. "Can you share what you found?"

Lasek unsuccessfully tried to hide a slight smile. "Detective Livingstone, I see no reason to proceed in that direction. As you are about to learn, you will be suspended, beginning at 5 pm today. The results of our search, at least at this time, should be of no concern to you."

"With all due respect, I call bullshit," she replied. "Griffith and I have been investigating this vigilante nightmare, and it could be relevant. At least until 5 pm tonight, I deserve an answer."

Syd noticed Pratt nodding in agreement. "Commissioner, I believe she has a point. May I?'

Lasek looked at Syd. "What the hell? Why not?"

Pratt proceeded. "We found a container of mole killer that contained strychnine. And one of the missing suitcases with some money inside."

"You showed me the video of Detective Montenegro purchasing the item. Right?"

Rearranging his chair to face her better, Lasek replied. "You are correct."

"I believe you only located one container in his garage."

"That's also correct," said Lasek.

"I've been racking my brain and finally remembered you telling me the container was unopened. Is that accurate?"

"Let's go with that."

"So, Commissioner, that container wasn't used to poison anyone. Would you agree?"

"Yes, maybe that particular container, but we know he purchased the product. Maybe he'd already used the other containers."

"But the tape showed that he purchased only one."

"Okay, so he probably bought others at different times."

"But you don't have him on video buying any additional ones, do you?"

"No. At least not at this time. But he is familiar with the product."

"Granted, he's familiar with it," said Syd. "But for argument's sake, Commissioner, that video doesn't prove a damn thing, does it?"

Lasek turned to look at Pratt, who shrugged his shoulders in response. "All right, I see your point," said Lasek. "You have good instincts. But we found a missing suitcase with money inside."

"Let's hope you've done your homework correctly," said Syd. "You can suspend me, fire me, or whatever. I can find another job. But taking down a good cop like Montenegro and threatening to incarcerate him is some serious stuff. Are you sure you know what you're doing?"

Pratt cleared his throat. "The evidence we've uncovered is overwhelming and, I believe, will stand up in court."

Syd nodded her head and sat back in her seat. "Well then let's proceed with my suspension paperwork," she said. "At least before I leave at five."

"You'll be out of here by noon," said Lasek. "Twelve... fifteen tops."

A few minutes after noon, Syd's phone buzzed as she sat in Lasek's office. The caller ID displayed the name Stacey Montenegro. Lasek had his back to Syd, digging in a file.

"Hi, Stacey," said Syd. "Can I call you back? I'm a little busy right now."

"This can't wait," said Stacey. "Stuart has gone crazy, completely out of his mind. He says they're trying to pin this vigilante thing on him. I thought he was going to harm himself, right here in our house. But he grabbed a handgun, got into his car, and flew out of here."

"Do you know where he's going?" asked Syd. "I'm going to put you on speaker."

Lasek spun around from the back of his desk to listen. Pratt, sitting across the room, was also listening.

"I'm not sure, but he may be going to his dad's farm in South Canton," said Stacey. "I'll text you the address. His best years as a child were spent there. His dad has dementia and lives alone with his caretaker."

"We'll send a team there," said Syd. "I'd suggest you stay home in case he returns. By the way, are you able to track him?"

"Normally, yes," she said. "But apparently, he's turned his phone off. I'm getting no signal."

Lasek rose to summon help from available officers.

"I need to go with you," said Syd to Lasek. "Stuart's my friend. He may listen to me. Even if this is the last thing I do as a detective."

"Hand your gun to me," said Lasek. "I could get in trouble, but I'll allow you to go."

As several squad cars pulled into the driveway of Mr. Robert Montenegro. Syd spotted Stuart's four-door blue sedan parked partially on the grass near the house. After knocking and receiving no answer, the detectives broke through the front door.

Syd followed Pratt through the front door. In the living room, they located Robert Montenegro staring at a blank television screen. "Where's your son?" asked Pratt. "We just want to talk with him."

A weak moan escaped the old man's mouth as he pointed

toward a window on the east side of the house. Outside the window was a pond with a large tree. All of the leaves were now gone, but Syd remembered Stuart telling him that it was his favorite getaway spot as a young boy.

On their way to the pond, they spotted a middle-aged woman shoveling snow off a stone paver patio. She seemed shocked to see the contingent of people moving toward her.

"We're the police," shouted Syd. "Where's Mr. Montenegro's son?"

"He was headed to the pond a few minutes ago," she said. "Is something wrong?"

"Official police business," said Lasek, showing his badge. "We'll take it from here."

The woman dropped the shovel and ran toward the house.

As the group moved closer, Stuart's silhouette became visible under the tree. He sat facing the pond on a patch of ground covered with snow.

Despite the rustle of the group approaching from behind, Stuart did not turn. Syd made out the shape of a revolver in his right hand.

"Stuart!" screamed Syd. "Everything's okay. We're here to help."

"Leave me alone!" he responded. "I can't go to prison. I'll die right here, on my terms."

"I won't let that happen," said Syd. "I believe in you, and so do plenty of others."

Stuart turned to face Syd, the gun still in his right hand. Mitsoff stepped up from behind them, pointing his gun. "Drop your weapon, or you're going to die on my terms. I'm not playing with you, you sonofabitch!"

"Screw off!" yelled Stuart. "If you want me dead, then go ahead and pull that trigger. It doesn't matter anymore."

"It matters to me," said Syd. "And more important, to Stacey. Don't do this to your wonderful wife."

Syd pushed Mitsoff's barrel toward the ground, then looked at Lasek for permission to approach Stuart. He nodded reluctantly.

The rest of the officers hung back as she walked slowly toward Montenegro, her feet crunching the snow. "I'm going to sit down next to you," she said. "I only want to talk to you as a friend."

Still holding the gun, Montenegro pointed to a spot next to him. "Are you sure you want to do that?' he asked. "Aren't you concerned that I'm The Enforcer?"

"Never entered my mind."

"Do you know who I'm thinking about right now?" asked Montenegro. "You'll probably never guess."

When Syd didn't answer, he continued. "I'm thinking about Fosterno. A man who seemed too big, strong, and self-assured to die. But now he's gone. Forever."

Syd caught Lasek's eye and saw the impatience etched on his face. She subtly shook her head.

"It was tragic," she said. "We all miss him."

"He was smart," Montenegro stated. "He didn't put much trust in anyone at the department except for you. He relied on his instincts."

"If there's a rogue officer in the department, we'll find him," said Syd. "But I know that you're not the one, Stuart. You're my friend."

"Tell those guys that," he said, nodding at the group behind him. "The evidence they've uncovered will put me away for life."

Montenegro raised the revolver and placed it under his chin.

Syd stole a brief glance back at the group. They were beginning to press forward. "Stuart, you told me that you and Stacey are trying to have a baby. Suppose she's pregnant right now and doesn't know it."

Montenegro turned to look into Syd's eyes. She noticed a tear running down his cheek.

"How would she feel giving birth to a little baby who doesn't even have a father?" she asked. "Are you willing to check out on the two most important people in your life? Even if it's not for you, you need to be there for Stacey. And for your future family members."

Montenegro closed his eyes and dropped his head. He released the gun, which fell to the snowy ground.

Syd quickly grabbed the weapon and tossed it several feet behind her. It was immediately retrieved by a detective. Lasek, Pratt, and Cataldi reached Montenegro simultaneously and helped him to his feet.

Syd placed her hand on his shoulder. "Stuart, everything will work out," she said. "I'm going to be in your corner. Please trust me."

Montenegro attempted to hug her, but several officers moved between them. "I've always trusted you," he said. "Syd, please don't allow them to take me down."

Before Syd could respond, Cataldi began reciting *Miranda* Rights. They walked him to a squad car parked in the driveway, several hundred yards away.

With Stuart now in custody, Syd approached Lasek. "Would you please have someone call Stacey Montenegro and tell her that her husband is safe?" she asked. "In the meantime, I'd like to request a brief meeting with you and others who are still here."

"The suspect has been neutralized," said Lasek. "That was the reason we're here. Why would we have a meeting?"

"I've become aware of additional facts about this case that you - and everyone else here - should know. Would you please indulge me, if only for a few minutes?"

"Well, if this was a lengthy standoff, I would have said absolutely not," said Pratt "But you did good, and this is your last day. However, if this turns out to be a waste of time…"

"I promise I won't waste anyone's time."

Syd pointed to a barn situated over a hill. "Stuart told me there haven't been animals there for a while. I don't think we'll be overwhelmed by the smell. Let's walk there?"

Lasek shrugged and motioned for the rest of the group to follow. The contingent - which included Lasek, Pratt, Griffith, and Mitsoff, as well as a couple of uniformed patrol officers - entered the skeletal remains of a once large barn. Gray paint peeled from splintered wood. Inside, the scent reminded Syd of the musty odor from her grandmother's attic. Rough, uneven boards creaked loudly as the group arranged themselves in a circle near several bales of hay.

Once everyone was assembled, Syd placed her hand on Griffith's shoulder. "Captain?"

Griffith stepped forward as Syd continued. "We all know that Captain Griffith harbors deep resentment about criminals who only receive a wrist slap from our court system. Sure, she uses humor to get her point across, but we know how she feels. I started thinking about her connection with the gangs from Indiana, like the guys Fosterno killed after that car chase. As Fosterno's partner, she could have been the first person he called after an intoxicated gunfight with two criminal gang members. Perhaps she would've jumped at the chance to take at least half of that money. Maybe she rationalized that she wasn't stealing, but rather putting money raised through criminal activities to a much better use."

Griffith stared at Syd, expressionless.

"And what else do we know about the captain? She uses her talents as a master of disguise to modify her appearance. She's also a stage actor. I hate to use the word 'chameleon' because that has negative connotations, and Wilma is both a partner and friend. However, that doesn't change the fact that she could have disguised herself to look different during the vigilante murders. Remember how The Enforcer seemed to blend in so well that no one could even determine their sex? And don't forget, she was present when someone served Fosterno that last tainted pitcher of beer. Plus, she drove a motorcycle during her early years as an officer.

Griffith looked at Syd and shook her head. "Partner, you're way off base. I thought we were friends."

Mitsoff stepped forward. "I drive a motorcycle too, but that doesn't mean shit. I think you're doing everything in your power to divert the blame from your buddy. The evidence is irrefutable."

Lasek tugged Mitsoff's sleeve. "Detective Livingstone is on a roll. I suggest we all let her finish her speech."

Syd smiled. "Thank you, Commissioner. And I'll get over the condescension of you calling this a 'speech'." She didn't care if it sounded insubordinate now. "Anyway, I was with Griffith at the Silver Salamander when Fosterno was poisoned. As clever as she is, I think I would have noticed her placing that pitcher on the table."

Griffith's stern expression relaxed into a grin. "Damn, Livingstone, that was quite a case you presented against me. Until your last statement, you almost convinced me that I was behind all of this."

"Like I said, Captain, you're someone I can trust. And I desperately needed to trust someone because I was on the brink of suspension, unable to access the department's computer system."

Syd crossed to Mitsoff. "You hate Montenegro. The two of you have never gotten along, and you certainly had a reason to set him up. Also, you like things - fashionable clothes, a sports car, and even a new motorcycle. People might wonder where you get the money."

There was a scattering of nervous laughter, but Lasek didn't appear pleased, and Mitsoff's jaw was tightening. She smirked. "Personally, I think you're a raving egomaniac with debt up the ying-yang. How many credit cards have you maxed out, Detective?"

"Shit, I don't know," he huffed. "Maybe two or three. But that doesn't make me a thief or killer."

"It doesn't," said Syd. "But I saw your face when you pointed your gun at Montenegro a few minutes ago. You would've loved nothing more than for him to make a move. I bet maybe you would have enjoyed terminating him."

"Only if he acted first," said Mitsoff. "Not liking someone versus wanting to kill them are two different things. Give me a little credit."

She looked at Lasek. "Like I should have given Chief Pratt? Pulling that winning lottery ticket out of his desk? What are the odds of that happening?"

"Livingstone, you're a real genius," said Mitsoff. "You're eliminating all of us, great. We already know it isn't any of us because it's Montenegro!"

Lasek chimed in. "Mitsoff has a point. I've given you some latitude, but I'm starting to regret my decision. If you've come up with something, please reveal it. If not, I've got a shitload of paperwork awaiting at the precinct."

Syd turned to him. "You know, Commissioner Lasek, there's something extremely liberating about knowing you're going to be fired. For example, I can point out that you've got a dark side too. Your wife was brutalized in your home when you lived in Arizona. It's on the record - no secret to anyone willing to do the research. No arrests were made for three months, but there was a suspect. But there never was a trial. And why? Because the suspect was found deceased under what some would call 'mysterious circumstances'."

Pratt interrupted. "I've heard enough. I can't let you attack our commissioner, who has only made positive contributions to this department."

"Appreciate the support, Chief Pratt," said Lasek. Then he looked toward Syd. "Are we done here now?"

"Just about," said Syd. "I doubt you'd be the guy Fosterno called in a crisis, so I don't think you are his accomplice. But since we know Fosterno had one, that raises an interesting question. What if these vigilante murders weren't revenge? What if they were only made to look that way?"

"For what reason?" asked Mitsoff. "To unite the criminals of the world against the law-abiding?"

Syd gave him a withering look. "Your sarcasm is charming, Mitsoff. It's been a nightmare living without it for these past few weeks."

Griffith approached Mitsoff, shoving him in the chest. "One more interruption, and you'd better develop a taste for hospital food."

"Okay, I think we're done here now," said Lasek.

Syd barked. "What if the other murders were just meant to conceal the motive for the most important one? We know whoever took the money was smart enough not to flaunt it, although they probably needed it."

Pratt laughed. "That lets me off the hook. I obviously don't need it."

"That person who took the money was Montenegro," said Lasek. "We've found the other briefcase in his possession, a large sum of money in his account, and he has a damn motorcycle hidden in a storage facility."

"I came to terms with the fact that it could be. I may have misjudged his character. Lord knows I've been wrong about friends before. But then I started thinking about that tape Fosterno made. He was clearly a reluctant participant. Kevin felt bad about letting himself be talked into taking that money, and he was preparing to turn himself in. He said he wouldn't reveal his co-conspirator, but in law enforcement, we all know how that shit works. Lawyers promise a sweetheart deal if you spill the names of everyone involved. His conspirator couldn't let that happen. Still, just killing Fosterno could have opened a Pandora's box, and investigators might find out what really happened after that shootout."

"Are we going anywhere with this?" said Pratt. "This barn's drafty, and I'm freezing."

Syd pressed on. "So what if the perpetrator's plan was to make these murders appear to be a vendetta against criminals when, in fact, the target was just one person?"

"Kevin Fosterno," interjected Griffith.

"Correct," said Syd. "McBride and Babson were really just collateral damage. And hounding Penny was intended to keep us convinced that the vigilante killer was still pursuing unpunished murderers."

There was a long silence, and then Lasek spoke. "Detective Livingstone, this is a great story, possibly one that belongs in a crime novel, but it's pure conjecture. We've got our perp - your friend Montenegro. He's already in custody."

Syd shook her head. "The Enforcer is among us, right here and now." As the others stared, she turned to Griffith. "Captain?"

Griffith pulled a folded paper from her pocket and handed it to Syd. Focusing on Lasek, she unfolded the sheet. "In your office earlier, you told me that in your experience, wild coincidences simply don't happen."

"Yeah," he grunted, "and Montenegro proved my point. The hidden motorcycle, the strychnine, the suitcase. The money in the bank."

Griffith broke in. "Yes, but if someone was framing Montenegro, then those occurrences wouldn't be coincidences, would they? They'd be part of a carefully crafted plan to divert attention away from the guilty party."

So what coincidences are we talking about?" asked Lasek.

"The fact that Chief Pratt was able to pull a winning lottery ticket out of his desk at a moment's notice."

"You're crazy, Syd," sneered Mitsoff. "The department checked the legitimacy of the ticket."

"You're right, Mitsoff. It certainly belongs to him. But do you know the odds of winning a super large jackpot? Well over one in a million."

"But he fucking won it," said Mitsoff.

She turned from Mitsoff to Pratt. Let me ask you, Chief, do you have a gambling problem?"

Of course not," Pratt said. "I used to like an occasional trip to the casino, but once I won the lottery, I figured I'd used up my good luck."

Syd looked around the group. "A quick hypothetical. If two people are fishing in a pond, and one is using a single line while the other has eight hundred lines baited and underwater, who is more likely to catch a fish?"

"Stupid question," Mitsoff snorted. "The one with more opportunities."

Now Griffith stepped forward. "Exactly. In the South Carolina lotto, he purchased 24,000 tickets. The previous month in Illinois, he bought more than 47,000. In states like Minnesota and Kentucky, he purchased 50,000. There are probably other states. I'm still waiting to hear back."

"How much did each ticket cost, Captain?" Syd asked.

"A buck or two each."

This time, Pratt's laugh sounded nervous. "Okay, I might have *had* a slight gambling problem," he said. "But after I won, all that changed."

"You know," Syd replied, "I believe you knew that your major purchases would eventually come to light. But you covered your ass nicely in buying enough tickets to transform a minuscule chance of winning into a realistic possibility. You used the money in the briefcase to do it. As they say, 'Easy come, easy go'."

Lasek looked at Pratt and, in a thoughtful voice, said, "Nice behind-the-scenes work to both you and Captain Griffith. But all you've proved is that Pratt may have had gambling issues at the time. So what?"

"I have uncovered another piece of information that you might find interesting, Commissioner," Griffith said. "I haven't even disclosed it yet to Detective Livingstone.

"We've just received some data back from the lab on the suitcase found under those wooden planks. Fosterno's fingerprints and DNA were all over it. No surprise there. But on one part of the suitcase, we discovered more DNA. None of it was Montenegro's. It belonged to Chief Pratt."

"That's impossible," said Lasek. "Why wasn't I notified?"

"I just received word on the way here," said Griffith. "It's definitive, Chief Delvin Pratt's DNA. My guess is that he wore gloves but probably touched the suitcase while searching the van with Fosterno. It's amazing how easily we leave DNA behind."

All eyes fixated on Pratt.

Syd spoke again. "I don't mean to pile on, Chief, but I have even more breaking news, courtesy of my cop friend from Columbus, Gil Trent. His text came through while we were in the process of apprehending Montenegro. The mysterious bank account that revealed more than one hundred grand in Montenegro's name was recently changed. It was originally in Mitsoff's. Same with the storage unit. Seems once you realized you couldn't pin this vigilante crap on Mitsoff, you decided to target Montenegro."

Mitsoff's mouth fell open. "Pratt, you were the one trying to frame me? All along?"

"I thought it was a little too convenient that he had a copy of his lottery ticket available inside his desk," said Syd. "It was almost as if he was expecting someone to ask."

Pratt's eyes locked with Syd's. His face was red, like he was having trouble breathing.

"Chief, since the cat's out of the bag, why don't you tell us the rest?" said Syd. "Like how you hunted down McBride on that motorcycle, how you broke into Babson's home after stalking him, and especially how you placed that necklace in Mitsoff's car for his girlfriend to find. And I'm curious, did you pay someone to slip that pitcher of beer on the table, or did you do it yourself?"

Pratt glared at Syd, saying nothing.

Griffith interjected. "Commissioner Lasek, I remember

you mentioning that Pratt was the one who talked you into allowing Fosterno to guard Penny Cefalo. That was probably so he could kill him while making it appear that Penny was the real target."

Pratt was now staring at the floor. Lasek signaled to Mitsoff, who stepped forward, reaching for the handcuffs at his belt. Before he could be cuffed, Pratt swung a wild roundhouse punch at Mitsoff, clipping him on the jaw. As Mitsoff fell, Pratt pulled his weapon and stepped close to Griffith, placing the gun at her head.

"If Fosterno wouldn't have been such a damn pussy, none of this would have happened," he spat. "That group of Indiana thugs was threatening to kill him slowly unless he returned all of the money. It would've only been a matter of time before he spilled the goods and incriminated me."

"Delvin," said Lasek. "You really don't have to say any more. Be smart. Let us take you in, then you can make bail and go home to your family. Just release Captain Griffith."

Ignoring Lasek, Pratt continued. "I have a sick child at home. Insurance doesn't cover the experimental procedures that might save him, and we've spent four hundred thousand so far. That money made all the difference. Now they're saying there's a slight chance he could be saved. But he needs another treatment. He's just an innocent kid. His life is worth more than those gangbangers or those murderers."

All officers had their guns pointing at Pratt, but he held Griffith in a chokehold with the gun still firmly pressed against her temple.

"I took that money in a last-ditch effort to save my son," said Pratt. "How would any of you react in that situation? It's easy to judge when you're not in my shoes."

Lasek interjected. "Delvin, we'll find a way to get your

son the treatment he needs. No matter how much it costs, we'll get it done."

Griffith was beginning to gasp under Pratt's arm, but he kept a firm grip. "Do you believe in a higher being, Commissioner?" asked Pratt. "Do you believe there's more after you die?"

"I'm a practicing Catholic," said Lasek. "I was an altar boy in the third grade."

"Then I need you to swear right now, in front of whoever you deem to be your god, that you will make sure my son has the funds he needs to complete his treatment."

"Please!" interrupted Syd. "You're going to kill Griffith!"

"Not until the Commissioner responds," said Pratt. "I want to hear his answer in front of the Almighty."

"He will get the treatment he needs," said Lasek. "Even if I have to cash in my 401K. You have my word."

Pratt released his grip on Griffith. She fell to the ground, coughing. As Syd rushed to her side, he raised the gun to his own temple. Looking up, she noticed his trigger finger twitching.

"You were kind enough to give Detective Livingstone a little extra time. Now I'm requesting a few seconds," he said. He looked down at her. "Kudos to you, Detective. You're a fine officer. You truly think outside the box. If Commissioner Lasek terminates you, he's doing the entire department a disservice."

With that said, Pratt fired.

EPILOGUE

Syd, Enzo, Stuart, and Stacey Montenegro, along with Griffith and her wife, lounged in the swimming pool at the Top Coast Resort and Casino in Las Vegas. Enzo was there competing in a new tournament, and everyone felt they were long overdue for a vacation.

Sipping her pina colada, Syd looked around at her friends. "If you would've told me I'd still be employed by Walsh County ninety days ago, I would have told you that you were insane. When Pratt pulled out that lottery ticket, my first thought was 'oh well, my career's over.'"

"That would've stopped me in my tracks," said Griffith. "But once we found that he won the lottery *after* that money was stolen, things looked a little different."

Syd nodded. "As my father always said, having money is the key to making even more."

Enzo smiled widely, pulling Syd's left hand from the water

to display the glittering stone on her finger. "Lord knows I'm gonna need every cent I can scrape up after buying this."

"So, Enzo, how are you feeling?" asked Stacey. "Will you be ready to go tomorrow?"

"Ask me that again after this drink," he responded. "You guys can imbibe for the rest of the night, but I'm one-and-done."

Stuart turned toward Syd. "Has Lasek mentioned that promotion again?" You know, the one he promised after you solved one of the biggest cases in the city's history?"

"Hell no!" said Syd. "That cheap ass probably still has his First Communion money. But don't worry, I'll keep leaning on him."

"You know," he went on, "Pratt planted a ton of incriminating evidence against me. How could you have been so certain I was innocent?"

Syd hopped up to the pool's edge, leaving only her legs in the water. "I've had a gun held to my head on two occasions," she said. "The first time was by a lunatic who was stalking me after a tournament. I truly feared for my life. I was terrified because I knew that person was ready to pull the trigger. But when Cutter held that gun to my head in the interrogation room? I was scared shitless, but there was something in his eyes that told me he couldn't do it."

"But what does that have to do with my husband?" asked Stacey.

"It all comes back to character. I know good people when I'm around them. I sense it. I figured if my instincts were truly wrong about Stuart, then I had absolutely no business continuing my career in law enforcement."

As everyone raised their glasses, Syd's heart sang. Her

career was intact, with a major promotion looming, and, soon she and the love of her life would be enjoying the blackjack table.

But better than anything, she knew she was surrounded by the best people ever.

AFTERWORD

If you're reading this, you've likely completed "Serves You Right." I want to express my heartfelt thanks for choosing to spend your precious time with me. Like most people, you probably face common life challenges: job and money pressures, health issues, and relationship problems. I hope this book offered you a momentary escape from such concerns. You might have read it while on vacation, perhaps finishing it on the beach or in a cozy cabin in the woods. Or maybe you enjoyed it in the comfort of your own home or during those too-short breaks at work. Regardless of the setting, completing an author's novel is one of the sincerest compliments you can give them

After finishing "Serves You Right," you might feel you know me more than you thought. As authors, our perspectives subtly emerge through the actions of our characters. Sydney Livingstone, the central figure in both of my novels, has essentially become part of our family. After writing more than 150,000 words with her as the protagonist, I almost expect her to walk through our front door and join us for dinner. (If she ever does, she is more than welcome.) She takes her job very seriously and does her best to work towards her strengths. However, like anyone, when facing insurmountable obstacles, she frequently doubts herself and becomes frustrated. She understands that trusting others is essential for fully enjoying life. As Confucius said, "It is more shameful to distrust our friends than to be deceived by them." And while we've all been let down by people we believed in, a life without trust is not a life well-lived.

Sydney and fellow officer Stuart Montenegro sustain a strictly professional relationship and friendship throughout the story. While many narratives introduce romantic tension between main characters, I believed it was important for them to stay committed to their partners as they focused on their mission to stop The Enforcer. This novel emphasizes the value of monogamy and demonstrates how men and women can collaborate effectively in a professional environment.

While you navigated through "Serves You Right," your thoughts likely branched out in various directions as you tried to uncover who The Enforcer was, along with any accomplices. Lasek had anger issues and logically would have had a vendetta against criminals after his wife's attack. Pratt's wealthy lifestyle didn't correspond to his level of employment. Mitsoff seemed to be in the middle of every controversial development, and he was certainly someone you loved to hate. Griffith was a professional actor and master of disguise. Since no one ever seemed to get a good look at The Enforcer, it would have been reasonable to assume that she was behind this mess, especially since she was Fosterno's partner. Even the likable Stuart Montenegro and/or his wife Stacey may have aroused your suspicion. Sometimes the nicest people are the most dangerous. And how about Penny Cefalo, who certainly had the temperament and was no stranger to violence? Or perhaps you ventured farther off the grid to suspect Mitsoff's girlfriend Michelle, or Coroner Pennington.

On a humorous note, one of my developmental editors noticed that I had inserted my favorite NFL team, the Cleveland Browns, into the playoffs. "Are you writing fiction or fantasy?" they asked.

Here's a glimpse into my plans for the future. I aim to dedicate my remaining years to writing more thrillers featuring Sydney Livingstone as the main character. She made her debut in my first novel, "Faults," where she was pursued by a mysterious attacker during her professional tennis career. I encourage you to revisit "Faults" and continue following my upcoming works, which are currently underway. Please also check the back of this book for my website. I enjoy sharing stories and ideas with readers. Thank you once more for allowing me to be a small part of your life's narrative.

ACKNOWLEDGMENTS

There are so many people I need to thank who have made this novel possible. Let me start with my best friend Ron Wukeson, an editor who freely and, without judgment, patiently answered any grammatical question I ever posed to him. Ron is now reaping his heavenly reward, and I'm sure he will be one of the first individuals to greet me when I make the final transition.

This endeavor would've never been completed without the immense contribution from developmental editor Carolyn Roark, who owns a media company called "The Writing Texan." She was supportive and encouraging when I needed her to be, but never afraid to knock me into the dirt and say, "Give me fifty!" I'd also like to thank Lynn McGinnis, a seasoned marketing professional who helped bring this novel to the forefront and taught me more than I could've ever imagined. The technical advice provided by my friend and neighbor Barry Wisecup, whose occupation involves training police officers, was also invaluable to this effort.

I could never even come close to thanking my family enough (my wife Fran, and daughters Carli and Jillian) for their encouragement and support. Without them, I never would've had the courage to begin this task, let alone finish it. And an obscure fellow I knew in college named Mike Hosier, who I lost track of many decades ago. After a writing class, he approached me and told me that I was talented enough to do great things. He has no idea he made such an impact. (This is proof that when you offer an honest compliment, you may change someone's life.)

I want to express my gratitude to the friends and family who have allowed me to use their names as characters in my stories. I can assure you that they are not as terrible as their fictional counterparts, but not always as wonderful either (wink wink)!

I had a great experience collaborating with Frank Eastland and his team at Publish Authority, especially Raeghan Rebstock and Teresa Evans. Their exceptional work on the cover and interior made it possible for my project to be realized. They are genuine professionals in the field, and I feel fortunate to have worked with them.

About the Author

Orion Gregory graduated from Wright State University with a B.A. in Communications. He received several prestigious awards as a writer in the newspaper and advertising industries. As a young boy, he received a life sentence to become a Cleveland Browns fan. He still serves that sentence to this day, with no chance of parole. He lives by the motto that the only bad pun is the one that remains unspoken. He resides in Southwest Ohio with his wife Fran, and daughters Carli and Jillian.

For more about the author, scan the QR code below or visit his website at OrionGregory.com.

THANK YOU FOR READING

Publish Authority

If you enjoyed *Serves You Right*, we invite you to leave a review and share your thoughts and reactions online and with friends and family.

www.ingramcontent.com/pod-product-compliance
Lightning Source LLC
Chambersburg PA
CBHW060854210726
48293CB00006B/1789